A TRIAL OF INNOCENTS

Michael Andrew

Dear Melanie,
May the Lord continue to bless your efforts on behalf of the unborn. I hope this book helps you in your sacred work.

Michael Andrew
December 22, 2003
Proverbs 31:8

First printing

ISBN: 1-58851-803-5
PUBLISHED BY AMERICA HOUSE BOOK PUBLISHERS
www.publishamerica.com
Baltimore

Printed in the United States of America

Dedicated to my Father and Mother

* * * * * * *

You gave me life and constant love
Both in me thru and thru.
Whatever of each has left my pen
I'm sending home to you.
My book is done and comes to greet
The parents it longs to see –
It would be my gift to both of you
If it weren't your gift to me.

Acknowledgments:

My grateful thanks to Dr. James Dobson whose work and ministry at Focus on the Family have revolutionized my thinking on the social issues addressed in this book and who lit the fire in my soul to write about them.

My thanks to Christen Beckman, Senior Editor, along with the rest of the staff at AmErica House for believing in this book and giving me a chance.

My special thanks to Jeff Haught, B. Akridge, and "J.D." Dile for their constructive criticism and feedback while I worked on the rough draft. To Erik Halgrimson for suggesting the final title. To L. Nevels for his spiritual guidance (II Tim 1:4).

A very special thanks to David Hickman who not only offered helpful suggestions during the final rewrite, but who also undertook the daunting task of re-typing the manuscript on my electric typewriter.

To Frank and Kelly for all their help on final manuscript preparation.

My most heartfelt and sincere thanks to Bill Wilder without whom the publishing of this book would have literally been impossible. He did everything from proofreading and copying and mailing to helping me with the marketing preparation. More importantly, he dedicated the last ten years of his life to mentoring me into the man I am today.

Thanks to my mom and dad for always believing and making me believe that I could do anything.

To Aunt Sarah and Uncle Ed, for your lifelong support and love – I'll call you on Sunday.

To my muse, for your faithful and devoted love; you inspire me.

Finally, all glory and honor goes to God, for truly in me "He chose the lowly things of this world and the despised things – and things that are not – to nullify the things that are, so that no one may boast before him." I Cor. 1:38,29.

1

August 4, 9:35 P.M.
Steubenville, Ohio

"You mean to tell me this psycho picks his victims by going through the obituaries." Sergeant Gates shot a dagger-like glare at the handcuffed perpetrator who was bent over spread-eagled on the hood of the patrol car.

"It sure looks like it, Sarge. I found these crumpled up papers in his back pocket," Officer Sharps said while holding out his find. "One is from the phone book and the other is the obituary section from today's Herald Star."

"Lemme see that."

Gates snatched the papers from the rookie's hand and held up his flashlight to get a better look. The page from the phone book had an entry circled in red - John and Dorothy Bernhart, 303 Lovers Lane. Gates twisted his neck to look over his left shoulder past the meticulously cut lawn, past the perfectly manicured shrubs, past the six white pillars to the three white numbers affixed to the two-story, brick Colonial.

Gates shuffled the pages and said, "The obituary is for Dr. John Bernhart. It says that he died in a car accident three days ago. Tonight is the last night to view the body; the funeral is first thing in the morning."

Gates paused as the hellish nature of the crime sank in. "That pregnant woman this sicko just beat unconscious is the newly widowed Dorothy Bernhart."

An awkward silence begging to be filled. The rookie gave in.

"He probably didn't expect to find anyone home if he was robbing the place."

Sergeant Gates stared down at the crumpled papers in his trembling hands, completely oblivious to the rookie's comments. His mind replayed the heinous scene. A pregnant woman lay on the floor clad only in a thin nightgown. A bear of a man kneeling across her waist savagely beats on her chest. Blood trickling from her nose and mouth.

Gates looked over at the heartless criminal and shook his head. He wadded the papers and slammed them against the hood of the car. He spewed a stream of colorful obscenities then in one swift motion spun around and thrust his knee deeply into the perpetrator's groin.

The huge man exhaled and winced in pain.

Gates pounced. He laced his fingers through the back of the degenerate's long, greasy hair and snapped his head back.

"You're a big tough guy beatin' up women, you wanna go a few rounds with me, punk?"

"Let him go, Sarge, let him go! Wait till we get him back to the station."

Gates redoubled his grip and pulled even harder.

"The paramedics are comin' out of the house, Sarge, let him go."

Gates let go of the thug's hair and stepped back as if nothing happened. The paramedics rushed the unconscious Dorothy Bernhart into the awaiting ambulance.

* * * * * *

"It's ten o'clock on a Friday night, Andy. What's wrong with the court appointing an attorney?"

"Danial, you don't know what it's like down here. I've never seen so many people all worked up. You'd better get down here right away." Andy Lewis sounded unusually rattled. "I'm afraid some hotheaded cop may kill this guy if he thinks he could get away with it."

“All right. Meet me in front of the courthouse in fifteen minutes.”

“Thanks, I owe you one.”

“You owe me more than one,” Danial Solomon said. “Ever since you’ve been volunteering down at the jail, I haven’t had a minute of rest.”

“That may be true, but look at all the business I’m bringing you.”

“I define business as paying customer,” Danial said in a condescending tone. “I’ll see you shortly.”

Andy Lewis nervously paced along the sidewalk at the base of the Jefferson County courthouse steps. A few minutes later the silhouette of a new Dodge Intrepid pulled into the attorney’s parking lot. Andy watched Danial Solomon step out of the car and straighten his five foot eight inch frame. Danial waved then ran his finger through his thick mop of chestnut hair. The prematurely gray shoots stood straight up. Even at a distance Andy felt comfortable when he looked into Danial’s ocean blue eyes. Danial’s full lips stretched into a disarming smile.

The two men shook hands, entered the building, and headed for the jail in the courthouse basement.

“So what’s this guy’s name?” Danial asked.

“I don’t know.”

“What’s he in for?”

“I don’t know.”

“Where’s he at now?”

‘I don’t know.”

“What do you know?” Danial asked.

“All I know is he supposedly beat up a pregnant lady, and he hasn’t said a word since being arrested.”

“Have you seen him?”

“Only at a distance, they wouldn’t let me near him.” Andy paused. “To be honest, he didn’t look quite right to me . . . a little off.”

"Off? What do you mean a little off?" Danial asked. "Off like crazy?"

"No, off like a little slow . . . I don't know . . . it looked like something is wrong with his head. You'll see."

The jail sat in the basement of the courthouse, the oldest part of the building, built prior to the Civil War and smelled like it. The two men climbed down the worn marble steps and stopped at the booking desk. Danial put down his briefcase and turned toward the female deputy wearing a black uniform and sitting behind the old Formica counter.

"I'm attorney Danial Solomon, and I'm here to see . . . um . . . um. . ." He looked over at Andy for help.

Andy leaned forward and said, "The weird looking guy who beat up the pregnant lady."

Danial rolled his eyes. "Thanks Einstein, I would never thought of that one on my own."

"Are you his lawyer?" the deputy asked.

"Not officially. I'll need his consent before it will be official."

"Good luck. He won't even say his name." She picked up the phone.

"Hold on, and I'll call the detective handling the interrogation."

A couple minutes later a short, stocky man turned the corner of the long hallway leading toward the booking desk. He wore a wrinkled brown suit. His baldhead and pudgy face were red and glistening with sweat.

"I'm detective Demus. What can I do for you?"

"I'd like to see the suspect arrested for allegedly assaulting the woman on Lovers Lane."

"Allegedly? That's a good one," Demus said, not trying to hide his agitation. "First of all, we allegedly caught him in the act, and Mrs. Bernhart is more than *allegedly* unconscious. Besides, what's a big shot lawyer like Danial Solomon interested in a psychotic scum-bag like this for anyway?"

"The Constitution guarantees the right of psychotic scum-bags to be represented by counsel at trial."

"At trial – you've got to be kidding. Even you couldn't get this guy off. Did I mention he had the obituary section of the paper in his pocket? Yeah, it seems he goes and robs families while they're out burying their dead. He should be a real media darling with that M.O."

"Nevertheless, I would like to see him."

* * * * * * *

10:30 P.M. – University Hospital

In spite of the emergency staff's best efforts, Dorothy Bernhart slipped into a coma. The doctors were now faced with a dilemma. The severe head injuries Dorothy sustained left her in critically unstable condition. Meanwhile, the tiny life of her unborn baby ebbed away with each tick of the clock.

"We've got to move now," Dr. Davies said. "The baby won't survive if we wait any longer. We've got to go in and get it."

"It's too risky," Dr. Parks, Chief of Staff said, "the mother is too unstable. She can't take anymore trauma."

"The mother may die no matter what we do. Let's at least give the baby a chance."

"We can't sacrifice one for the other. And we can't be sure they both won't die in surgery."

"They both could die if we do nothing," Davies said. "It would be a lot easier for the hospital to explain that we lost both mother and child in surgery than if they both died while we sat here twiddling our thumbs."

The white-haired, over-weight Chief of Staff rubbed his jowls. He nodded his head and said, "All right, do what you've got to do.

But if anything goes wrong the blame will fall squarely on your shoulders."

"I can live with that," Davies shouted as he dashed off to the operating room.

* * * * * * *

10:45 P.M. – Jefferson County Jail

Demus led Danial Solomon down the dimly lit corridor. Multiple layers of paint chipped off the walls, and a thick musty smell of rotting timbers lingered in the air. The hallway led to a dead-end with two doors on either side of the hall. Demus picked up the phone outside the door on the right.

"Access interview room one."

The latch buzzed and the door swung open.

Dingy blue paint covered the walls, floor, and ceiling of the claustrophobic cube. A single light bulb hung from a wire over a small square table. Sergeant Gates stood behind the suspect who sat slumped over the table with his face buried in his folded arms. He looked up when the two men entered the cramped room, his face swollen and a generous stream of blood ran down the corner of his mouth.

The suspect flinched as Demus reached near to gather up the paperwork.

"What happened to him?" Danial asked, his anger beginning to burn.

"Our friend here suffers from self-defense injuries inflicted by the victim," Demus said with a smirk on his face. "Looks like she did pretty good for herself, huh?"

Demus flashed a knowing smile over at Gates. Danial snatched Demus by the wrist and glared at the detective's bleeding knuckles.

"What happened here?" Danial asked through barely parted lips. I suppose you cut yourself shaving."

"How'd you guess?"

The two men locked eyes. Demus tugged his arm free. Danial took a step forward and stood nose-to-nose with the shorter man. "If my client so much as said a mumbling word, I'll get the statement thrown out, and I'll have your badge."

"Relax, counselor. We couldn't get his name out of him."

Demus backed out, and Danial found himself alone with the disheveled young man. Danial took a good look at him. *He can't be more than twenty years old, probably six feet or so, maybe two hundred-twenty pounds.*

Danial opened his briefcase and took out a legal pad.

"I guess we'll start at the beginning. In order for me to represent you, I'll need to have your consent. Do you want me to be your attorney?"

No answer.

"Well, I'm going to take your silence for consent. So if you don't want me to be your attorney, speak now or forever hold your peace."

No answer.

Danial walked behind the large man to get a closer look at the scar running down his forehead from under his hairline. *Looks like a gruesome injury. Andy was right; his head is definitely lopsided.*

"What's your name?"

Still no answer.

"No matter. After they plaster your face across every television station in the area there will be hundreds of people eager to tell your whole life story."

* * * * * * *

10:50 P.M. – University Hospital

"We're losing her!" shouted the trauma team chief as the gurney burst through the operating room doors.

"We're not losing anyone around here," Dr. Davies shouted as he ran to meet the frantic group. "Get her on the table! Stat!"

Immediately four pairs of hands grabbed the battered, comatose woman and flopped her on the operating table. The trauma unit scurried out of the way as the awaiting surgery team dashed into action.

A blur of hands sliced away Dorothy's nightgown, strapped down her arms and legs, and scrubbed her bulbous mid-section. A ring of purplish discoloration encircled the base of her protruding abdomen.

"She's slipping, doctor. Her pulse is fifty-four and dropping. Pressure is fading too."

"Damn! Damn!" Davies said. "It's now or never. Scalpel."

Davies traced the instrument a few inches below Dorothy's belly button.

"Retractors. Get me some suction over here," Davies said. "Dr. Hayes, clamp here and here."

Hayes clamped open the incision.

"How's she doing?" Davies asked.

"She's fading. Pulse is down to forty-eight."

"She'll make it. Man, there's a lot more blood in here than there should be. More suction here — no —here by my little finger."

Davies reached in through the incision and lifted out the limp body of the premature baby girl, her left eye black and blue and swollen shut, her tiny body riddled with bruises.

"Oh my God!" shouted one of the nurses when she got a glimpse of the child.

Davies cleared the baby's airway, his hands moving with intricate precision. He pressed his ear against the baby's chest.

"She's not breathing! No pulse!"

The surgical team divided its attention. Dr. Hayes took half the team and attended to the mother, while Davies and the rest of the team frantically tried to revive the baby.

2

7:25 A.M.
Saturday, August 5

The bright morning sun broke over the West Virginia foothills of the Appalachian Mountains and illuminated the eastern side of the Jefferson County Courthouse. Crews from all three local television stations pushed and shoved outside the main entrance while reporters from the various newspapers jockeyed for position near the bronze statue of Edwin Stanton, Abraham Lincoln's Secretary of War. Once the story broke, interest in the case was instant and fierce. They all clamored for an official announcement on the case of the decade. Such brutal things didn't happen often in Jefferson County, and they never happened on Lovers Lane.

From his third-floor office window, Anthony DiAngello watched the frenzy on the street below. This case could easily catapult the four-term prosecuting attorney to the Attorney General's office, and he knew it. This opportunity could not be squandered.

Anthony DiAngello stood five feet ten inches tall and stayed in remarkably good shape for a man in his early fifties. His curly hair, dyed black, projected a youthful appearance. Bushy eyebrows and deep set, dark brown eyes gave him a permanently intense expression that turned menacing when he was angered. He had a large pointed nose, covered with tiny black hairs; a narrow mouth with thin lips and a strong chin. Anthony DiAngelo always wore a double-breasted suit. It had become his trademark.

DiAngello turned away from the window and shuffled toward his desk. His administrative assistant, Bill Jenkins, who also served as his campaign manager, sat in the worn leather chair across from the oak desk.

"What's your take on all this, Bill?"

"I think if we handle it correctly this could be the best thing that has ever happened to your political career."

"I couldn't agree more." DiAngello cracked his knuckles and plopped down in his chair. "But we've got to be cautious, everyone will be watching on this one."

"The timing couldn't be better. With the election four months away, all this free press is worth a mint."

"Maybe I should try this case myself?"

"Definitely not," Jenkins said without a second thought. "We need you to look judicial at all times. And if anything goes wrong, it's always good to have a scapegoat."

"You're probably right. Maybe I'll give the case to Franks."

Jenkins perked up and his cheeks flushed at the mention of Lori Franks. "She's a good choice. A woman's touch is just what a grizzly case like this needs."

"A woman's touch, you've got to be kidding me. She's mean as a snake."

"But what about Danial Solomon? He's taken the case Pro Bono."

"Danial Solomon . . . huh. . . . well, I can't see how that Bible thumping prodigy could possibly win an open and shut case like this; I don't care how sharp he's supposed to be."

"I went to Ohio University with him chief," Jenkins said. "He graduated Summa Cum Laude. He's no slouch."

* * * * * * *

7:35 A.M. – Mt. Pleasant, Ohio

Andy Lewis rubbed the sleep out of his eyes to the smell of bacon frying in the kitchen. Marianne liked to surprise her husband with breakfast in bed the morning after a long night at the jail. After what she saw on the news last night, she knew Andy needed all the support she and their daughter Erin could give him.

Andy's lanky frame stretched out under the covers. His arms were a little longer than they should have been. He had no chin to speak of, his long narrow head tapered into his long narrow neck. In fact, if it wasn't for the oversized Adam's apple and long pointed nose, it would have been impossible to tell where his head stopped and his neck began. His dark brown eyes were almost black, and his thinning brown hair always looked a little too oily. Andy gave off the appearance of awkwardness. His students referred to him as Ichabod Crane.

Andy feigned sleep when he heard his wife and seven-year-old daughter making their way up the creaking steps. Marianne carefully balanced a tray of fried eggs, bacon, toast, and orange juice while Erin prodded her along by pulling on the waist of her nightgown. As soon as they reached the bedroom door, Erin took off on a dead run and leaped on the bed and her unsuspecting father.

"Daddy! Daddy! Wake up, Daddy!" Erin squealed as she jumped up and down on the queen-sized bed.

"I'm awake, Precious, I'm awake."

Erin giggled and took one last spring into the air, then flopped down on the bed. She crawled over to her dad and perched on top of his chest. She grabbed his stubbly face in her chubby, little hands and gave him a sloppy kiss on the lips. Marianne stood watching, her heart welling up with love. *Thank You, Lord, for giving us this little angel and finally making our family complete.* She watched for a moment longer then said, "I'm going to get jealous if you two don't cut it out. Breakfast is getting cold."

Erin wiggled over next to her dad as he sat up. Marianne placed the tray across Andy's legs then sat on the edge of the bed next to him. Andy held his wife's hand and put his other arm around Erin.

"Let's have a word of prayer."

All three closed their eyes and bowed their heads. Andy prayed.

"Our most gracious and heavenly Father, we thank you for providing this food for us once again. We also thank you for blessing us with good health and happiness. Dear Lord, we ask to look over the woman injured last night. We ask your healing hands be upon her. Your Word says that by your stripes we are healed, so we pray that you grant her a speedy and complete recovery.

Dear Lord, we also ask you to watch over the young man arrested last night. We don't know exactly what happened, but you do. So we ask you to forgive him and prepare him to receive the Gospel of Jesus Christ into his heart. We ask these things in Jesus' name – Amen."

The loving little family paused for a few moments of silence. Andy turned toward his wife. "I didn't get home till after midnight. Did you happen to catch the news?"

Marianne opened her mouth to answer when Erin caught her eye. "Erin, could you go out to the kitchen and get Mommy the milk and a spoon?"

Erin climbed off the bed, but before she took a step Marianne added, "And don't run."

Erin looked back and started walking as fast as her spindly legs would go. Marianne watched the black-haired girl scamper out of the room, then she turned toward her husband.

"The news said that a recently widowed woman eight months pregnant was savagely assaulted and in surgery at the time of the broadcast. They also flashed the suspect's picture and asked for anyone with information about the man to call the station at once."

"I wouldn't think a man like that would have many acquaintances." Andy shoveled a heaping bite of eggs into his mouth.

"You'd be surprised how many calls they got. By the end of the telecast the anchor man said they received hundreds of calls, and someone even made a positive identification of the suspect."

"I'm sure Danial will be delighted to hear that. He spent two hours with the guy and couldn't get him to say anything." He picked up a piece of bacon and popped it in his mouth. "Did you happen to catch his name?"

"I wrote it down so I wouldn't forget it. Let me think where I put that piece of paper."

She rummaged through the nightstand as Erin walked through the door with both hands on the milk carton and the spoon in her mouth.

"What will happen to that guy next?" Marianne asked.

"Well, Monday morning is the arraignment when the charges will be officially entered against him, and he'll enter a plea. I'm going down to support Danial since I'm sort of responsible for getting him into this mess."

"Don't forget you're taking Erin to her first dental appointment at noon on Monday."

Erin put the milk on the tray and climbed back in bed; she snuggled up next to her dad. Andy kissed the top of her head.

"That's all right. I'll take my little princess with me."

Erin smiled.

Marianne stood up and put her hands on her hips. "I know I put that paper someplace where I wouldn't lose it." She smacked herself on the forehead. "That's right – I put it on the refrigerator door."

She hurried out of the room and returned a few moments later with a tiny piece of paper in hand.

"Here it is. The man's name is Archie Kisner."

* * * * * * *

Monday, August 7
7:55 A.M. – Jefferson County Courthouse

Danial Solomon took a deep breath and said a quick prayer before pushing open the heavy oak door; cases like this made him thankful for the attorney's entrance into the old courtroom. At this stage of the game it's best to avoid the gallery filled with reporters, politicians, family, and friends of the victim. When defending the enemy, the defense attorney becomes the enemy as well.

Danial made his entrance and looked around the courtroom. The high vaulted ceiling, inlaid with hand-carved wooden reliefs, looked simple yet majestic. The oak-paneled walls had darkened over the years to an antiquated charcoal hue. A portrait of Baron Friedrich von Steuben, for whom the city was named, hung on the wall over the jury box. On the facing wall hung a portrait of Thomas Jefferson for whom the county was named. A hand-painted seal of Ohio covered the wall behind the judge's bench.

Danial made his way over to the mahogany table reserved for the defense. He placed his briefcase on the table then walked over to the prosecutor to introduce himself. County Prosecutor DiAngello sat behind the table tapping his gold pen on a stack of files. A woman in a blue business suit stood with her back to the table talking to someone in the gallery. Danial extended his hand.

"Good morning, Mr. DiAngello. My name is Danial Solomon. We met a couple of years ago at a death penalty conference."

DiAngello stood and firmly clasped the outstretched hand. "Mr. Solomon, your reputation precedes you. Allow me to introduce you to Lori Franks. She'll be handling the Kisner case for the State."

Lori turned around at the mention of her name to see Danial reaching out to shake her hand. They locked eyes.

She's gorgeous, and look at those eyes.

"Ms. Franks, it's a pleasure to meet you."

Lori grabbed his hand and in a sarcastic tone said, "So you are T-H-E Danial Solomon. I hope you'll take it easy on us non-geniuses."

A few seconds of awkward silence ticked by.

"They say there's a fine line between genius and insanity, and most of the time I find myself on the wrong side of that line."

Danial chuckled; no one else did.

I'm dying here.

A commotion at the back of the courtroom saved him from any further unpleasantness. Two deputies brought in the defendant dressed in a blaze orange jumpsuit. Flash bulbs lit up the courtroom like a fireworks finale on the Fourth of July. The din of the crowd turned into a roar when the expressionless defendant reached the waist-high, wooden gate, which separated the gallery from the attorneys. One of the deputies unfastened the handcuffs and escorted Kisner to his seat. Danial walked over to him and whispered in his ear.

"Don't worry. This will only take a couple of minutes. I'll do all the talking." Danial chuckled. "Yeah, as if I have to worry about you saying anything."

Danial felt a hand on his shoulders. He turned to see the smiling face of Andy Lewis.

"I just wanted you to know that I'm here for you. I've got Erin saving me a seat in the back row. We'll be praying for you."

"Thanks," Danial said. "As you can see, this is not going to be easy."

The bailiff emerged from the judge's chambers and shouted, "All rise. Here ye! Hear ye! Hear ye! This court is now in session. The Honorable Judge John Williams presiding."

Judge Williams entered the room and climbed the three steps leading to his high-backed, leather chair. He grabbed the gavel, slammed it on the bench.

"Please be seated."

Judge Williams, a large man in his early sixties, stood six foot two with thick curly white hair. He combed it straight back revealing a dramatically receding hairline. Two deep wrinkles ran across the width of his forehead, parallel to his thick, white eyebrows. His eyes were hidden behind thick, round glasses that sat on his narrow, pointed nose. Folds of loose skin now swallowed his once prominent chin. The years had not been kind to Judge Williams. In a deep baritone voice the old judge opened the session.

"I understand we're here this morning for the purpose of arraignment."

"That's correct, Your Honor," Lori said. "The State is set to bring charges against the defendant, Archie Kisner."

The judge peered over the top of his glasses at Kisner. The young man stared at the floor as if not paying attention.

"The defendant will rise for the reading of the charges," Williams said.

Kisner stood up; Danial stood next to him. Judge Williams glanced over at Lori. "The State may proceed."

"Thank you, Your Honor." Lori consulted a stack of documents on the table in front of her. "The State of Ohio charges the defendant, Archie Kisner, with one count of aggravated burglary, one count of aggravated assault, and one count of aggravated murder."

"Murder." Danial said, his face soured by indignation.

A wave of murmuring swept the gallery.

"Order!" Judge Williams slammed the gavel on the bench. "Order in the court!"

"May we approach the bench, Your Honor?" Danial asked.

"Approach."

The old judge plopped heavily into his seat. Lori and Danial walked up to the edge of the bench. Williams turned off his microphone and leaned forward.

"Your Honor, I was under the impression this was an assault case," Danial said in a hushed tone. "The latest information I received reported Mrs. Bernhart in stable condition. If it pleases—"

"I would hardly say a coma is considered stable condition," Lori said. "However, the murder charges don't stem from Dorothy Bernhart's death, but rather from the death of her baby. The medical report states that baby died prior to delivery, doubtless from the injuries sustained in the assault."

"Your Honor, the State has conveniently withheld this information, and it's put the defense in a very compromised position."

Lori glared at Danial then turned back toward the judge. "Your Honor, surely the astute Mr. Solomon is aware that the defense has no right to discovery until the indictment is on file at the Clerk of Court's office. Besides, this is only the arraignment. He has plenty of time to prepare for trial."

Judge Williams leaned a little further forward and spoke in a slow whisper. "Today is the beginning of a long process. I expect things to go smoothly between the two of you. Do I make myself clear?"

"Yes, Your Honor," they said in unison.

"Good. Then you may step back, and we'll continue." Judge Williams returned to his seat and turned the microphone back on. He waited until the two adversaries were back in place then looked over to the defendant.

"You have heard the charges brought against you. How do you plead?"

Kisner made no attempt to answer.

"The defendant pleads not guilty," Danial said.

"Let the record reflect the defendant has entered a plea of not guilty. I bind the defendant over to the Court of Common Pleas, and the case will proceed to the Grand Jury."

"What about bond, You Honor?" Danial asked.

"You're not serious, Mr. Solomon."

"Indeed I am."

"All right then, bond will be set at two million dollars cash."

"What?"

"Court is adjourned."

"But Your Honor . . ."

"I said Court is adjourned." With that Williams stood up, rapped the gavel, then returned to his chambers.

The deputies slapped handcuffs on Archie Kisner's wrists and hustled the stone-faced defendant out of the courtroom. Danial gathered up his papers and stuffed them in his briefcase. He started to leave along with the rest of the crowd, but then turned back and walked over to the prosecutor's table where Lori stood reviewing some papers.

"Excuse me, Ms. Franks, I know we sort of got off on the wrong foot this morning. We both have a difficult job to do, and I hope it doesn't become personal."

"Mr. Solomon, I'm a professional; I never allow cases to get personal." She flashed a plastic smile.

"I'm glad to hear that." Danial took a deep breath. "By the way, have we met before? You seem familiar to me for some reason."

"No."

"You have very memorable eyes." Danial leaned closer to the petite woman. "They appear to be violet blue. I know I've seen them before."

Lori shoved a stiff-arm into Danial's chest and stepped back. "I warn you the only thing flattery will get you with me is slapped with a sexual harassment suit."

Andy Lewis pushed his way through the crowd and sidled up next to Danial. He held his daughter by the hand.

"I wasn't trying to flatter you." Danials cheeks flushed. "I was just being honest."

"Being honest, huh? Well, I guess that makes sense. I've heard you were some sort of religious fanatic or something."

"I'm a Christian if that's what you mean."

"Well, I'm an atheist, and I really don't trust anyone who is weak-minded enough to need a crutch to get through life. Now if you'll excuse me."

Lori pushed past him and bumped into Erin. She didn't notice the little girl.

3

Tuesday, August 8
Steubenville, Ohio

Danial arrived at the two-story, Victorian brownstone building that housed his modest law office just before seven-thirty A.M. He climbed the three concrete steps leading up to the white front door. A wooden placard hung above the door by a wrought-iron support, which simply read: Danial Solomon, Attorney at Law. Sixth Street may not have been the most desirable part of town, but it was conveniently located close to the courthouse.

Danial walked into the office and took a deep whiff; the inviting scent of Hazelnut coffee pulled him toward the kitchenette like a homing pigeon returning to its roost. He nodded to Jennifer, his middle-aged, heavy-set secretary who sat behind and L-shaped desk in front of the door to his office. She smiled and pretended to be busy, but followed him with her eyes. He poured himself a cup of coffee and walked straight into his office without saying a word. Jennifer waited until she heard his computer booting up before she finally spoke.

"I placed this morning's Herald Star on you desk. I think you'll be interested in the front page story."

She heard the sound of the newspaper rustling, followed by the sound of hot coffee being sprayed through tightly pressed lips, followed by a series of coughs.

"Jennifer, get that . . . that . . . woman on the phone! Now!"

She obeyed; her fingers raced across the phone's touch pad as if she worked the Rubik's Cube. Over the years she had developed a friendship with the switchboard operator at the courthouse, so it didn't take long to track down the woman in question. Jennifer held her hand over the mouthpiece.

"Danial, Ms. Franks is on the phone. Pick up line two."

He pushed the appropriate button on his console and the battle commenced.

"What's the big idea leaking to the press you intend to seek the death penalty?" Danial said.

"The public has a right to know."

"The press is already in a feeding frenzy, and there you go throwing more blood in the water."

"Don't blame me, I'm just doing my job."

"You job isn't to exploit the press and trample over my client's civil rights. It's already going to be next to impossible to have a fair trial in this county."

"His rights! What about Dorothy Bernhart's rights? What about that innocent, defenseless baby's rights? Who protected them from your retarded, mute, client?" Lori said, her voice an octave higher than normal and quite piercing. Danial winced and pulled the phone away from his ear.

"He hasn't been convicted of anything yet. Besides, he may not be competent to stand trial; he's had a severe head injury."

"You must be out of your mind, Solomon. You're sadly mistaken if you think you can get him off. He was competent enough to hunt down his victims. Who knows how many times he was competent enough not to get caught. They invented the death penalty for cold-blooded mutants like Kisner."

"Assuming you're right and he's competent to stand trial — and that's a big if — the way the State subjectively applies the death penalty is wrong. You know the statistics better than I do; nearly everyone on death row is black, and they're all poor."

"Hey, I don't make the laws, I just enforce them."

"That doesn't make it right. Slavery used to be legal and that didn't make it right."

"Slavery was a part of the culture at that time. Besides, I thought all you Bible thumpers were in favor of the death penalty. Capital punishment comes right out of the Bible, doesn't it?"

"The Bible does indeed advocate capital punishment, but in the Bible God is the ultimate authority in the government. When an infallible God is the judge, the wrong person never got executed. I think we both can agree that God certainly isn't the ultimate authority here in America. And as far as that goes, the Old Testament also says that homosexuality, adultery, fortune telling, and being disrespectful to parents are also capital offenses. I haven't seen the State try to fry anyone for any of those crimes. But then again, if they did I suppose there wouldn't be anyone left in your office to prosecute the cases."

Danial paused for a moment and since Lori didn't fill the gap, he continued the sermon.

"And since you brought it up, the Bible also has a New Testament. You've heard of the New Testament haven't you? You know, where Jesus Christ died on the cross for the sins of the world. Oh yeah, by the way, the crucifixion is probably the most famous example of an innocent man being wrongly put to death."

Silence.

"Nice speech, Scripture Boy," Lori said, each word dripping with sarcasm. "But allow me to throw this little tidbit at you. I *AM* going to seek the death penalty . . . simply because I can!" Lori paused for effect then added, "What do you think of that, Scripture Boy?"

She slammed down the receiver.

Danial leaned back in his chair still holding the phone in his hand, Lori's words stinging his ears.

* * * * * * *

8:00 A.M.

Mt. Pleasant, Ohio is one of the state's rare historical treasures and a wonderful place to live. The town is situated on top of a hill, which commands a beautiful view of the Ohio River valley. The Lewis family owns a 19th Century, brick Victorian row house just up the street from the old Quaker Meeting House. In the summer they enjoy eating breakfast on the back patio.

Erin sat on the end of the picnic bench, her feet dangling. She fished around in a bowl of pink colored milk trying to capture one final, elusive marshmallow. After getting frustrated at her multiple failed attempts, she tipped back the bowl and slurped down the marshmallow along with the milk. She picked up the bowl, walked over to her daddy and gave him a milky kiss, then hurried into the house.

"What's on your agenda for today?" Marianne asked as she cleared off the table.

"Danial has a psychiatrist coming in to put the Kisner boy through some tests. I'd like to spend a little time with Kisner before they get started. Maybe I can get him to loosen up some."

"Has he said anything yet?"

"No, not yet. If I could just get him to understand that he can be forgiven for his sins, no matter how terrible they may be. But how do you do that when the man will not or cannot talk to you?"

Marianne put down the dishes and walked up behind her husband. She wrapped her arms around his long neck.

"Honey, this whole situation is in the Lord's hands."

Andy tipped his head back; he could see an upside-down view of his wife, her shoulder-length, reddish-brown hair waving in the early morning breeze.

"I know," he said. "But with school starting in a couple of weeks, I feel like I need to reach him now or I never will. You know how hard it is for me to get down to the jail once I'm teaching."

"You can only do what you can do," she said with a smile. "Just plant the seed and allow God to make it grow in His own time."

Andy stood up, his lanky frame dwarfing Marianne. He gave her a hug. "How did you get so smart?"

She gave him an extra squeeze. "Hanging around you."

"What are your plans for the day?" he asked.

"I'm taking Erin to the Fort Steuben Mall to do some back-to-school shopping. Would you like us to met you at the courthouse for lunch?"

"Sounds like a winner to me. How could I pass up lunch with the two prettiest girls in the world?"

* * * * * * *

In the seven years since graduating from law school, Lori Franks had become a confident and aggressive prosecutor under the tutelage of a very prominent mentor, Judge Spitzer-Clark. Prior to making a successful bid for the bench seven years earlier, Spitzer-Clark had formed the *Society for the Advancement of Women in the Legal Profession.* The group was not much more than a thinly veiled fund raising machine for Spitzer-Clark.

Twice each month the small group of devotees would meet with the judge to discuss fund raising strategies or bring up any legal concerns for her input and advice. As a result, Lori would not make any important decision without checking with Spitzer-Clark first. And now with the high-profile Kisner case brewing, Lori felt anxious for this evening's meeting, and to make matters more stressful, Lori's mother was due to arrive any minute for an extended visit.

Lori checked her look in the full-length mirror behind her office door. She stood only five feet two, but her forceful personality made her seem much bigger. She looked petite in a curvaceous sort of way. Her jet-black hair framed her narrow face and long, elegant neck. Her creamy smooth skin had a porcelain quality to it, not so much as a large pore to reveal a flaw. With a button nose and full lips, she could have easily been a model had she been taller. If it weren't for her eyes, she would have looked like a black and white version of a Renaissance painting. Her eyes were unique and quite remarkable, almost perfectly round and violet blue. When the light hit them just right they looked lavender.

Lori straightened her skirt then headed for the third-floor conference room where all the key players in the Kisner case were assembling for a strategy meeting. She walked in the room to the pungent smell of burned coffee. The sound of forced air whirled overhead through the air conditioner vent. The room held a long, rectangular table and six plastic chairs, stained from years of abuse. She walked to the coffeepot and poured herself a cup and knocked an empty box of doughnuts on the floor. She kicked it toward the garbage can.

She glanced at the back of the uniformed officers. *I guess I don't have to ask who brought the doughnuts.*

She took her seat at the head of the table. To her left, Officers Gates and Sharps devoured their doughnuts like ravenous wolves. At the far end of the table sat Detective Demus digging into both nostrils with his thumb and forefinger. To her right sat DiAngello's assistant, Jerry Jenkins, with a lovesick look in his eyes. And next to him was Dr. Washburn, the resident capital punishment guru.

With this group of morons, I'd be lucky to prove the sky is blue.

"All right gentlemen," Lori said, calling the meeting to order. "I don't need to reiterate how important this case is to the State of Ohio, to the citizens of Jefferson County, and to the people who live up on Lovers Lane. I want to use this case to send a strong message to the potential Archie Kisners of the world — if you commit a heinous crime in our community then we will kill you. After all, I live up on Lovers Lane myself."

* * * * * * *

8:05 A.M.

Danial Solomon took a few minutes to calm down following his conversation with Lori Franks, then he turned his attention to tracking down everything available on Archie Kisner. He swiveled his chair around to the computer hutch and logged on to the Internet. He navigated his way through multiple web pages until finding the desired search engine. He typed in his client's name and instantly three hits popped up: Children's Services, University Hospital, and Juvenile Offenders. He clicked the mouse twice and the screen flashed "Access Denied: Records Sealed."

He tried again getting the same results.

"I can see this is going to be one of those days."

He grabbed his keys and headed for the door.

"Jennifer, I'll be gone for the rest of the morning."

"Where're you going?"

"I've got to get a court order to unseal some records."

At 8:25 A.M. Danial arrived at the office of Probate Judge Gary Trent, a long-time friend of Danial's father, John Solomon. At 8:45 A.M. Danial raced out the door with court orders in hand. He drove directly to University Hospital to do battle with the records department.

A young college intern noticed the good-looking attorney having a difficult time in the cramped records office.

"May I help you, sir?" the pretty young coed asked as she stepped uncomfortably close to Danial. "My name is Kay, and I'd be more than happy to assist you in any way possible."

Danial retreated a step. "I'm looking for the medical files for one of my clients, Archie Kisner. I have a court order."

"Oh, you must be a lawyer." She beamed a toothy smile and stepped forward again, backing Danial to the wall. "What did you say your name was?"

"I didn't, but my name is Danial Solomon. And I don't mean to be rude, but I really have to get back to the courthouse."

"Yes, of course. What's your client's name again?"

"Kisner, Archie. That's K-I-S-N-E-R."

"Gotcha." She scribbled the letters on the palm of her hand.

She pressed past Danial, brushing her breasts against his arm with a wry smile. A few minutes later the dark-haired girl returned. She grabbed Danial by the arm and squeezed his biceps.

"Here you go. I wrote my work number on the outside cover of the file in case you need my help again." Her lips curled up in a seductive grin. "I wrote my home number on the inside cover in case you . . . well, you know."

Danial felt trapped. He needed to read the file as soon as possible, but he had to put some distance between him and the aggressively flirtatious coed. He took a few steps toward the door with the young girl right on his heels.

"Could you tell me where I can find the men's room?" *At least she can't follow me in there; I hope.*

"Down the hall and to the right," she answered in a disappointed tone. Her prey had somehow managed to wiggle through her fingers once again.

* * * * * * *

10:25 A.M.

"Do I make myself clear to you two?" Lori directed the question to the two uniformed officers. "Before you turn in your *official* arrest reports, I want you to go over them with a fine tooth comb; no inconsistencies whatsoever. If so much as a comma is out of place, Solomon will find it.

"Washburn, find me every capital case ever tried anywhere in the country involving an unborn baby, and I mean every case. Leave no stone unturned —."

The telephone in the corner of the room interrupted Lori's train of thought. She hurried over and snatched the receiver from its cradle.

"Franks here, what do you want?"

"Ms. Franks, I'm sorry to bother you," the switchboard operator said. "But your mother has just arrived. What do you want me to tell her?"

"Tell her to wait in the lobby. I'll be right down."

Lori hung up the phone.

"Gentlemen, I've got another pressing appointment, so if you'll please excuse me."

Lori gathered her papers and slid them into her gold-handled, black leather briefcase. She rushed out of the room heading for the elevator.

* * * * * * *

10:26 A.M.

After another frustrating stint at the Juvenile Court's record office, Danial rushed to the courthouse to receive his first pleasant surprise of the day; Dr. Clay was still testing Archie.

Danial took the opportunity to review the fruits of his morning's labor. He opened the medical file first and began scanning its contents.

This is some rough stuff, he thought. Blunt force trauma to the skull by a long cylindrical object, possibly a baseball bat. Deep skull fracture, fracture to the forehead and eye orbital, brain damage but extent unknown. Patient exhibits slurred speech and loss of memory. What else do we have here? Date of birth: June 19, 1977. That would make him just over twenty. I would have guessed him at close to thirty. Here's something that may come in handy, his next-of-kin is a brother named Ralph.

Danial pulled out a legal pad and made himself a note to find Ralph Kisner. He closed the medical file and picked up the Juvenile record and began to read. This is not good, assault at age fourteen. He did time in the detention center for burglary at age sixteen. Not good, not good at all.

* * * * * * *

10:27 A.M.

Marianne and Erin Lewis enjoyed any excuse to go shopping and today was not exception. They purchased the typical back-to-school fare of notebooks, pens, pencils, glue, and the like, and then they had some fun. They tried on everything from matching dresses to matching hats. They left the mall with only two pairs of jeans and a pair of tennis shoes, but they certainly had a blast.

They walked into the courthouse hand-in-hand, and stood in line behind a short, pudgy woman at the receptionist's desk in order to have Andy pages. Erin stood a bit too close to the woman in front of her; the lady stepped back and the heel of her shoe mashed Erin's big toe. Erin let out a blood-curdling scream. The woman jumped forward, Erin began to cry, and the woman opened her purse and pulled out a handkerchief. She squatted down to Erin's level.

"I'm so sorry little girl, I didn't mean to step on your foot."

"I'll – be – O – K," Erin said between sobs.

Marianne stepped forward to have her husband paged while the lady patted Erin's tears dry. The woman's mouth fell open when she looked into the little girl's eyes.

"Your eyes are exactly the same color as my daughter's. As a matter of fact, you look just like she did when she was small."

* * * * * * *

10:28 A.M.

Dr. Clay walked out and shouted to no one in particular, “You may return Mr. Kisner to his cell. I’m finished with him.”

Danial stood up from the chair directly behind the psychiatrist and caught the overweight doctor by surprise. Danial reached out and shook his hand as an uniformed deputy squeezed in behind the two men.

“Thanks for coming on such short notice,” Danial said. “As you can see, I’ve got my hands full. What do you think?”

“I can’t give you the official report until I can go over my notes and evaluate the test results, but I can tell you this much, I believe he *can* talk; he simply chooses not to. It’s almost like he has taken a vow of silence or something.”

The deputy escorted Archie Kisner out with his arms handcuffed behind his back. Danial studied the scar that ran down the left side of Archie’s forehead as they walked past. Archie’s hair looked greasy and uncombed, his beard thick and unkempt.

I’ve got to do something about his appearance. He looks like someone a jury will want to execute.

Danial turned back to the doctor. “Well, give me the bottom line. Is he competent to stand trial?”

“He’s definitely no rocket scientist, but at this point I have no evidence to say he can’t stand trial. I’ll give you my full report tomorrow morning.”

Danial shook his head. “That’s not what I wanted to hear, but thanks for your time. I’ll probably have more questions once I go over your report. Thanks again for your help.”

“Don’t mention it,” Dr. Clay said, walking toward the smoking lounge.

Danial closed up the files and placed them in his briefcase. He walked to the elevator with his mind a million miles away. He accidentally bumped into a small woman already waiting for the elevator; he nearly knocked her down.

"Excuse me, ma'am. I didn't see . . ." *Unbelievable, what else could go wrong this morning?*

"Danial Solomon. Imagine bumping into you here," Lori Franks spit out as she regained her composure. "Don't you have some Mensa Society meeting to attend somewhere?"

"I'm glad we have this chance to chat. I wanted to apologize for my tone with you this morning on the phone. I was way out of line."

"I accept your apology," Lori said. "But it doesn't change anything. I'm still going to seek the death penalty."

"You can seek anything you like, but I have a feeling that the Grand Jury will see things my way and won't issue a death specification on the indictment."

The elevator door opened. Danial placed his hand on the black safety lip. "After you."

Lori stepped in and pushed the button for the lobby. Danial walked in and prayed silently.

Lord, please don't allow this elevator to get stuck.

4

10:40 A.M.

Lori and Danial stood as far apart as the elevator walls would allow. A suffocating silence filled the tiny compartment. When the doors opened in the lobby, the two anxious rivals rushed out of the elevator. They bumped hip-to-hip and stumbled out into the lobby making quite a scene.

Three people sat in red vinyl chairs to the left of the elevator, Joanne Franks with Erin on one side and Marianne on the other. Joanne held out her wallet to the two strangers, proudly displaying childhood pictures of Lori as if they were long lost relatives. Lori could not believe her eyes. Could this be her antisocial mother?

"What are you doing?" Lori asked, embarrassed to see half-naked pictures of her being shown to complete strangers.

"Oh, don't get yourself all worked up," Joanne said. "I have your pictures out because this beautiful little girl looks so remarkably like you."

Lori examined Erin's face.

"I must admit the resemblance is remarkable." Lori leaned forward to get a closer look at Erin's eyes.

"Even her eyes are violet blue," Joanne Franks said. "What are the chances of that?"

"I knew it," Danial said, feeling vindicated. "I knew I had seen those eyes before." He bent over, and Erin wrapped her arms around his neck.

"Hello, Uncle Danial."

"Hello, Sweetheart. You look beautiful today."

"Uncle Danial?" Lori asked. "This little girl is related to you?"

"I'm just a good friend of the family."

Danial waited for some kind of snide or sarcastic remark. When it didn't come he looked over at Lori as if disappointed. She stared at Erin, obviously deep in thought. A painful expression draped across Lori's face.

Lori shook her head to snap out of that old haunting train of thought. She stood up and grabbed her mother by the arm.

"Come on mother, let's go. We can't be late for our meeting."

Joanne Franks was not the kind of woman who took orders from anyone. Her eyes narrowed with annoyance. This behavior was rude even by Lori's standards. The two women walked toward the main entrance. Joanne attempted to reorganize her purse as they went.

"What's got into you?" Joanne asked. "Could you have possibly been more rude? You'll never get elected to the bench with public behavior like that. Those were potential voters."

"Mom, you wouldn't understand."

"Do you think I'm an idiot? Of course I understand. That little girl brought back some difficult memories for you. Deal with it. You're a grown woman."

"I'm not sure I want them to pass. That little girl looked a bit too much like me to be a coincidence. And what about those eyes? It disturbed me to look into the face of another human being and see my own eyes."

"Well, they say everyone has a twin someplace in the world."

Joanne had not seen her daughter like this in almost seven years.

"I'm not one who believes much in coincidence or superstitions," Lori said. "I'm going to look into this a little further. Did you happen to catch her last name?"

Joanne laughed and turned her face away. "This may not be a good thing. If it doesn't work out the way you expect, you could be opening a lot of old wounds for nothing."

"Just give me the last name. I may never get around to doing anything with this anyway," Lori said.

"I believe her name is Lewis, Erin Lewis."

* * * * * * *

10:42 A.M.

Andy walked up the well-worn marble steps that led from the old jail to the first floor lobby and saw two women storming away from his group of loved ones. He approached the bewildered group and asked, "What happened here?"

"I don't know," Marianne said. "The nice older lady showed us pictures of her daughter – who looked a lot like Erin – when all of a sudden her daughter staggered out of the elevator and pulled her away."

The confusion on Andy's face intensified. "What do you mean she staggered out of the elevator?"

"It's a long story," Danial said. "But this should clear things up. Those two were Lori Franks and her mother."

Andy chuckled. "I guess that explains it."

Danial's face turned deadly serious. "Andy, do you think it's possible the Bible is wrong?"

"What do you mean by that? You *know* that every word in the Bible is breathed by God; it cannot be wrong."

"Well, the more I'm around that woman, the more I'm convinced the anti-Christ is a woman, and her name is Lori Franks."

"Oh, come on now," Marianne said, "she can't be that bad."

"Oh yes she is," Danial and Andy blurted out in unison.

"You two are terrible." She looked at Danial. "Would you like to join us for lunch? It's our treat."

"I wish I could, but I've got to drive over to Children's Services. I'll just grab a bite on the way. But thanks for asking."

"At least join us for dinner tonight. You haven't been over in ages. I'm making meatloaf – "

"And it's just the way you like it," Andy said. "Hot and free."

They all laughed.

"Very funny, very funny," Danial said. "I'll try to make it, but no promises."

They said good-bye and parted company. Andy lifted Erin onto his shoulders. She wrapped her arms around his neck and pressed her cheek on top of his baldhead.

"I love you, Daddy," she said tenderly.

Andy's heart melted.

Danial walked toward the attorney's parking lot at the rear of the building. He stopped off at Burger King and devoured a Whopper with everything, then he parked his midnight blue Dodge Intrepid outside the Children's Services office on the north end of Steubenville. This time he tried a new strategy before leaving the safety of his car. He bowed his head and prayed.

He got out of the car and walked into the building. He had no trouble finding help or securing the file he needed. In fact, the clerk showed Danial into a small conference room so he could review the file before making a copy. Prayer does indeed change things.

Danial opened the tattered manila folder and began to read. At the age of six, Archie's mother died in a car accident. Two weeks later his father committed suicide. Archie found his father's body in the garage in a pool of blood, what a horrible thing for a child to live through.

Danial dropped the file on his lap and rubbed his eyes with his thumb and forefinger. After a few moments he flipped to the next section. Archie lived in a series of foster homes until the age of twelve when his older brother, Ralph, took custody. *There's that name again. I've got to find him. Let's see what this is.* Children's Service attempted to regain custody on two occasions for suspected abuse by the older brother, but each time they could not prove anything because Archie refused to talk. *Boy, that sounds familiar.*

Danial flipped to the last section of the file and wrote down some notes: educational background – almost straight D's and F's; Archie is definitely no rocket scientist. His I.Q. is listed as 68 before the head injury. *I might be able to use this.*

****

Lori dropped her mother off at her townhouse on Lovers Lane then rushed back to the courthouse. Instead of going straight to her office, she stepped off the elevator on the second floor and paid a visit to the Jefferson County Records Office. She walked up to the old wooden counter.

"Excuse me, sir. Could you give me a copy of the birth certificate for one Erin Lewis."

"One minute, ma'am," the young clerk said. He turned to the computer terminal, typed in the name and executed the search code. He shook his head. "I'm sorry but the computer lists no such name. That doesn't mean we don't have the record, the information probably hasn't been entered into the system yet. I'll have to do a manual search."

"Super, how long is that going to take."

"Not to long. Do you have the Social Security number?"

"No."

"Do you have the date of birth?"

"No . . . wait a minute . . . try June 6, 1990."

The clerk jotted down the information. "Very good, I'll get right on it. I can see from your I.D. you work in the building. Why don't you give me your extension, and I'll give you a call as soon as I find what you're looking for."

"I'm at five-four-two. Try to make it snappy."

"Yes, ma'am. I'll get right on it."

Lori walked out of the office with her stomach tied in knots and mumbling under her breath.

"Is it possible? Could the hospital have made a mistake?" She unconsciously moved toward the elevator. "What if they did? If nothing else it'll relieve this guilt I've been carrying around for all these years. This is giving me a headache."

During the seven years since going into University Hospital for her late-term abortion, Lori's conscience constantly singed her soul with agonizing guilt. She tried hard to suppress it, and on the surface it looked as though she succeeded, but underneath it ate her alive. Judge Spitzer-Clark had suggested she become involved in the Pro-Choice movement as a form of therapy. So Lori became an avid Pro-Choice advocate and vocally denounced everyone who disagreed with her position as bigots and self-righteous, religious fanatics. She single-handedly brought Planned Parenthood to the Ohio Valley and served on its local board of directors.

Pangs of regret and guilt overwhelmed her at the most inopportune times. A child playing in the park or a television commercial showing children eating ice-cream on a hot summer day would trigger an explosion of raw emotions. Melancholy doldrums would set in and tortuous thoughts raced through her mind: that could be my baby; she would probably look something like that; what would he be doing now?

Nightmares plagued her sleep. Lori had the same recurring dream. She would be shopping at the mall, and all of a sudden a mannequin would come to life and ask, "Why did you kill me, Mommy?" Lori would turn to see violet blue eyes staring back at her. Sometimes it would be a boy, sometimes a girl, but those haunting eyes and that mocking question was always the same: "Why did you kill me, Mommy?"

This whole Kisner case irritated her to no end. Ever since being asked to prosecute the case of a murdered unborn child. Lori found the parallels quite disturbing. Lori's baby was eight months old when she went in for the abortion, the same age as the Bernhart baby. Why is one situation considered murder and the other a legal abortion? Wasn't the outcome the same? These were hard things to reconcile in her mind. And to make matters worse, in order to prosecute this case Lori would have to argue against the dogmatic position she firmly held for so long, namely, that an unborn child is not a person. It wasn't that Lori had a problem being hypocritical, it just annoyed her to be dealing with these emotions again.

Lori arrived at her office and shut the door. She closed the Venetian blinds and sat anxiously by the phone. After twenty minutes of silence, she slid open the bottom desk drawer, and pulled out a well-hidden flask of Southern Comfort whiskey. She didn't make a habit out of drinking at work, but during times of great stress she would turn to her old reliable comforter. And now was one of those times she needed a little bit of help. She took two large gulps of the burning tan liquid, and tipped the flask a third time when her phone rang.

"Yes – hello – what did you find?"

"I didn't know I was supposed to be looking for anything" Joanne Franks said.

"Ah, it's you, Mom. I was waiting on an important call."

"In that case, I won't keep you on the line. I called to see if you wanted me to start dinner, or if you planned on eating out tonight."

"Let's just eat in tonight. It's been a long day."

"Okay then, I'll let you go."

"See you tonight."

"Ba - Bye."

Lori hung up the phone. She ran her fingers through her shoulder length, black hair. "What is keeping that incompetent fool. If I don't get that information in ten minutes I'll have his job!"

Instantly, the phone sprang to life as if afraid of her threat.

"Ms. Franks, I found the birth certificate you asked about. Erin Lewis was born on June 6, 1990 at – "

"Let me guess," Lori said. "She was born at University Hospital."

"That's correct. How did you know?"

"Lucky guess."

Her stomach felt squeamish. The room began to spin. She hung up the phone and slouched back in her chair completely wiped out. Lori's mind raced back through seven years of agonizing memories. The events that changed the entire course of her life now seemed so cloudy and vague. It took every ounce of strength she had just to reach out and pick up the flask. The remaining whiskey didn't last long as Lori took a staggering walk down memory lane.

5

SEVEN YEARS EARLIER

In the heart of Silicon Valley, research engineers toil in the lab for hours without end in search of the miracle breakthrough. Such a cutting-edge discovery could mean millions of dollars in bonuses and royalties to the first person to reach the patent office. However, Shawn Perry had more riding on his experiment than mere money. In fact, the very future of his life depended upon the results of these secret tests, and the strain clung to his face like an old T-shirt.

The tension in the environmentally controlled room was thicker than a London fog. No smell in the air and no sound other than the whirl of the air conditioner, which kept the lab colder than comfortable. In spite of the chilly temperature, beads of sweat formed on Shawn's brow. His brown eyes intently focused on his work. Lori laughed at the bizarre expression on his face.

"Silence, I need silence! The slightest slip of the hand could taint the results and then where would we be?"

Shawn returned to his work. He poured a translucent, yellowish fluid into a vial of chemicals and shook the amalgamation vigorously. He stepped back and took a deep breath. The moment of truth had arrived. His hands trembled so much he could barely pick up the litmus stick from the stainless-steel counter top. After what seemed like an eternity, Shawn composed himself enough to complete the task at hand. He inserted the stick into the vial, quickly withdrew it, and held his breath while he waited for it to change color. And change it did – to bright red.

"Oh no."

He dropped his head, a defeated man. He put the stick down next to the other three bright red sticks on the counter. He gathered himself, and put on his best game face. "No doubt about it, you're pregnant."

Lori showed no reaction.

"How could this happen?" he asked. "You've been on birth control pills for as long as I've known you."

Silence.

Silence.

The extreme stillness had the retching effect of someone running their fingernails down a chalkboard.

"It doesn't matter what you think, I'm having this baby."

"What!?"

"What do you mean *what*?"

"You never really struck me as the motherly type."

"What are you trying to say, Shawn?"

"You're always obsessing about your career — "

"Obsessing! I've never obsessed a day in my life. Since when did wanting to get ahead become a crime?"

"There's nothing wrong with wanting to get ahead, but cheating on the bar exam — "

"There you go, I knew you couldn't wait to throw that in my face."

"I didn't mean it."

"I could have passed that exam with my eyes closed – "

"I know."

"I don't know what drives me to do these things." She shook her head. The expression on her face softened as tears welled up in her eyes. "I just wanted to be first, had to be first."

"Lori, I don't – "

"Look, Shawn. I may have screwed up my life in a lot of ways. But I'm not gonna blow this one." She placed her right hand on her belly.

"Well, if that is how you feel then I guess the thing to do is get married. At least you and the baby will be covered by my hospitalization."

Shawn walked around the counter like he was heading to his own funeral and in a half-hearted gesture of chivalry, he got down on one knee. He looked up into those tear-filled, beautiful eyes and said, "Will you marry me?"

Lori bit her lip and nodded her head.

Shawn stood and coolly embraced her. For the first time all night when she knew that it would not be seen, she allowed the corner of her mouth to smirk out a devious smile. *I love it when a plan comes together!*

* * * * * * *

The Ohio Valley is littered with steel mill towns, and Tiltonsville looks much the same as the rest. The town was built on the narrow flat land between the base of a long chain of hill and the Ohio River. The houses are generally the same size and style, and they surrounded the mammoth, rusting mill like worker bees around the queen. The mill dominated the landscape.

Andrew and Marianne Lewis had been trying to have children ever since they were married ten years earlier. They had come close once, but the fertilized egg had become lodged in the Fallopian tube, and just as they believed their prayers were answered, the developing baby burst the tube and nearly killed Marianne in the process.

Andy and Marianne were advised by their doctor not to attempt another pregnancy. They were also told it would be practically impossible to conceive again due to Marianne's advanced endometriosis. (Endometriosis is a condition where the uterine walls become hardened with the abnormal growth of endometrial tissue. It makes it difficult for a fertilized egg to attach itself to the uterus and begin to develop.) Nevertheless, their desire to have children outweighed the risks. Three years later, and against all odds, the home pregnancy test sat on the kitchen table once again.

"Before we do this, I believe prayer is in order," Andy said, his voice, normally a deep baritone, cracked at least two octaves higher.

Andy stood and took his wife's tiny hands in his own. He closed his eyes, bowed his head and in a hushed tone began to pray.

"Dear Father God, we thank You for this opportunity to humbly come before You once again. Lord, we know that You can do all things and make a way where there is no way. So now we ask that You allow Marianne to be with child. We know that such an answer would bring glory to Your Name as many have repeatedly told us that this would be impossible. But nevertheless, not our will, but Your will be done. In Jesus' precious name – Amen."

"Amen," Marianne said.

She paused for a moment to look up into her husband's eyes. Then like a giddy schoolgirl she swooped the pink box from the table and darted off to the bathroom.

The minutes seemed like years to Andy as he sat at the table alone with his thoughts. Memories of their life together came racing from the past, and just like that he was back at the campus of Ohio University on the day they met.

Andy nervously paced the length of the classroom, his first year of teaching undergraduate history. He looked at his watch, time to start. He introduced himself to the class, and reached to close the door when Marianne burst in the room at a full sprint. They collided. Books and papers flew everywhere. They both bent over to pick up the same book and smacked foreheads. A hollow thud echoed through the room along with a chorus of laughter from the other students. Both their faces flushed with embarrassment, and Andy fought to regain his composure. Marianne made a strong impression on him that day, and Andy had the bump on his forehead to prove it.

She was the most beautiful girl he had ever seen; she stood a full foot shorter than his six foot one inch frame. Reddish-brown hair surrounded her perky round face, and her blue eyes and freckles made her appear younger than her years. He always thought her too pretty for him, and he was probably right.

His walk down memory lane came to an abrupt halt by the slamming bathroom door. Out bounded Marianne carrying a plastic stick in her hand.

"The instructions say the little window will either show a plus sign if I'm pregnant, or a minus sign if I'm not."

"What does it say?"

"I don't know," Marianne said, looking as if she would burst. "I wanted for us to see it together. Are you ready?"

"Ready as I'll ever be."

She opened her clenched fist.

"It's . . . . a plus!" Marianne squealed.

They jumped up and down and attempted to high five, but in all the excitement their aim was off by at least a foot; Andy nearly smacked Marianne in the face. They hugged each other tightly and continued to jump around.

Tears streamed down both their cheeks; they dropped to the floor in one another's arms and thanked God for His gracious answer to their prayer.

* * * * * * *

Bakersfield, California

Lori Franks sank into her old couch, the only comfortable piece of upholstery in her meagerly furnished, studio apartment. And right now that old couch seemed like the only friend she had in the world. Dirty dishes were stacked in the sink, law books strewn all over the apartment, and she presently wore the only pair of clean clothes she owned.

The phone rang. She took a deep breath before picking up the receiver; she knew who it was.

"You're what!!" screamed Joanne Franks. Her shrieking voice made Lori pull the phone away from her ear. Joanne's voice had a whining quality that made it difficult to endure for long. It made Lori want to scratch her ear.

"Lori, please tell me that was a joke you left on my answering machine."

"Mom, I know what I'm doing. Just trust me for once in your life."

"If you're trying to see how many ways you can screw up your life in two months, then I'd say you've succeeded wonderfully. What kind of idiot does something this stupid? Didn't I teach you better than this?"

"You taught me to succeed no matter what the cost, and that's precisely what I'm trying to do. The pregnancy is a short-term fix to my present financial problem."

"What are you talking about?"

"You do recall that I owe you over one hundred-thousand dollars in student loans?"

Joanne spoke slowly; her comment meant to sting. "Yes, I'm well aware of your financial trouble, and you would have had your pick of jobs if you hadn't been caught cheating on the bar exam. How can someone so smart be so stupid?"

"Mom – "

"I guess I should be glad you didn't rob a bank."

"Would you let it go already. I made a mistake, and now I'm trying to recover. If I hadn't gotten pregnant, I could never have talked Shawn into making my loan payments."

"But you were on the pill – "

"I've been flushing them down the toilet since the exam."

"But you hardly know the guy."

"I know how much he makes, and that's enough for now."

"You should have come home. We could have figured something out. You can still pass the bar in Ohio."

"Return to Fly, Ohio, population five-hundred? Be real. I didn't go to Stanford to practice law in Mayberry, R.F.D.!"

"Do you at least have any leads on a job?"

"I've got over a hundred resumes out from here to New York. But as soon as news gets out about my cheating on the exam, I'll be blackballed for sure. Why don't you give your judge buddy a call and see if she can pull some strings for me? You're always raving about your feminist sisters. It's about time we cashed in on their political connections."

"Well, I just might do that. But let's keep this pregnancy thing quiet. If word got out it would only make things worse."

"Mom, if I get a job anywhere, I'll make this pregnancy thing go away."

Lori heard Shawn's keys rattling in the front door.

"I've got to go. Shawn is here to take me to the doctor's office. Now I've got to play the cheerful mother."

Lori hung up the phone, put on her best Hollywood smile and walked to meet her only means of financial support.

* * * * * * *

Steubenville, Ohio

"You're what!?" Dr. Merashoff shouted. He stood up and paced around his office, which looked like a print from a Norman Rockwell painting. "We went through this three years ago in this very room. You know how dangerous this is. What were you thinking?" His Russian accent became more heavy and pronounced. "How dare you defy me!"

"Doc, it's nothing personally against you, " Andy said. "We just want to have a baby."

"I've got to be very frank with you, those home pregnancy tests aren't always accurate. Marianne, with you endometriosis it's nearly impossible for you to get pregnant."

"Doc, what is impossible to man is quite possible with God. Go ahead and test me yourself."

"Well, I intend to do just that, and if you're pregnant then you can thank that God you're always telling me about. Because in my forty years of practicing medicine on two continents, I've never seen a clinically infertile woman conceive."

Dr. Joseph Merashoff had been born and raised in Communist Russia, but had immigrated to the United States with his wife and two daughters just after World War II. He was educated in the first generation to be soundly indoctrinated with evolutionary science. He long ago ruled out God being compatible with medicine or science. But in spite of his atheistic beliefs, Marianne and Andy attempted to share their faith with him every chance they could. While he didn't agree with them, he certainly admired their persistence.

Joseph Merashoff was a large, burly man in his early seventies. White hair ringed his round, balding head. His ears were too big for his face, and thin red veins were spattered over his cheeks and nose, the result of too many years of Vodka. Merashoff had very kind blue eyes that were nearly hidden by a single, prominent, bushy white eyebrow that ran the full width of his forehead.

Joseph Merashoff amassed a small fortune delivering babies over the years, but money had nothing to do with why he continued to work. He truly loved bringing life into the world. Even though he continued on staff at University Hospital, he kept his caseload light so he could give his few patients the personal attention he believed they deserved. In a lot of ways, these were the best years of his career.

"What are you grinning about?" Merashoff said, turning toward Andy. "You look like the cat who ate the canary."

"Nothing," Andy said, but his grinning face revealed something else was cooking in his mind.

Well, my good Doctor Joseph, when the results of the test come back you'll see first hand the mighty power of Jesus Christ. And, then we'll see if you can still say there is no God.

6

Seven months later Marianne and Andy Lewis were back in Dr. Merashoff's office; the results of the latest ultrasound had just arrived.

"How could something be wrong?" Marianne asked as water filled her swollen blue eyes. "For seven months I've done everything by the book. I quit my job, I've rested, I've taken vitamins . . ." Her words became more halting and her breathing more pronounced as each syllable tumbled off her quivering lip. "I've played classical music . . . not too loud. What else could I have done?"

Tears streamed down her face leaving black streaks of mascara in their wake. Andy pulled his wife close, her face pressed against his chest. His white shirt absorbed her tears; he felt the dampness against his skin. He bowed his head to whisper in her ear.

"Everything is going to be all right. God is still in control. It's not your fault." Andy looked over his wife's ponytail.

"Doctor, please explain exactly what's wrong?"

The normally stoic Russian looked visibly shaken at the emotional scene unfolding before his eyes. His face flushed and his large chest heaved. He chose his words carefully.

"The ultrasound shows there isn't enough amniotic fluid being produced to support the baby's growth. This is usually caused by the baby having a bladder or kidney blockage, which prevents the normal discharge of bodily fluids.

"In healthy developing babies, the urine and other discharges make up the amniotic fluid in which the baby is floating. Without the proper amount of fluid, the baby won't have the cushioning or the room to grow." Merashoff paused and rubbed his temples. "Of more grave concern . . . toxic fluids are backing up inside the baby. This could cause a fatal infection to spread throughout the baby's body. I'm sorry."

The young couple sat perfectly still.

"This is not anyone's fault," Merashoff said. "These things just happen. I know this is a difficult time, but we need to talk about your options."

"Options?" Andy said, his face contorted by pain. "I don't understand."

"Time is of the utmost concern, because with each passing hour the baby is retaining more and more toxins. You have basically two choices: one, abort the fetus; or two, attempt an extremely risky prenatal surgery which would put both the baby and mother in great danger."

"ABORTION!" Marianne shouted. "Are you crazy!?" Tiny hairs stood up on the back of her neck. "That is not an option, do you understand me? That is not an option!!"

"You understand Ohio Law requires I give you all the options," Merashoff said, his voice very apologetic.

"I don't care what the law says, I will not murder my own baby. I would rather die first!"

"I thought you would choose the surgery so I took the liberty to check around for the nearest hospital equipped with the specialist you need."

"It doesn't matter where or when," Andy said.

"How about the Cleveland Clinic first thing tomorrow morning?"

"Tomorrow morning!" the pair said in unison.

"Right now time is the enemy. It's now or never. And still there's no guarantee the baby will survive the operation. The survival rate for this new procedure is only about five percent," he lied. The rate was closer to one percent.

This new revelation filled the room with oppressive silence.

"Just to make sure we understand you correctly," Marianne said, "if we do nothing the baby is definitely going to die?"

The old doctor nodded his assent, then lowered his eyes to the floor. "As I said, this procedure is also risky for the mother. A million things could go wrong. The infection could spread throughout your body, and there's always the danger of toxic shock. And the procedure will have to be done while you're awake. Anesthesia and babies don't mix." He paused. "Are you sure this is what you want to do?"

"I told you before I would die for my baby, and I meant what I said. Besides, God isn't going to let anything happen to me. Right honey?"

"Right," Andy said. Her question interrupted his silent prayer.

Marianne looked back to Dr. Merashoff. "So it's settled then; we'll have the operation in the morning."

Marianne sounded a lot more confident than she felt inside. The magnitude of the situation had not yet set in.

* * * * * * *

A light blue BMW sped toward Los Angeles and the exclusive Hollywood Children's Hospital. The couple inside the car argued fiercely.

"Lighten up, Shawn, and stop nagging me. I'll smoke if I want to. I've been smoking since high school, and if my mother couldn't make me stop, you don't stand a chance."

"I thought we agreed you'd at least cut down during these last two months of the pregnancy."

"You and Dr. Dean agreed I would cut down. I believe I said I would do whatever I wanted with my own body."

"It may be *your* body, but right now *my* baby is depending on it."

Lori rolled her eyes and took an exaggerated drag off of her cigarette and blew the smoke in Shawn's face along with her words.

"Men are always trying to tell women what to do with their bodies. Anything that is inside of me belongs to me."

"What you seem to forget is that genetically I'm as much a parent to that child as you are. Therefore, my opinion counts for something."

"Your opinion does count for something all right," Lori said. Before she finished her sentence, the fact that Shawn paid all the bills came rushing to the forefront of her mind; it restrained her for now.

"For someone so adamant about having this baby, you sure don't act very maternal." He regretted his words even as they floated over his lips. He dared not turn to look at her.

Meanwhile, Lori's violet blue eyes burned a hole in the side of Shawn's face. It was amazing how someone so pretty could look so mean. Shawn could feel the weight of her glare pressing against his cheek, daring him to defy her. The fight had reached that critical point where Shawn could either back down, or face the full vent of Lori's rage. He chose to back down.

"Lori, you know the pressure I've been under trying to adjust to this whole father thing. And with the wedding coming up after the baby is born . . . this is a lot for me to deal with right now. I just want you and the baby to be healthy."

You had better back down you little coward. "I don't want to fight anymore either," Lori lied. "And, besides we're almost there."

Lori snuffed out her cigarette in dramatic fashion, then stared out the window until the car came to a stop in front of the posh Hollywood hospital. The stars came here to have their babies in style. Even though several hospitals were a lot closer and more convenient, Lori would settle for nothing but the best.

Shawn dropped her off at the front door, then drove off to find a place to park. From behind Lori didn't look pregnant. She had watched her diet very carefully and had only gained fourteen pounds. The old Italian lady who lived across the hall said she was going to have a boy since she carried the baby so low. However, during the rare moments when she actually thought about it, Lori believed it would be a girl.

For the past seven months Lori lived a continuous exercise in frustration. She moved into Shawn's apartment, which led to continuous fighting. Of the twenty firms that even bothered to respond to her resumes, all rejected her. Lori never experienced rejection at any time in her life, and now actually having people tell her "No" seemed beyond her comprehension. The void within her soul grew with each passing day. Even the alcohol she turned to when Shawn wasn't around didn't help anymore; nothing did. Her sarcastic personality took on new bite, and Shawn became her favorite target. At least it would be over soon.

An hour after the appointment, Lori found herself alone in Shawn's apartment. In spite of herself the baby was in perfect health. She reached for a bottle of Jack Danials in the kitchen cupboard when the phone rang.

"Lori, pack your things," Joanne Franks said. "You're coming back to Ohio. Jane got you in at the Jefferson County Prosecutor's office."

Joanne Franks and Jane Spitzer went to college together at Oberlin University in the early seventies, a radical time on most college campuses across the United States, and Oberlin led the way. Joanne and Jane were at the epicenter of the radical feminist movement at Oberlin. The duo was the first to lead protest marches and to organize bra-burning campaigns. During their years of undergraduate studies, they had formed a feminist group that has remained on campus to this day.

Being the ever vigilant feminist, Judge Spitzer-Clark had been continuously pressuring the Jefferson County Prosecutor's office to hire more women, and when the last female on the staff left for private practice the door swung wide open.

"Excellent!" Lori shouted. "Where's Jefferson County? And when do they want me to start?"

"Jefferson County is just north of Wheeling, West Virginia on the Ohio side of the river. It's about an hour north of here. They want you to start in two weeks."

"But what about the bar exam thing?"

"I explained the whole mess to Jane, and she said it won't be a problem. All you need to do is pass the bar in Ohio within the next six months."

"Fantastic!" Lori felt a knot develop in the pit of her stomach. "What about my other problem here? I'm already in my third trimester, and it's a bit too late for an abortion now."

"Not necessarily," Joanne said. "Late term abortions are legal in most states, including Ohio. Jane has a friend at University Hospital in Steubenville who is taking care of all the arrangement." Joanne paused for a moment. "What about Shawn? He could throw a major monkey wrench in the works here."

"Don't worry about him. He won't even begin to know where to look for me."

"Come on now Lori, Shawn isn't a complete idiot. Ohio is the first place he would look for you. He knows I live in Ohio, doesn't he?"

"As a matter of fact he doesn't. I told him we were from Pennsylvania. Do you think I want anyone to know I was born in West Virginia and grew up in a town called Fly?"

"All right, pack whatever you can carry and take a cab to the San Francisco airport. I'll have a ticket waiting for you under the name Jane Austin."

"San Francisco?" Lori said. "That's three hours away. I can get to L.A.X. in thirty minutes."

"L.A.X. would be the first place Shawn would look if he came home early from work and discovered you were gone." Joanne's voice took on a condescending tone. "Just do what I tell you and do it quickly. You'll have a direct flight to Columbus, and I'll pick you up at the airport."

"Thanks Mom, I'll never be able to repay you for this."

"Repay me by hanging up and getting out of there."

Lori hung up and scurried around the well-furnished apartment, grabbing whatever clothes and valuables she could stash in her two gray suitcases. She paused when she came to Shawn's underwear drawer. He always kept a large amount of cash in there in case of an emergency.

"Well, if this isn't an emergency, I don't know what is," she said. "Besides, I've had to put up with a lot from that man. He owes me this and a lot more."

She snatched a wad of bills totaling over three hundred dollars and stashed it in her purse. Twenty minutes later she sat in the back seat of a beat-up yellow cab with two over-stuffed suitcases on her way to San Francisco. The sound of whining tires crept up through cracks in the floorboards.

Everything is happening so fast. It took eight months to get used to the baby thing, and now this. I've never heard of aborting a baby – I mean a fetus – at nearly eight months.

The cab drove on for another twenty minutes.

I need something to distract my thoughts for awhile. This is too much to deal with. "Excuse me sir. I've never been to San Francisco, could you tell me a little about the city?"

"Me Englais he no too good," the driver said.

"Never mind."

An hour ticked by.

I could always have a child later when I want one. Every child should be a wanted child anyway. Aside from that, life doesn't really start until the first breath, so it's not like I'm doing anything wrong or illegal.

No matter how hard Lori tried to justify her decision, a twisted feeling in the pit of her stomach just would not let go.

This is my body, and I am entitled to do whatever I want with it. I worked too hard to make it through law school to have something stand in the way of the career I've always wanted.

And so the battle raged on for three straight hours. When the cab finally reached the airport, Lori felt as if she had received a last minute reprieve from death row. She picked up her ticket and checked her bags at the desk. Now that the necessities were out of the way, Lori pushed through the crowd and found the nearest lounge to her departing gate. She drank herself into oblivion.

At least I don't have to feel guilty about getting drunk anymore.

* * * * * * *

Cleveland, Ohio
8:00 A.M.

Marianne and Andy were on the road early to make the solemn three-hour trip up from the Ohio Valley. Marianne tried to sleep but had no luck; her mind wouldn't slow down. Andy prayed silently for most of the trip. Several times during the journey Marianne placed her hand on her belly and said, "Don't worry little one, everything is going to be just fine."

The sight of the sprawling mirrored Cleveland Clinic looked impressive with the early morning sun reflecting off the eastern side of the main building.

"Being a High School History teacher may not pay much, but thank God for the benefits," Andy said. "I could never afford a place like this."

They parked the car and received their first surprise of the day at the registration desk.

"Dr. Merashoff," Andy said. "What are you doing here?"

"Did you actually think I would allow my favorite patients to go through such a delicate procedure without me?" Merashoff flashed a smile. "I'm going to observe and assist Dr. Snider. Maybe this old dog can learn a new trick or two."

Marianne walked over to the old Russian and gave him a hug. Her little arms didn't reach around to his back. "Thank you so very much for coming," she said. "I feel better just knowing you're here."

"What do you know about Dr. Snider?" Andy asked. The thought of his wife and unborn child in the hands of a total stranger wasn't very comforting. Andy needed something tangible to hold on to.

"I've only met Dr. Snider once at a lecture she gave last year on prenatal operative procedures. She impressed me." He lifted a Styrofoam cup to his lips and took a sip. "By the way, I believe the biographical information from the lecture said she was a Christian."

Andy and Marianne looked at each other and smiled.

"Praise the Lord!" Andy shouted and then caught himself. "For almost twenty-four hours I've been looking for someway to discern the Lord's will in this situation. And now to discover that the only doctor in the state available to operate on a moment's notice is a Christian – "

Just then, Dr. Brenda Snider walked into the room dressed in surgical scrubs; she couldn't have been over five feet tall. She wore her salt and pepper hair pulled back in a neat ponytail. Thick round glasses sat on top of her small pug nose and concealed her eyes. With thin lips and a pointed chin, she looked professional and remarkably wide-awake for this time of the morning.

"Mr. and Mrs. Lewis, I'm Dr. Snider. I'll be performing the operation this morning. Dr. Merashoff has informed me that he has already gone over the general points of the procedure. Please allow me to fill in the details and answer any questions you may have."

"I have a question," Marianne said. She looked over at her husband for approval. "Could we skip all the gory details and have a word or prayer?"

"Well . . . uh . . ." Dr. Snider looked over at Merashoff. The old Russian shrugged his shoulders. "You got me. It's your call."

Snider stammered for a moment and said, "I guess it's all right but you may have to sign some sort of waiver. It's standard procedure for me to inform you of all the contingencies."

"Dr. Snider, all the contingencies are in God's hands," Andy said. "We would feel better agreeing with you in prayer than hearing about a whole bunch of stuff we wouldn't understand anyway."

Brenda Snider smiled. "Prayer sounds great to me. I would like that very much."

Andy stretched out his hands; Marianne took hold of his right hand. Merashoff looked as if he had been asked to jump into a vat of boiling oil. However, he reluctantly reached down and took Andy's bony hand and bowed his head. The group formed a tight circle, and with all heads bowed and all eyes closed Andy began to pray.

"Most gracious and heavenly Father, we come to You today with thanksgiving in the mighty name of Jesus Christ. Lord, we ask You to guide and anoint the hands of Dr. Snider as she seeks to correct whatever problems she encounters with our baby. Give her the wisdom to deal with whatever she finds.

"We ask Your powerful hands of protection be with Marianne as she goes through this operation. We ask You to show mercy and kindness to us in this hour of need, and we seek Your peace. Nevertheless, Father God, allow Your will to be done and not ours. We trust you completely with our lives and our souls. In Jesus' precious name – Amen."

Merashoff caught himself slip out a quiet "amen" along with the rest of the group.

Snider and Merashoff hustled out of the room; Snider headed for her office and a last minute review of the data, and Merashoff walked to the elevators. He felt relieved to find one empty.

"What are these people doing to me," he said out loud. "I've never prayed in my life. I'm a man of science." But for some strange reason he had never felt better in his life. A touch of peace poured into his heart.

Prayer does change things.

Back in the room, orderlies prepared Marianne for surgery, then whisked her away. Andy found himself alone.

"Now I will pray like never before."

He knelt down beside the strange bed and began to commune with God. A tear ran down his cheek – the tear of a prayer warrior.

7

8:03 A.M.

Marianne Lewis watched the ceiling tiles flutter past as her gurney rolled into the operating room. A strong scent of antiseptic chemicals stung her nostrils. Two orderlies transferred her to the operating table then left with the gurney. A nurse in pink scrubs strapped her arms and legs to the table and began the preparations for surgery. Two enormous overhead lights hung from directional support arms and poured blinding illumination over the table. Marianne could see two large, round clocks on the wall nearest her head.

A few moments later Drs. Snider and Merashoff came in wearing blue surgical scrubs, green caps, and white masks.

"How're you holding up?" Snider asked Marianne.

"So far so good."

"Since we're doing the procedure under local anesthetic, you're going to be awake. So we're going to put a headset on you playing classical music. You don't need to hear all the gory technical stuff."

"Fine with me."

"I'll be starting the procedure in a few moments, any questions?"

"I'll be praying for you," Marianne said. "And me."

The nurse in pink placed the black headphones over Marianne's ears. The strains of Strauss were instantly relaxing. Another nurse pushed over the television-like monitor and the laparoscopy equipment. Dr. Snider pulled up Marianne's gown to reveal her bulging mid-section.

"Scalpel," she said.

Merashoff handed her the instrument. She made a keyhole-sized incision near the navel, and inserted a small stainless steel nozzle.

"Pressure please."

Merashoff pressed the preset button and discharged carbon dioxide gas into the incision causing the abdomen to distend and separate from the internal organs. Snider withdrew the nozzle and worked a small stainless steel tube into the opening.

"Laparoscope," she said, holding out her right hand.

Merashoff handed her the thin, telescope-like instrument with a tiny video camera and light on the end. She ran the instrument in through the tube and immediately a red and yellow image flashed on the screen. She gently pressed the scope down into the amniotic sac. An eerie picture of the infant filled the screen, its eyes wide open and skin pure white.

"Why is the skin so pale?" Merashoff asked.

"That's normal," Snider said. "All infants are covered with a protective coating at this point of gestation; it's called vernix."

She worked the instrument down to the baby's torso.

"Good God," Snider said. "He's swollen to twice his normal size. His kidneys are visible here. See?"

Merashoff nodded. "Do you think there's an obstruction in the urethral pelvic junction?"

"Could be" she said. "Or maybe he's got congenital hydronephrosis. That would explain why the kidneys are so distended."

She pressed the scope against the baby's stomach, his arms and legs flinched.

"This is going to be tricky."

* * * * * * *

3:15 P.M.

The effects of the sedation began to wear off. She placed her hand on her protruding stomach.

"I must still be pregnant."

Her head pounded and throbbed at the temples. Her mind sluggishly fought through a slough of haze. She opened her eyes to see the fuzzy outline of a smiling woman wearing a white uniform.

"I must have made it. Thank God."

The voice of the lady in white came into focus. "Ms. Austin, we've just landed in Columbus. It's time to disembark."

"Oh yeah, all right. Thank you very much." Lori shook off the cobwebs and started grasping the situation while the other passengers filed past. "Man, what a hangover. And who is Ms. Austin?"

Lori stood and attempted to straighten the wrinkles out of her hot pink maternity dress. She joined the procession of passengers exiting the plane.

Lori had not seen her mother in almost two years; their last meeting resulted in continuous arguments. The two women butted heads like rams, and when they got together it was like sparks and gunpowder – an explosive combination. Lori regretted this meeting more than any she could remember; she regretted placing herself in a position of weakness. Any wisdom Lori had seen in her decision to get pregnant seemed like sheer foolishness now, and she knew her mother would rub her nose in it. Worst of all, she could say nothing in her own defense.

Lori stepped off the plane and scanned the crowd but couldn't find her mother. She scurried down the ramp.

"Lori, where are you going?"

Lori startled. "I didn't see you."

The two women hugged shoulder-to-shoulder in a distant and cold manner. Lori stopped and gave her mom the once-over.

Joanne Franks was a short, dumpy woman in her early fifties, and over the past couple of years she really packed on the pounds. She kept her red hair short and combed in a masculine style. Deep crow's feet dug in the corners of her hazel eyes. She had no neck to speak of, and her double chin tucked right into her collar.

"You look great," Lori lied. *Thank God I must take after my father, whoever he is.*

Lori's birth resulted from a well-timed one-night-stand Joanne Franks orchestrated in order to get pregnant. Artificial insemination was not readily available in the mid-seventies for a woman who wanted children without the burden of a husband. Joanne felt proud of herself for such a clever plan.

"You look pregnant," Joanne said. She stepped back in order to get a better look at her bulging daughter.

"Thanks for noticing, I see you still have a firm grasp of the obvious."

The two women walked toward the baggage claim area.

"Lori, I'm going to say this once and then let it go. This has got to be the dumbest, most idiotic thing you've ever done. Next time, please talk to me before you do something stupid."

"There won't be a next time, okay. I admit this was stupid." Lori's head throbbed from the alcohol. She tried to restrain her normally sharp tongue. This would not be a good time to snap.

"There better not be, I called in all my favors on this one."

"Speaking of favors." Lori patted her hand on her belly. "When will this be taken care of?"

"If all goes well, at the end of next week." Joanne stopped walking on seeing the large crowd in the baggage area. "Go pick up your bags. I'll get the car and meet you out front."

"It figures that I get stuck carrying the bags."

The two women pushed their way through the crowd in opposite directions. Lori arrived at the baggage claim area just as the conveyor started to rotate. Before long the first of her over-stuffed gray suitcases made its way around to where she stood. She struggled to lift the heavy bag over the knee-high, aluminum ledge lining the conveyor.

"Allow me to help you with that," a tall man in cowboy boots standing to her right said. His accent must have been from somewhere down south – Texas perhaps. He hoisted the bag with his left hand. "Do you have anymore comin'?"

"Just one more, it's turning the corner there." Lori pointed at the bag. Ordinarily, she despised the idea of a man doing anything for her out of perceived weakness. But the hangover combined with jet lag suppressed her feminist zeal.

"Thank you, sir."

He smiled as he looked at her belly. "No problem at all, ma'am. If you don't mind me askin', when are you due? It looks like your ready to go any minute."

"Ah . . . ah . . . well, next month."

The unexpected question stung her heart.

The tall Texan reached over and grabbed the second bag; he struggled with its weight. "Is it a boy or a girl? I have two boys myself."

"I'm really not much of a conversationalist." She reached over and snatched the suitcase from his hand. "I can make it from here. Thanks."

Lori pressed by the man like the building was burning down. "Some people can't mind their own business," she said. "Imbecile!"

* * * * * * *

"Honey, can you hear me?" Andy Lewis said while gently brushing the reddish-brown strands of hair out of his wife's closed eyes. Monitor wires snaked and tangled all over her chest and stomach. One monitor beeped in synch with Marianne's heart. The second monitor silently showed the baby's rapidly beating pulse.

Andy had watched the baby's monitor go from the dangerous range to just above normal in the three hours following surgery. He wasn't a doctor but he knew that must be a good sign.

While Andy attended to his wife, both Snider and Merashoff walked into the room. They both looked like they had been run through the ringer.

"Mr. Lewis we need to talk," Dr. Snider said with absolutely no expression on her face. It came from years of breaking bad news. "Things went remarkably well, but we're far from being out of the woods. We weren't able to install a shunt because of the infection; we can't be sure the ureters will stay open." She rubbed the corners of her mouth with her thumb and forefinger. "The infection is worse than we expected."

"Is Marianne going to be all right?" Andy's narrow face went pale. His large Adam's Apple disappeared momentarily while he swallowed.

"Marianne is going to be just fine," Merashoff said. "She's a little wiped out from the surgery. Our major concern is for the baby."

"Anytime an infection is left untreated for such a long period of time, a number of complications can arise," Dr. Snider said.

"Complications? What do you mean complications?"

"We're not sure if the infection has caused any permanent damage to the baby's organs. We also don't know if the urinary tract will stay open. We'll know a whole lot more in the morning."

"What's . . . ah . . . what's the worst case scenario?" Andy asked.

Dr. Snider looked directly into Andy's bloodshot eyes and said, "Worst case scenario is the baby has suffered permanent organ damage that could ultimately lead to miscarriage and death. But let me add that developing infants are quite resilient." She paused. "As I said, we'll know more in the morning."

"What do we do now?"

"We wait and pray," she said.

For the first time since entering the room, Dr. Snider smiled. She reached over and patted Andy on the elbow before turning and walking out of the room. Merashoff nodded and followed her out.

Andy scooted the stiff-backed chair over to the side of Marianne's bed and lowered the railing. He didn't care how long it took, when she opened her eyes she would see his loving face looking back at her. Andy leaned over and kissed his wife gently on the lips. He lifted her tiny limp hand, and he prayed until slumping into sleep on top of Marianne's right hand.

At 3:16 A. M. Andy awoke to a gentle poke in the eye. Pain shot down his stiff neck and back from the hours of having his tall lanky body locked in the same contorted position.

"You're awake," Andy said, instantly alert. "How do you feel?"

"I feel okay, just a little sore," Marianne whispered. She looked at Andy then she giggled.

"What's so funny?"

"You have my hand print on the side of your face. It looks like I belted you a good one."

"I see how it is, I hold a twenty-four hour vigil, and I get repaid with a slap in the face!"

Marianne smiled. "I love you. Thanks for being here for me."

"I love you too. We're in this together no matter what."

They kissed.

A wave of pain swept over Marianne's face.

"What is it? Something wrong?"

"I'm all right, but what did the doctors say about the baby?"

Andy rubbed his chin. He wanted to be truthful, but at the same time he didn't want to worry his wife.

"Everything is going to be all right. The doctors said they would know more in the morning. There really isn't anything else to do. It's all in God's hands."

"We're in good hands then. I was really scared for a while. But I do feel at peace now. God has been so good to us."

A few hours later Snider and Merashoff made the early morning rounds. They exchanged pleasantries, and made a beeline for the charts. The doctors looked confused as they checked and re-checked the data. All of Marianne's vital signs were normal, and even more remarkable, all the baby's vital signs were perfectly normal as well.

"With numbers like these, I don't see why you can't be released tomorrow," Snider said.

"The power of prayer, huh Doc?" Andy said.

"Indeed."

Dr. Merashoff went over the charts a second time; he scratched his head and paced around. Then he went over them a third time. He couldn't stop shaking his head.

"In all my years of medicine I've never seen anything like this. It's just not statistically possible. That baby had less than a one percent chance of surviving the surgery; a complete recovery was totally out of the question, much less in twenty-four hours . . . no explanation for this."

"Oh yes there is, Doc" Andy said.

"Maybe there is something to this God thing," said Merashoff. "After all, eight months ago science said it was impossible for you to conceive."

8

6:08 A. M.
Fly, Ohio

Lori Franks lay in bed watching the red digital lights on her radio alarm clock mark off the hours she couldn't sleep. She wrestled off the covers and rolled onto her left side. It didn't matter, no sleep could be found on that side of the bed either.

The baby kicked.

"Dammit! I hate it when it does that. I can't wait to get this little parasite out of my body."

Parasite? I'm your own flesh and blood. I'm a part of you, Mommy."

"Shut up, I told you not to talk to me."

She gave up the fight for sleep. In a few hours the anesthesiologist would take care of the insomnia. She rocked herself out of bed and shuffled down the hall to splash some water on her face and brush the sour taste out of her mouth. She looked in the mirror.

"I'm not doing anything wrong. This procedure isn't any different than a face-lift."

A face-lift wouldn't snuff out my hope and future.

Lori shook her head trying to rid herself of that condemning voice. But the voice of human conscience dies slowly. She returned to her room and dressed in front of the full-length mirror, then brushed her long, black hair.

Why not give me up for adoption. I'm old enough to survive on my own you know.

"Shut up!"

"Who are you talking to?" Joanne Franks asked from across the hall.

"Go back to sleep, mother. I'm on my way out the door."

****

9:45 A. M.

Marianne Lewis received a clean bill of health and was released from the Cleveland Clinic the day following her surgery. Merashoff gave her an electronic blood pressure cuff and thermometer and told her to closely monitor her vital signs. The slightest change could indicate an infection or complication in the developing baby. Several times each day Marianne diligently charted her vital signs. For five straight days everything proceeded normally, then came day six.

She sat at the kitchen table while Andy prepared his special recipe for pancakes. He waltzed over to the table with a wash cloth draped over his left arm doing his best impression of a French waiter. He placed the steaming plate of pancakes on the table and Marianne doubled over in pain.

"What is it? Are you all right?"

"I . . . I don't know, but whatever it was it feels like it's easing up." Marianne winced again. "Wow, like a hot poker."

"Is there anything I can do?"

"Go get the thermometer off the night stand in the bedroom."

Andy hustled off to retrieve the instrument; he returned and set it on the table in front of Marianne. She placed the probe under her tongue and pressed the button. They bumped heads trying to get a closer look at the numbers racing up the scale; it finally stopped at one hundred degrees.

"Andy, I think you should call Dr. Merashoff."

"Yeah, yeah . . . all right."

He trotted to the phone hanging on the wall a few strides away. He flipped through the Yellow Pages and found the number to University Hospital. He dialed the number and began to pace.

"Hello . . . yes . . .I would like to speak to Dr. Merashoff please. Yes . . . he's in obstetrics. Sure I'll hold."

Andy placed his hand over the mouthpiece and looked at Marianne. "They've got me on hold; they're paging him."

He uncovered the mouthpiece. "Yeah . . . he's what? Yeah, put me through then. Hello doctor, this is Andy Lewis. I'm calling about my wife. She's eight months pregnant and has just experienced a sharp burning pain in her side . . . ah . . . ah . . . well . . . yes we did . . . it's a hundred right now. Yeah . . .I understand. Thank you."

Andy hung up the phone with a frustrated look on his face. "Dr. Merashoff was in some kind of meeting."

"Who was that on the phone?"

"The attending physician in the obstetrics department. He said these pains are not uncommon at this point in the pregnancy. He said to continue monitoring your temperature, and if it continues to rise call him back."

"I've got a better idea," Marianne said. "Let's pray."

* * * * * * *

9:45 A. M.
University Hospital

"You want me to do what?" Merashoff said. "I should choke you little man for asking me such a thing. If we weren't standing in the hallway, I would choke you."

"Dr. Merashoff, I know full well how you feel about this procedure, but with Dr. Jarvis out of town you're the only doctor on staff who is trained to perform it." Banko tried to sound as authoritative as possible. It wasn't working.

Allen Banko, a slightly built man in his early thirties, stood barely five foot five and suffered from a Napoleonic complex. He always dressed in expensive suits. On any given day it looked as if he stepped off the cover of *Gentlemen's Quarterly* magazine. He had jelled his light brown hair perfectly in place.

The hospital intercom blared to life: "Dr. Merashoff line one. Dr. Merashoff line one, please."

Banko took a few steps back and grabbed the phone hanging on the wall behind him. "Dr. Merashoff is in a meeting with the hospital administrator at the moment. Please tell the caller to try back later or patch them through to the attending physician." He hung up. "Sorry about that. Where were we?"

"I'm trained for these abortion procedures because you threatened to fire me if I didn't get certified."

"Hey, don't kill the messenger. These decisions come from higher up than me," Banko lied.

"Why can't this wait until Jarvis gets back; it's an elective procedure."

"The powers that be have their reasons. The young lady will be here shortly. We're handling this as a Jane Doe."

"That explains it. Some rich girl or politician is trying to save face. I'll have you know that I'm doing this under protest. I became a doctor to save lives, not to take them."

"Believe me, if I could get someone else I would. But unfortunately, you're the only game in town at the moment. I'm sorry to put you under the gun."

Merashoff opened his mouth to dig into the smaller man once again when a nasal female voice blared over the hospital intercom: "Mr. Banko, please report to Admissions. Mr. Banko, report to Admissions please."

Banko turned to the fuming Russian and said, "That must be her. Go ahead and get ready for surgery. I'll take care of all the paperwork and escort her to Pre-Op myself."

Banko picked up the wall phone. "Yes, very good. Show her to my office. I'll take care of everything from there." He hung up the phone and trotted down the hall and stopped at the elevators. Merashoff watched the little man scamper away.

"Only in America does a doctor get paid to kill a baby because it is politically correct." Utterly disgusted, he turned and headed for surgery.

* * * * * * *

10:01 A. M.

Lori wore a tan raincoat, a matching broad brimmed hat, and sunglasses. Her disguise made her stick out like a sore thumb.

The secretary ushered her past the Admissions office and escorted her directly into Banko's office. The mahogany-paneled wall gave the room a dark and formal appearance. The couch and matching chairs, covered with burgundy leather, added a touch of elegance.

"Good morning, Miss Franks. I am Mr. Banko, the hospital administrator. Welcome to University Hospital."

"I was told my real name wouldn't be used."

"No one outside of this room will know who you are. However, for legal purposes, you must be admitted under your real name. I'll list the operation as an elective cosmetic procedure."

"Sounds good to me."

"Believe me Miss Franks, Judge Spitzer-Clark stressed to me the delicate nature of your situation. I'll walk you through the necessary forms, and everything from this point forward will be handled under the name Jane Doe."

Banko swiveled to his computer console and typed in the necessary information on the computerized forms; he could hear Lori fidgeting in the high-backed leather chair.

"Reason for the abortion?" Banko asked without turning around.

"What do you mean by that? Obviously I don't want to have a baby."

Banko swiveled back around to face her, and with as much fraudulent compassion as he could muster said, "Whenever a late-term abortion is conducted, we prefer the documentation reflect the procedure is needed to protect the health of the mother."

"I see."

"So would you say the abortion is needed for your emotional or possibly financial health?"

"Emotional health."

"Of course. I can take care of the rest from here. Now let me show you to your room, and we'll get the ball rolling."

"How long will this take?" she asked.

Banko looked at his watch. "It's about ten-fifteen, if all goes well, you should be ready to check out by six o'clock this evening."

Banko led Lori on a maze-like journey through the hospital. They stopped at the outpatient ward where Lori changed into the customary hospital gown. From there Banko pushed her by wheelchair to the operating rooms dedicated for maternity and birthing.

"I'm going to leave you in the capable hands of Nurse Lander. I'll stop by and see how you are doing in recovery." With that Banko walked away.

Nurse Lander helped Lori onto a waiting gurney where she became the focus of a flurry of activity. First a nurse walked in and inserted an I.V. into her left hand. Another technician came in and attached sensors to her chest and abdomen. Next, the anesthesiologist entered and injected a tranquilizer called *Twilight* into her I.V. port. An orderly came and wheeled Lori into the operating room and transferred her to the birthing table. Landers strapped her legs in the stirrups, and finally, Dr. Merashoff walked over to give the pre-surgery briefing.

"Ms. Doe, I'm Doctor Merashoff. I assume you know why you're here, so I'll simply explain what's going to happen. First, we'll induce labor. You'll need to be awake for this part so you can push as needed. Since you're at the beginning of the eighth month, the fetus hasn't yet inverted into the normal head-down delivery posture. Basically, this will be a breach delivery so it may take a little while. Once the fetus travels down the birthing canal, I'll ask you one last time if you want to change your mind and fully deliver the baby. If you decide to continue with the abortion, I recommend that you be anesthetized at that point."

"I've never been put to sleep before, so if it is all the same to you I'd like to stay awake," Lori said. "I'm tough."

"Toughness has nothing to do with it," Merashoff said in a condescending tone. "Once the fetus is delivered to the neck and begins to kick and squirm, you may bear down and complete the delivery. You can imagine the complications for both you and the hospital if the baby is inadvertently delivered. Also, the sound of the cerebral extraction is quite gruesome. It would probably be best to spare you the unpleasantness of hearing your own baby's brains sucked out."

Having said his piece, Merashoff walked over to have Nurse Lander help him on with his surgical gloves.

"Quite a grizzly display of bedside manner, doctor. Don't you think?"

The burley doctor looked directly into her eyes. "Killing a perfectly viable baby is a grizzly thing, nurse, don't you think?"

"Well, I – "

"They may be able to force me to do it, but they can't force me to like it."

He turned and walked back over to the birthing table and injected the I.V. port with a labor-inducing drug. Within minutes the contractions began, Lori dilated to four centimeters, and everything progressed normally. Then the door crashed open and a young nurse rushed in looking terror-stricken.

"Dr. Merashoff, we need you across the hall! Stat!"

"What are you doing in here without a mask? Can't you see I'm already engaged? Someone else will have to handle it."

"But doctor, the patient is one of yours – Marianne Lewis."

His rosy cheeks went pale. He turned to the Surgical Resident. "Snelling, stabilize her. Notify me when the baby reaches the birthing canal."

He ran across the hall as fast as his seventy-four year old legs would allow. He rushed over to the table where Marianne's eyes were glazed and barely open; her red hair matted to her ashen face by a cold sweat; she looked cadaverous.

"What's the situation?" Merashoff shouted.

"The patient is in premature labor and hemorrhaging," said the Emergency Room nurse still holding the I.V. drip bottle she had carried on the sprint through the hospital.

Merashoff leaned over so that only Marianne could hear. "Don't you worry. Everything is going to be all right. I'm here now."

He took the young attending physician aside.

"What do we have here?"

"It's not good," Dr. Davies said. "Her blood pressure is one-eighty over one-twenty, and her temperature is one-hundred and three. If we don't do something quick we stand to lose both the mother and child."

We are *N O T* going to lose anyone," Merashoff said, glaring at the young doctor. "What are the infant's vital signs?"

"We're just now hooking up the monitor."

Merashoff glued his eyes to the display; his heart sank when the numbers appeared: forty beats per minute. *Something is terribly wrong. The baby is not going to make it.*

"What're we going to do?" Davies asked.

"We're going to operate right now. An emergency C-Section is the only chance we have to save the baby."

"But doctor, the patient is too weak. She may not survive the anesthetic. Shouldn't we attempt a radical extraction first?"

"The birthing canal is too small. The baby hasn't had the chance to naturally widen the bone structure. We don't have that kind of time. We'll do the procedure with a local anesth-"

A yelling Nurse Lander burst into the room.

"Doctor Merashoff, the fetus has entered the birthing canal. You must come at once!"

"Davies, prepare the patient for surgery. I'll be back as soon as possible." He glanced at the baby's heart monitor as he rushed out of the room: thirty beats per minute.

He won't live another two minutes.

The nurse held the door open. Merashoff ran as fast as his aging body would go, sweat poured through his green surgical scrubs.

"She's dilated to eight centimeters," Snelling said. "The infant has traveled into the birthing canal feet first."

"Are you sure you want to proceed with the abortion?" Merashoff asked Lori.

"Certainly," Lori said, her speech slurred.

The irony of the situation hit Merashoff square in the head like a ton of bricks. *Ms. Doe has a perfectly healthy baby she wants me to kill, and Marianne is going to deliver a stillborn and would give her own life for a healthy baby. This just isn't right. If I could somehow switch them without being detected, everyone would be happy. As long as there is one live baby and one dead baby, why would anyone care?*

He looked over at Dr. Snelling. "Put her out. I'll be right back."

The old doctor lumbered out of the room.

Diversion, I need a diversion. Something. Anything!

He found the answer in the hallway, just above the biohazard storage container – a fire alarm. Across the hall sat the incubator gurney used for prematurely born infants. Merashoff looked at the alarm then looked up and down the hall.

"Here goes everything."

Instantly the siren let go a deafening series of shrieks about two seconds apart.

Merashoff burst into the operating room and found Marianne strapped down, and people running everywhere in chaos.

"Everyone calm down. This is probably a false alarm. You know the procedure. All non-essential personnel must leave. Davies and I will stabilize the patient. Everybody out, NOW!"

The room cleared.

"Davies, give her the local and hold down the fort. I'm going to check on the patient across the hall. When I get back be ready to make the incision."

Merashoff had never felt so alive, the adrenaline rush surging through his veins was incredible.

The siren continued to blare. The old Russian ran back across the hall and found Dr. Snelling attending to Lori.

"Snelling, you will leave at once. All non-essential personnel must leave the building."

"I'll stay. You may need my help."

"You will leave now! I am ordering you. GET OUT!" Merashoff's thundering bass voice spurred Snelling to action. He ran out of the room.

Forty-five seconds had elapsed since Merashoff pulled the alarm, and he knew time was quickly running out. In fact, deep in the bowels of the hospital the security staff ran the computerized diagnostics on the high tech alarm system.

Ordinarily, a breech delivery is a complicated and time-consuming procedure. However, time was not a commodity Dr. Merashoff could waste. In order to deliver the baby quickly, he would have to violate every prenatal technique known to medicine.

Using a pair of forceps, he reached in and searched for the baby's foot.

"Got it. I hope I don't dislocate the hip."

He jockeyed the instrument to firm up his grasp and gave an aggressive tug. Both feet broke into the air together.

"The first bit of luck I've had today."

He grabbed both feet in his bloody rubber gloves and gave a powerful pull.

Lori moaned.

Merashoff's stomach twisted. He glanced up at the head of the table. Lori was sound asleep. He gave a second strong pull and the baby came out in one quick squirt. He cut the umbilical cord and ran for the door cradling the baby in his arms. The sound of the blaring siren drowned out the baby's first cries. It was a girl.

Out in the hallway, Merashoff put the newborn in the glass-covered incubator gurney, and ran for the crash doors on operating room three. He rushed over to the operating table and glanced over at the baby's heart monitor: zero beats; the monitor display flat-lined. The blaring siren kept Davies from noticing the monitor sounding its alarm. Merashoff pulled the lead wires off Marianne's bulging stomach.

"Scalpel."

Davies reluctantly placed the instrument into Merashoff's trembling hand. The old man gasped for air clearly exhausted.

"Are you all right?" Davies asked. "I can handle it from here if you want."

"I'll be fine. I just need to catch my breath."

At that moment the fire alarm stopped.

The staff will be back any moment. I've got to move fast. "I'll do it," Merashoff insisted.

He steadied his hand and made a twelve-inch incision along Marianne's waistline. He quickly separated the opening and lifted out the lifeless body of a baby boy. He looked directly into the young doctor's eyes and barked, "Cut the umbilical cord! Then call a Code Blue!"

Merashoff crashed through the operating room doors holding the tiny corpse like a football. He slung the little body into the biohazard disposal bin. He got behind the incubator gurney and pushed it toward the intensive care unit. He hadn't taken three steps before a squad of doctors and nurses turned the corner and ran directly down the hall towards him responding to the Code Blue.

I made it! I pulled it off!

He did indeed make the switch undetected, but those would be the last words to run through the old doctor's mind. The spirit was willing but the flesh could take no more. Doctor Joseph Merashoff died instantly of a massive heart attack at the age of seventy-four, dead before he hit the floor.

9

BACK TO THE PRESENT
8:15 A. M.
Monday, August 14

During the week following the Kisner arraignment hearing, Danial spent as much time as his hectic schedule allowed preparing for the upcoming Grand Jury hearing. He realized Lori Franks was deadly serious in her threat to seek the death penalty. So at this point, a victory for the defense may be nothing more than stopping the execution. After all, life in prison is a far cry better than taking a ride in the electric chair.

A good lawyer always keeps several irons in the fire, and Danial was a very good lawyer. He spent the early part of the week running between Estate Probate hearings and depositions for a few civil suits. He also had court appearances for other criminal cases. All the while he felt the mounting pressure of this potential death penalty case invading his every thought. He spent more than a few nights tossing and turning and staring at the ceiling.

It often bothered him that some of his clients were actually guilty. Danial's policy not to allow his clients to tell him their side of the story until just before trial prevented the added complication of sorting through lies. It also allowed him to fulfill his oath to provide his clients zealous representation within the bounds of the law, without violating his conscience. Sometimes his clients would volunteer a confession of guilt in which case Danial would withdraw himself rather than attempt to deceive a jury or the court into thinking his guilty clients were innocent.

Facts were facts. The police caught Archie Kisner beating an unconscious woman. How do you get around something like that? How do you reconcile in your own mind defending a guilty man? Danial perched at his desk grappling with these issues when Jennifer came in with the morning mail.

“Do you want to open it?” she asked. “Or should I go through and separate it according to case number?”

“Go through it yourself. I’m kind of deep in thought at the moment.”

Even if he is guilty, he still deserves the best defense I can provide. There must be some precedent in the law that will give me at least one leg to stand on.

“Danial, you’re not going to like this.”

“What is it?”

“It looks like an indictment – ”

“For who?”

“Archie Kisner,” she said. “I thought the Grand Jury hearing wasn’t scheduled until next week sometime.”

“It’s not supposed to be. Let me see that.”

Jennifer handed the papers to her boss and stepped around the side of his desk to look over his shoulder. Danial carefully read the document then ran his fingers through his wiry hair. “That woman is completely unbelievable. She went to the Grand Jury on her own and got them to issue a secret indictment.”

“What’s a secret indictment?”

“A secret indictment is when the prosecutor gets approval from a judge to go to the Grand Jury without notifying the defense when the hearing will be held. The results aren’t disclosed to the media until the indictment is served. It’s supposed to be used when the State believes the defendant poses a substantial flight risk.”

“Why would the State be afraid Archie might flee? He’s in the county jail, isn’t he?”

“This is Lori Franks’ way of trying to keep me off guard.”

“If you don’t mind me saying so,” Jennifer said as she nudged his shoulder. “It looks like it worked.”

* * * * * * *

8:20 A. M.

At University Hospital, Dorothy Bernhart showed no sign of improvement. Her pupils remained dilated and unresponsive. She had suffered two mild seizures over the past six days. The medical staff managed to stabilize her, and remove her from the ventilator. The neurologists determined the most severe damage occurred in the frontal lobe, the region of the brain that controls, among other things, eye tracking and self-awareness.

The M.R.I. revealed no sign of permanent head trauma. The electrical impulses in Dorothy's brain showed her mind functioning just below the conscious level in a profoundly deep sleep.

Dorothy Bernhart's parents didn't return to their home in Virginia following John's funeral. Instead, they took a drive up to Niagara Falls to get away from it all. It took the hospital three days to notify them of the assault on their daughter and then to secure the family's permission to install a feeding tube. And to make matters worse, arrangements had to be made for the infant's burial.

Maria Bonfini, a volunteer in the extended care wing of the hospital, took special interest in Dorothy. She stood only four feet, ten inches tall and had fluffy white hair. Her skin, weathered and wrinkled, looked leathery. She wore thick round glasses over her pale blue eyes and spoke in heavy broken English. Everyone called her grandma.

"I hope you like flowers," Grandma said as she walked into Dorothy's room. "I brought you some nice fresh daisies from my garden. I'll just put them here on the night stand."

She carefully arranged the bouquet and then glanced over at Dorothy. Most of the discoloration had faded from Dorothy's face, leaving her looking yellowish and swollen. Tubes were taped in her mouth and nose and a number of round electrodes were attached to her forehead. A myriad of wire and tubes snaked everywhere.

"They've got you wired up like a Christmas tree. I don't know whether I should talk to you or put some presents under you."

The old woman laughed.

"I hope you weren't offended by my little joke. I was just funnin' with you. I didn't mean no harm."

She leaned over the bed to get a closer look at Dorothy's face.

"You sure are a pretty thing. Back in the old country all the boys thought I was a looker myself."

A middle-aged man dressed in white entered the room. "Sorry to disturb your visit, but it's time for Dorothy's physical therapy."

"Do you want me to leave?" Grandma asked.

"No, you can stay. Have a seat for a few minutes. This won't take long."

The therapist proceeded to flex and bend Dorothy's arms and legs vigorously.

"Is all that necessary?" she asked.

"Don't worry, she can't feel a thing. Besides, the more work we do now, the easier her recovery will be later when she wakes up.

A few more twists and contortions and the therapist left. Grandma stood with a groan and made her way to the side of the bed. She looked around to make sure they were alone then reached out her bony, liver-spotted hand and placed it on Dorothy's forehead and began to pray quietly in Italian.

"Dear Lord, Your Word says that the power of life and death is found in the tongue. And You command that Your children speak words of encouragement to build up one another. So right now I speak the words of life over this woman. I plead the blood of Jesus over her wounds.

"I pray emotional healing as well as physical healing, because I know when You do open her eyes, she'll be facing not only the death of her husband but now the death of her child as well. Dear God, You and I both know the painful sting of losing a child, so I pray You will comfort her in the midst of her pain. I ask these things in the name of the Lord Jesus Christ."

* * * * * * *

8:30 A. M.

The more Danial thought about the way Lori Franks went about getting the death specification added to the indictment, the more agitated he became. He always distrusted secret indictments. It was too easy for an unscrupulous prosecutor to type up an indictment and have some lackey scratch a signature in place of the Grand Jury Foreman without a Grand Jury even voting on the case. He carefully examined the indictment line-by-line and read through the legalese out loud.

"COUNT ONE: On or about the 4th day of August, 1997, in the State of Ohio, County of Jefferson, Archie Kisner did, by force, stealth or deception, break into an occupied structure at 303 Lovers Lane, with the purpose to commit therein any theft offense or any felony where the offender inflicted, or attempted, or threatened to inflict physical harm of another – to wit Dorothy Bernhart. Whoever violates this section, § 2903.11, is guilty of aggravated assault, an aggravated felony of the third degree.

"COUNT TWO: On or about the 4th day of August, 1997, Mr. Archie Kisner did, while under the influence of sudden passion or in a sudden fit or rage, did knowingly cause serious physical harm to Dorothy Bernhart. Whoever violated this section, § 2903.11, is guilty of aggravated assault, an aggravated felony of the third degree.

"COUNT THREE: On or about August 4th, 1997, Archie Kisner did purposely cause the death of Baby Jane Doe Bernhart, while committing or attempting to commit an aggravated burglary. Whoever violates this section § 2903.01, is guilty of aggravated murder, and shall be punished as provided in section § 2929.03 of the Revised Code.

"Specification to Count Three: The above offense was committed while the offender was committing, attempting to commit, or fleeing immediately after committing or attempting to commit aggravated burglary – a crime punishable by death."

Danial flipped over to the last page to examine the signatures and filing date, and it nearly jumped off the page at him.

"There's no signature; no one signed the indictment. No signature means the indictment is invalid. I caught her at her own game." Joy welled up in his heart. "She tried to be slick and avoid facing me at the hearing, and now we will see how well she likes being caught in her own trap."

Danial smiled like the proverbial cat that ate the canary until Andy Lewis staggered into his office white as a ghost. The look on his face made Danial's stomach sink. He stood up and raced over to his friend.

"What's wrong? You look like death warmed over."

Andy couldn't muster the strength to say anything. He reached in his back pocket and handed Danial a letter from the court. Andy nodded for Danial to read it and then slouched down in the love seat next to Jennifer's desk. Danial's eyes raced over the documents, his face turned red and veins bulged out of his neck. Every few sentences he muttered, "Unbelievable."

* * * * * * *

8:45 A. M.

Monday mornings were never a cheerful time for Lori Franks, but this Monday had to be one of the worst she could remember. The past week turned in to one continuous, acrimonious argument with her mother. The topic occasionally changed but the outcome remained the same.

Lori sat in her office, head pounding, allowing the final argument of the weekend to replay in her mind.

"Lori, you're so predictable it sickens me. You make a habit out of compounding your mistakes."

"Mom, I've lived for a lot of years just fine without you. I regret asking your opinion."

"Sought my opinion! That's a laugh. You've never sought my opinion in your life. You simply tell me what you've done when it's too late. And usually I have to break my back to get you out of trouble – "

"Mom, you act like my entire life has been one big failure. If you haven't noticed, I'm doing quite well for myself. I don't recall you driving a Volvo when you were twenty-nine."

"You seem to forget, my sweet little girl who got you this job."

"My memory works just fine. And I don't see how I'm compounding anything."

"How can you not see what you're doing? Every time you make a mistake, you immediately react, and your reaction is what gets you in trouble. You found out the little girl was born on the same day as your abortion, and you file for custody and sue the hospital. What were you thinking? You'll be laughed out of town if the child isn't yours."

"Yeah, that may be, but what if she is mine? The hospital will make me a millionaire – "

"It doesn't matter how much money is involved," Joanne shot back. "You act before you think. If you're right, what're you going to do with a daughter?"

"I'll cross that bridge when I come to it. I simply filed the suit. I can withdraw it without prejudice at anytime. I now have access to information that would otherwise be confidential. And besides, I filed a request for a *Gag Order* so none of this will get out." Lori paused. "I'm a lot brighter than you give me credit for mother."

"Well, I'm telling you now. I will not lift one finger to help you. Do you understand me? I've already packed, and I'm leaving." Joanne Franks stormed out of the front door and drove away.

Lori shook with venting rage as these bitter scenes flashed through her mind. And now she regretted turning to the bottle for help. The room spun out of control, and her head pounded so loud she could barely concentrate. The steaming black coffee didn't help a bit.

The phone rang. Lori forced herself to focus.

"Prosecutor's Office. Lori Franks speaking."

"Ms. Franks, this is Derek Norton, the Court Administrator. I received a message you called my office late Friday after I left. What can I do for you?"

"You may not be aware yet, but I've filed a joint civil action against University Hospital and Mr. and Mrs. Andrew Lewis. I'd like to know who the case will be assigned to."

"Allow me to check the docket." Lori could hear the clicking of computer keys over the phone. "The case is assigned to Judge Myrtle."

"Oooh . . . I see."

"Is there something wrong with Judge Myrtle?"

"No, there's nothing wrong with him. It's just I believe a case dealing with such sensitive issues may be better handled by someone with a domestic background. Maybe someone like Judge Spitzer-Clark."

"Let me check her docket."

Lori tapped her fingertips on the desk while the middle-aged bureaucrat searched the computer for the information.

"It doesn't look good. Spitzer-Clark's caseload is full. She would have to trade cases with Judge Myrtle in order to get you in."

Instantly, a scene from last year's Christmas party flashed before Lori's eyes. Derek Norton, in spite of being married, had spent almost the entire night hitting on her. She decided to play a new angle.

"Could you look into it for me?" Lori asked, sounding incredibly seductive for this time of the morning. "I would consider it a personal favor, and I always repay favors."

"Well . . . ah, since you put it that way. I do know the bailiffs for both Judges. I'm sure I could arrange for your case to be assigned where you want it."

"Thank you ever so much."

"Don't mention it. But remember, you owe me one." His words dripped with insinuation.

"Anything at all. Just let me know."

She hung up the phone. "Men are such pigs, and much too easy to manipulate. Now let him even smile at me wrong, and I'll sue him for sexual harassment."

* * * * * * *

8:50 A. M.

Tears streamed down Erin Lewis' face, but she really didn't know why. Erin was an exceptionally bright little girl; she seemed to perceive things very deeply for a child of such tender years. She saw the look on her father's face when he opened the morning mail. Then when her mother started crying after he rushed out of the house, Erin knew something was wrong – terribly wrong. And now she just couldn't stop crying.

"Mommy, how come we're crying?"

"Everything is going to be just fine, sweetheart. Daddy got some unexpected news this morning, but it's nothing to worry about. Okay?"

"Mommy, it scares me when you cry."

"Erin, Mommy is crying because she loves you so much. It's hard for you to understand right now. But God loves us, and He isn't going to let anything bad happen to us. Daddy went down to see Uncle Danial. He'll know what to do."

* * * * * * *

8:55 A. M.

The color returned to Andy Lewis' face. He still felt sick to his stomach. A flood of emotion overwhelmed his senses. What if some doctor made a mistake? Mistakes happen all the time. Andy had to be honest with himself, Erin didn't look like either he or his wife. Marianne had red hair; he had light brown hair, and Erin had jet-black hair. And what about those eyes? No one on either side of their families ever had eyes like that. Somewhere deep inside Andy had always wondered where those violet blue eyes came from. But the possibility of Erin not being his daughter had never occurred to him. Or had it? Didn't he question why Erin had no kidney problems, even though she nearly died in her mother's womb from kidney failure. And why wasn't there a scar from the operation? At the time, the answer seemed obvious to him — God had worked a miracle. But now things didn't seem so clear. These and a thousand other questions and doubts tormented Andy's mind.

Jennifer made a fresh pot of coffee. For whatever reason, Jennifer thought the solution to any crisis was a fresh pot of coffee. Danial read over the papers again.

"Andy, all this really amounts to is an official notice that a civil action has been filed against you. At this point, there's no danger you'll lose custody of Erin."

"What happens now?"

"I'll file an answer to the complaint and move for discovery. We'll exchange interrogatives and depositions. By the time we get to trial, we'll know exactly what Ms. Franks is up to."

"What kind of evidence could she possibly have?"

"It's hard to say. I'd bet she'd request a DNA test. Other than that, your guess is as good as mine."

"That's not very reassuring."

"I'm sorry, Andy. But it's just too early to tell. She requested a Gag Order. So she isn't seeking publicity."

"Be brutally honest with me; what's the worst case scenario?"

"If things break bad, she could prove she's the biological mother. But before you panic that still doesn't mean the court would automatically give custody to Franks. You and Marianne are the only parents Erin has ever known. I can't imagine any court in the country taking a child out of such a stable environment."

"What should I tell Marianne?"

"Reassure her, comfort her. There's nothing we can do at this point. The wheels of the legal system grind slowly. It could be months or even years before this case gets to trial, if ever. And allow me to remind you what you've taught me. God is completely in control, and now is one of those times you've got to sit back and let God be God."

"I know. But it sure doesn't make it easy."

"Do you want to pray?"

"How about you lead us this time, buddy," Andy said, his voice cracking. "I'm not up to it."

Danial wasn't used to being the spiritual leader in the group. After all, it was Andy who had led him to Christ some ten years earlier; and ever since that day, Andy had been a spiritual mentor to Danial.

Holy Spirit please give me the words to heal a broken heart.

Jennifer watched as the two men held hands and prayed.

10

9:25 A. M.

Andy Lewis left the building. Danial closed the door to his office and spent the remainder of the morning deep in thought. He kicked off his shoes, put his feet on the desk, and reclined back in his chair. He placed his hands behind his head and stared motionlessly at the ceiling.

It took Danial nearly a year to break Jennifer from interrupting these "brain storming sessions." She thought he was joking when he said he did his best work staring at the ceiling. It just didn't make sense to her how anyone could *think* for three hours at a time without so much as moving a muscle. But no matter how odd this behavior appeared, she couldn't argue with its effectiveness. Danial would emerge from these seclusions refreshed and focused.

Jennifer froze outside Danial's door with her fisted hand poised to knock. She hoped against hope that the door would magically open without her having to interrupt. But after nearly five minutes of waiting, she banged on the door.

"Sorry to bother you, but Mr. Stedman is here to see you. He said you spoke to him on the phone last week and were expecting him today."

The door swung open. Danial looked much more composed than when he went in, and his voice contained a sense of urgency.

"Jennifer, call Reverend Stone at the Greater Ohio Valley Pro-Life Association. See if you can get me in to see him this afternoon." He turned to Stedman and said, "Please step into my office."

Eugene Stedman stood six foot four and was bone thin; he wore an ill-fitting tan suit. He had thick, salt-and-pepper hair for a man in his sixties, but his face was so wrinkled he looked old enough to be one of the original Pinkerton detectives. After retiring from the Steubenville police department with thirty years of service, Stedman opened his own private investigation business. He didn't need the money; he loved excitement.

Danial walked around his desk, sat down and pulled out a fresh legal pad. Eugene Stedman sat in one of the two maroon leather chairs next to the desk.

"Mr. Stedman, it is an honor to make your acquaintance."

"Same here, sir. I've heard you're supposed to be some sort of F. Lee Bailey or something?"

"I don't know about all that." Danial crossed his feet and locked his hands behind his head. "So what do you have for me?"

"I've spent the past week tracking down every shred of information I could find on your Kisner brothers. I've got to say, they ain't what you would call model citizens." Stedman cleared his throat.

"I kind of thought that would be the case."

"They lived together in a rundown apartment on Fifth Street. However, the landlord said no one has been there since Archie got arrested. She let me look around."

"Meager?"

"Meager isn't the word for it. It looked like the final burial ground for old beer cans, almost no furniture, one bed. The landlord said Ralph slept on the bed, and Archie slept on the floor in the kitchen. She also said something else I think you'll find interesting."

"What's that?"

"She said it surprised her Archie was the one arrested, since she had all the problems with Ralph."

"What kind of problems?"

"She said Ralph had a lot of wild parties. A few times she had to call the police. Said Ralph was pretty much a bad seed."

"What's the landlord's name?"

"Kathy Ryrie. I thought you might want to interview her yourself. Her phone number is in my report."

"Very good, Mr. Stedman. I can see already that working with you is going to be a blessing. What else do you have for me?"

"Archie worked as a furniture delivery man for Cannery Furniture in Wintersville. I spoke to his boss. According to him, Archie worked hard, wasn't very bright, and was clumsy with the furniture."

"Any disciplinary problems with him?"

"A couple fights. Apparently, other workers picked on Archie quite a bit. They called him the Elephant Man – "

"So let me guess, Archie attacked them."

"No – at least not for picking on him – Archie beat up two guys for picking on the young girl who worked in the office. He beat them pretty good from what I understand. No charges were filed."

"More violence on his record."

"I also tracked down Ralph Kisner's watering hole. A place called *The Underground*. A real dive; the patrons weren't big on answering questions. But according to the bartender, Ralph hasn't been in since all the trouble with Archie jumped off. I find that hard to believe."

"It sounds like our friend Ralph Kisner has gone into hiding." Danial sat back in his chair. "I wonder what he has to hide?"

"It's hard to tell. I haven't found anyone to confirm it, but I suspect Ralph's involved in the drug trade here in town. I have a few leads."

"How about character witnesses? Anyone willing to say something nice about Archie?"

"Nope, that's going to be a tall order. The landlord said Archie didn't have any friends she could speak of. Basically, he either tagged along with Ralph or stayed home by himself."

The intercom next to the phone buzzed. Danial pressed the button on top of the black box. "What is it Jennifer?"

"You have a two o'clock appointment with Reverend Stone. Also, the Clerk of Court's office called. They said you had a question about an indictment being unsigned or something. I told them you'd call back."

"Thanks Jennifer. We'll be finished here in a moment."

Danial turned his attention back to Stedman. “Now, where were we?”

“You asked about character witnesses for Archie, and I said we had no luck.”

“Yes, that’s right. You mentioned something about a report for me.”

Stedman reached into his beat-up leather bag and pulled out a folder. He handed it to Danial.

“I like to give my clients a weekly progress report. You’ll see an outline of everything we discussed here, as well as the amount of hours I’ve spent so far.”

“Very professional.”

“I aim to please.”

“What’s your game plan from here?”

“Like I said, I have a few more leads to track down. I’ll do whatever it takes to find the elusive Ralph Kisner. It seems to me that he could shed a whole lot of light on all this. Unless you would rather I do something else?”

“No, not at all. Let’s get together again next Monday for another update. In the meantime, give me a call if you find anything earth-shattering.”

The two men stood up and shook hands. Danial walked him to the door.

* * * * * * *

9:55 A. M.

The Lewis family lived in a two-bedroom, brick Victorian. The front of the house had four windows with black, decorative shutters. Short hedges enclosed the small front yard, and a large magnolia tree grew just to the left of the living-room picture window.

Andy Lewis parked his car in the driveway and sat for a few moments before getting up the nerve to face his wife. Andy took his wedding vows seriously, especially the ones concerning protecting and cherishing. He didn't know how to explain all this to her without crushing her quiet and gentle spirit.

Andy prayed silently for a few more moments, then got out of the car. Marianne had seen the car pull up and stood waiting by the front door.

They hugged.

"I've been so worried since you left," Marianne said with tears streaming down her face. She tried to be strong but the safety of Andy's embrace released the floodgates once again.

"It's gonna be all right. Danial is taking care of everything."

"But what if they take Erin away?"

"It's okay. No one is going to bust up our family."

Erin ran in from the kitchen and squeezed between them. Marianne squatted down. "Sweetheart, your Daddy and I have some things to talk about, grown-up things. How about going outside to play for a little while?"

"I don't wanna! Can't I play with you?"

"It'll only be for a few minutes. As soon as we finish you can have some ice cream. How does that sound?"

"Can I have chocolate and vanilla both?"

Marianne smiled. "You drive a hard bargain, but I guess this time it'll be okay."

Erin trotted outside and climbed on the rope swing, which hung from the lower branch of a large willow tree in the backyard. Too bad ice cream doesn't have the same medicinal effect on adults. Andy sat down on the couch with his wife, and tried the best he could to relate everything Danial said.

They hugged a lot, cried a lot, and prayed a lot. When they both seemed to be in control of their emotions, Andy put his arm around Marianne and said, "You know, this isn't happening by coincidence. We're under spiritual attack and the good news is no matter how bad things look, the Lord Jesus Christ has already won the battle for us. All we need to do is keep our eyes focused on Him."

They kissed.

"I love you," he said looking into her tear-stained eyes.

She smiled. "Thank God for giving me such a spiritual and loving man."

Andy smiled back at her. "And all these years I thought you loved me for my good looks."

* * * * * * *

10:20 A. M.

Danial closed the door behind the old private detective and turned to see Jennifer crying. While Jennifer could be a bit scatter-brained at times, she wasn't emotional. Danial reached into his pants pocket and pulled out a handkerchief. He offered it to her.

"What's the matter?"

She took the handkerchief and blew her nose.

"I don't know what's gotten into me." She blew her nose again. "I'm not much of a religious person, but you and Andy kind of overwhelmed me today. I actually saw a difference in him when you prayed; like his batteries were recharged or something."

"Jennifer, I have always respected your privacy, but I'd love the opportunity to sit down with you sometime and share exactly what I believe."

"When I started working for you two years ago I wasn't too interested in spiritual things. But, after being around you day-in and day-out, I can see you have something I don't."

Jennifer held out the used handkerchief.

"No thanks, you can keep it," Danial said. "How about we talk for a few minutes right now?"

"I don't think now is the best time for me."

"Whenever you're ready then; you let me know. I don't want to be pushy." *Please Lord, allow the Holy Spirit to draw her to you now.*

"Well, maybe when you get back this afternoon," Jennifer said. "Don't forget your meeting with Reverend Stone, and the Clerk's office called."

"I almost forgot about seeing the Clerk. It'll be interesting to see his take on Archie's unsigned indictment." Danial looked at his watch. "If you'll give me just twenty minutes when I get back, I promise you won't regret it."

Jennifer felt an invisible, oppressive force enshrouding her, she could almost hear a voice telling her to flee and not listen to anything he said. At the same time, she felt an opposite force telling her to open up and accept.

"I'll give you twenty minutes, but I have the right to walk away at any time. Agreed?"

"Agreed." Danial flashed a disarming smile. It radiated a sincere joy and peace most people don't have.

* * * * * * *

1:35 P. M.

Dorothy's parents finally got the word and rushed in from Niagara Falls. They spent the morning at Dorothy's bedside. A short, thin man in a white coat stepped in behind then; they didn't notice him. He ran his hand through his thinning white hair and cleared his throat.

They still didn't notice him.

He pressed his index finger against the bridge of his glasses and slid them up his long, straight nose and cleared his throat louder. They both turned to look at him.

"Good morning, I'm Dr. Fritz, Chief of Neurology."

"Charlie Barcia, this is my wife Cindy." He stretched out his hand. "We're Dorothy's parents."

"I can assure you, your daughter is receiving the very best of care."

"How is she?" Mrs. Barcia asked. "I mean . . . look at my little . . ." Her voice choked by emotion.

"It's always difficult to diagnose the status of a coma patient. We've been following the standard protocol of raising her blood pressure in order to force oxygen to the brain. But to this point it doesn't seem to be working."

"How bad off is she?" Mr. Barcia asked.

"Dorothy's inner cranial pressure is at fifty-two. The normal range is zero to ten."

"Isn't there anything you can do?"

"We've had some success with a new procedure. It involves inserting a small tube between the two hemispheres of the brain that will monitor and slowly reduce the pressure."

"Then do it," Mr. Barcia said.

"Inserting the tube isn't too serious, but she has another problem."

"What is it?"

"A vascular malformation has developed."

"A what?" Mr. Barcia asked.

"Basically, it's an abnormal growth of veins and arteries."

"Is it serious?"

"Quite serious, and it puts us in a difficult position. On the one hand we need to keep her blood pressure high to keep her brain functioning, but at the same time the added pressure could cause the vascular malformation to explode. We need to operate as soon as possible."

"Isn't there any other way?" Mrs. Barcia asked.

"I'm afraid not. I wish I had better news for you."

"Do whatever you think is best," Mr. Barcia said, putting his arm around his wife. "We'll sign whatever forms or waivers necessary."

* * * * * * *

2:50 P. M.

"What do you mean, this is not the actual copy of the indictment?" Danial asked as he pointed to the certified stamp from the Clerk's office. "It says right here this is a true and correct copy of the indictment on file in your office. How is it the copy you have on file is signed, and my copy is not?"

"It must have been a clerical mistake," the nervous clerk said.

"Clerical mistake! You've got to be out of your mind. The rules of court say once the prosecutor submits the indictment to the Clerk it officially becomes part of the record. And now you're telling me the indictment in my hand is not official."

"That's exactly what I'm telling you. Someone made a mistake by sending you an unsigned indictment."

"How is that possible?" Danial's voice elevated. "Explain to me how an unsigned indictment can slip through all the proper channels, and when I bring it to your attention, it unaccountably comes up signed. What did they use, invisible ink?"

"I . . . ur . . ."

"It sounds a whole lot like someone tampered with the files. Has anyone signed out the Kisner file since I asked about the unsigned indictment?"

"Let me check the log book."

The clerk's hands trembled as he searched through the pile of papers on his desk and found the log sheet. He ran his finger down the list of case numbers.

"As a matter of fact, the file was checked out shortly after I notified the Prosecutor's office of your complaint. Lori Franks signed out the file about an hour after your phone call."

"Now, isn't that interesting," Danial said through clenched teeth. "An invalid indictment is submitted to you – clear evidence of prosecutorial misconduct which would set my client free – and I bring it to your attention. You notified the prosecutor's office. Lori Franks examined the files, and low and behold the indictment gets mysteriously signed. Doesn't that sound fishy to you?"

No answer.

"Well, I should have expected as much. I'll deal with this in court."

Danial stormed out of the office then out of the building. He took a walk around the block to regain his composure. As soon as his head cleared, he remembered his appointment at the Greater Ohio Valley Pro-Life Society with Reverend Stone. He hurried back to his car with just enough time to make the appointment.

Danial always made a point of being emotionally detached from his cases. It was easier to stay objective and sharp that way, but now he just couldn't help himself. Lori Franks was trying to put a man to death just to prove she could. To make matters worse, she now had her ruinous sights set on his two closest friends, Andy and Marianne Lewis. Times like these beckoned the old Danial Solomon to rise up and retaliate.

Growing up in a volatile home infused instability into the young Danial Solomon, and he knew his parents stayed together for his sake, which added a touch of guilt. They fought about everything, and showed no affection. His father was a hard-drinking steelworker. Danial's memories were filled with nights spent alone in his room listening to his drunken father vent frustration on his mother. Danial vowed to be different when he became a man, but in high school, he already displayed flashed of his father's temper.

In spite of being the most brilliant student to ever come out of the Steubenville School District – having scored a perfect 1600 on the SAT exam and a 38 on the A.C.T. – Danial incubated seeds of self-destruction. He began drinking beer at fourteen, and was prone to explode into fits of rage over minuscule irritations. On one occasion after an argument with a girlfriend, he pulled the door off his locker then smashed his calculator on the floor. Several teachers agreed Danial would implode before his intellect could blossom. That prediction would have come to pass if it wasn't for a chance meeting with Andy Lewis on the campus of Ohio University.

* * * * * * *

2:55 P. M.

Lori Franks sat in her cluttered office feeling pretty good about herself. While disappointed she hadn't covered her tracks better, she found it exhilarating to have stayed one step ahead of Danial Solomon. She only worried the ink hadn't dried on the forged indictment before Danial arrived at the Clerk's office.

Lori picked up the phone and hit the speed-dial.

"The Honorable Judge Spitzer-Clark's office, may I help you?"

"Hello, this is Lori Franks. I would like to speak to Judge Spitzer-Clark."

"One minute please," the receptionist said.

"Jane Spitzer-Clark speaking."

"It's Lori – "

"Oh, hello Lori. What can I do for you?"

"Have you had the chance to read over my brief?"

"Yes, yes, fine work. I'm looking forward to watching you make Solomon dance. I see where you're going with this; it's genius."

"Thanks Your Honor, but I'm – "

"You'll be able to tie him in knots between the two venues. Besides, beating Solomon in a death penalty case will make a nice feather in your cap."

"I'm actually calling to see if we can schedule the pre-trial hearing as soon as possible."

"I'll clear my docket for you," the judge said with a lilt in her voice. "I'm looking forward to getting a crack at the famed Mr. Solomon myself."

* * * * * * *

4:45 P. M.

Danial pulled his car into the space next to Jennifer's Chevy Cavalier. His body felt weary, his emotions wrung out from the day, but his spirit eager for his twenty minutes with Jennifer. He bowed his head.

"Most gracious Heavenly Father, I ask Your anointing upon me as I seek to share the wonderful message of your Son, Jesus Christ, with Jennifer. I pray You'll prepare her heart to receive this gift. I ask You to give me the words, and lead me by the Holy Spirit to boldly proclaim Your Words of eternal life to her. I ask this in Jesus' name – amen."

He checked his coat pocket to make sure he had his Gideon's New Testament. He took a deep breath and climbed the three steps to his office. Much to his surprise, two people were waiting for him on the love seat next to Jennifer's desk. They looked to be in their sixties. Danial closed the door and the couple stood. Before Danial could introduce himself the woman cut him off.

"Are you Danial Solomon?"

"Yes, I am."

"Are you representing this Kisner fellow?"

"Yes I am."

Wham!

She slapped him in the face.

He raised his hand to the spot where a red handprint already formed. He stammered, gestured, grimaced, and finally blurted out, "What'd you do that for?"

"I'm Dorothy Bernhart's mother."

11

6:15 P. M.

Dorothy Bernhart's parents stormed out of the office. Danial flopped down in the chair next to Jennifer's desk in disbelief. He knew they were hurting, and they had every right to be angry. Danial knew all too well that anger. Just ten years earlier, his uncle had been stabbed to death in a bar fight.

Jennifer watched her boss slouch over in the chair with his head in his hands. She spoke softly, "Rough day, huh?"

"That would be the understatement of the century."

"Is there anything I can do for you?"

"I'll be all right in a moment. I didn't expect to come back to the office and be assaulted by perfect strangers. I know they must be going through hell right now, but why take it out on me?"

He stood up shaking his head, then walked into his office.

He searched for a comfortable place to park his weary body. The couch looked inviting.

Jennifer made a fresh pot of coffee. She poured two cups of the piping hot liquid, and carried them into Danial's office. She sat on the couch near his feet and offered him a cup. He sat up and accepted it. Without looking up from her coffee she said, "If it would make you feel better, I'm ready to hear what you have to say about your faith."

"Are you serious?"

"I'm ready."

Danial perked up as if he had been hit in the face with a cold glass of water. "Thank you so much for giving me this chance. I promise you won't regret it."

"Sounds good to me."

Danial sipped his coffee, then took a deep breath. "If it's all right with you, I'd like to start by asking you a spiritual question."

"Go ahead."

Danial looked deeply into her eyes. "Have you come to the place in your spiritual life where you know with absolute certainty if you died today you would go to heaven?"

* * * * * * *

6:45 P. M.

Eugene Stedman did his best work after business hours. His many years as a police detective produced a myriad of contacts with people the average citizen considers the scum of the earth. The tip Stedman operated on said Ralph Kisner had several strong drug connections around town. So what better place than a Methadone Detox Clinic to find a suitable informant.

Stedman pulled his white, rust-stained pick-up truck in the vacant space in front of the clinic. The front tire hit a pothole and water sprayed up through the corroded floor boards. From this spot he had a clear view of the patrons entering and exiting the building. It wouldn't be long until a reliable source turned up. In the meantime, he pulled out a pack of Camel non-filtered cigarettes and fired one up. He took a deep drag and belted out a wet, body-wracking cough.

"I really should quit." He had been saying that for nearly forty-five years.

The old detective tapped his fingers on the wheel as sweat poured off his forehead. He thought back over the course of his life and the rocky marriage he shared with his ex-wife, Melinda. She endured the long nights he worked stakeouts; she endured his long nights drinking; but she left when he started to hit.

After a half-hour and a half pack of Camels, the object of his search materialized. Jack Webster, a die-hard heroin addict, walked out the front door of the clinic. He was short and exceptionally thin. In spite of the August heat, he wore a filthy yellow and green flannel shirt with the tattered sleeves buttoned at the wrist in order to cover the long needle scars lining his arms. Webster had dark, greasy hair that looked as though it had not been washed in ages. Life on the streets exacted a high toll on Jack Webster.

Stedman's face lit up when he saw the reliable source of information. For twenty bucks Webster would tell his own mother's deepest secrets.

Stedman leaned out the window. "Hey Webster, come here."

Webster goose-necked up-and-down the sidewalk, his eyes shifting rapidly as he walked up to the passenger side door.

"Get in. I'll give you a ride."

Webster looked around again and climbed in. He slouched down in the seat.

"Relax. I've been off the force for several years now. This is a personal call."

"What do you want, man?"

"I just want to chat a little while. Where you headed?"

"You can just drop me off a the park, man."

"Let me cut right to the chase here, Jack. What do you know about a guy named Ralph Kisner?"

"That depends," Webster said.

"How does twenty bucks sound?"

"Sounds like I might know him, man."

Webster reached out his hand. Stedman pushed it aside. "Not so fast my friend. You give me a little, I'll give you a little."

Stedman pulled out four, five-dollar bills and held them in plain view. "Let's start at the beginning."

"Kisner is a pack mule for a big dope boy out of Pittsburgh."

"Pack mule?" Stedman asked. His wrinkled face betrayed his confusion. "What's a pack mule?"

"A pack mule is a runner. He doesn't deal; he just delivers the stuff."

"What kind of stuff are we talking about?"

"He only moves the hard stuff: heroin, crank, coke – "

"What kind of people does he deal with?"

Webster didn't answer. He stuck his hand out. Stedman placed a five-dollar bill in the dirty palm.

"Who does he deal to?" Stedman asked.

"Old Ralph don't play with the little fish like me. Rumor has it, he has some pretty big clients up in the high rent district."

"Put some names to that statement."

Again Webster stuck out his hand, and again a five-dollar bill landed on it.

"Remember dude, you didn't hear this from me. But word on the street is Kisner delivered to Gus Gram and a few other big wigs from the hospital."

"Gus Gram! You mean as in County Coroner, Gus Gram?"

"That's the one."

"You better not be blowing smoke," Stedman said as he shot a glare at the fidgeting passenger.

"I'm not, I swear. I got that one straight from the horse's mouth. Ralph and me were pretty tight for a while there. I even went on a couple of runs with him, till he found out I was using again."

"Where can I find old Ralphy boy?"

"No one has seen him since his brother got knocked. My guess he's worried his brother may give up the grapes on some of his moves."

Stedman took one last deep drag off the dwindled cigarette and flicked it out the window.

"How do I find him?"

"Your best bet is his ex-old lady, Grace Showers. She lives over on Fourth Street."

"One last question and I'll give you the last ten bucks." He held out the money. "Was Ralph involved in that mess up on Lovers Lane?"

"I really don't think so, man. With all the money he's making from running, it doesn't make sense he would be involved in penny ante stuff like breakin' in houses."

Stedman held out the rest of the money. Webster grabbed it and stashed it in his shirt.

Stedman pulled the truck over to the side of the road.

"Get out."

"Hey, this ain't the park, man."

"And I ain't the bus. Now get out!"

* * * * * * *

Jennifer puzzled over Danial's question for a moment trying to come up with an honest answer. "I would have to say I don't think anyone can know for sure they're going to heaven. I would like to think I'll go there when I die, but I can't say for certain."

"I appreciate your honesty," Danial said. "But I can assure you, it is possible to know for sure you're going to heaven when you die. In fact, the Bible says, 'I write these things . . . so that you may know that you have eternal life."

"I never knew the Bible said that. I went to church for a long time and never heard that before."

"Don't feel bad. Most churches today don't do a very good job of communicating this simple message," Danial said. "But before we continue, could I ask you a second question?"

"Sure. Go right ahead."

Danial drank another sip of coffee. "Suppose you were to die today, and stood before God. And suppose he was to ask you why He should let you into His Heaven. What would you say?"

Deep furrows appeared on her forehead. "That's ah . . . ah . . . another tough question. I guess I'd say I've been a pretty good person all my life, and I've never tried to hurt anyone on purpose."

"Is there anything else you would say?" Danial asked softly.

"I'd say I tried really hard to follow the Ten Commandments, and overall I've done more good things that bad things. I guess that's what I would say."

Danial's blue eyes lit up, and a big smile spread across his face. "When we started this conversation I thought I had some good news for you. However, now that I've heard your answers to my two questions, I know I have the best news you have ever heard. Are you ready for some good news?"

"Lay it on me, Danial. I certainly could use some good news."

"Well, the good news is that heaven is a completely free gift. The Bible says, 'The wages of sin is death, but the gift of God is eternal life.' You see, if we receive what we deserve we would go to hell. But God offers us heaven as a free gift."

"That is good news," she said.

"The Bible also says, 'For it is by grace you have been saved, through faith and this not from yourselves, it is a gift of God, not by works, so that no one can boast.' To me this verse is like a summary of the Bible in a nutshell. So let's go through it carefully to make sure you have a good understanding of the key terms. First of all, it starts out with the phrase, 'For it is by grace you are saved . . .' Do you know what the word *grace* means?"

Jennifer rubbed one elbow. "Is it like receiving mercy from God?"

"Close, but not exactly," Danial said. "For years I thought the words *grace* and *mercy* were interchangeable, but I came to find out they're not. Mercy is not receiving the punishment you deserve when you do something wrong, whereas grace is receiving something good that you don't deserve. For example, if a police officer doesn't give you a ticket after stopping you for running a red light, he has shown you mercy because you deserved to be punished. If, on the other hand, the officer gives you a gold watch instead of giving you a ticket, now he has shown you grace. Do you see the difference?"

"Yeah, I think so – "

"Look at it this way. You couldn't perform enough good deeds or religious rituals to earn your way into heaven, so God offers it in a way you can receive it, as a gift."

She nodded her head. A strange calm enshrouded her body.

"I think this can be seen more clearly if we see what the Bible says about the nature of man. The Bible declares in several places very clearly that man is a sinner."

"I have heard that."

"In one place it says, 'All have sinned and fallen short of the glory of God.' When the Bible says all it means all. That means not only are you and I are sinners, but people like Billy Graham, Mother Teresa, and anyone else you can think of are sinners as well. We're all in the same boat."

"I never really looked at it that way before," Jennifer said. "But it does make sense."

"It makes perfect sense, and if you consider how easy it is to sin, we all sin several times each day. Let me give you an example. Say there was a man who lived a really good life. He never broke any Commandment, he always showed love to everyone he met, and he never told a lie or took the Lord's name in vain. Would you agree that he would appear to be without sin?"

"Yeah, I would say so."

"Well, let's say that three times a day he had a sinful thought – he never acted on the thought – but say he had a lustful thought a few times a day and then immediately repented. Do you realize with just three sins a day, he would have over one thousand sins in a year's time? And if he lived to eighty-five, he would have over eighty-five thousand sins to account for."

"Whoa."

"What do you think would happen if you went before Judge Williams with eighty-five-thousand prior offenses?"

"I'd get slammed," she said.

"You're right, you'd get slammed. And what do you think would happen if you stood before God, the Almighty Judge of the Universe, with all those sins?"

"I'd get slammed."

"Precisely. The trouble with us humans is we like to use a sliding scale to determine who exactly is a bad person, and usually a bad person is someone who is a little bit worse than us."

"When you put it that way, you're right."

"But when you consider all the sinful thoughts and actions and speech we engage in without even thinking about it, it's plain to see it's impossible for us to do more good things than bad. I used to think God would have a big scale, and on one side He would weigh out my good deeds, and on the other He would place my sins. And if the good outweighed the bad, I would go to heaven. It made sense to me, but the Bible says, 'There is a way that seems right to a man, but in the end it leads to death.' If I would have continued to trust in my ability to do more good than bad, I would have ended up spiritually dead."

"I would have too," Jennifer said, feeling convicted of her self-righteousness. "I was trusting in myself to get me to heaven."

"It's human nature, but this will come into sharper focus when we see what the Bible says about God. And this is very important because most people don't have a true understanding of the nature of God. Most people like to see God as being a merciful, loving Father. And that's true, the Bible says God is love. However, the same Bible says God is holy and therefore must punish sin. It says, 'He will by no means let the guilty go unpunished.' And this creates a dilemma in man's way of thinking. If God is only loving, then He would have to forgive everyone: you, me, Hitler, Charles Manson, and even the Devil. If God were only just, then he would have to condemn everyone since we all have sinned and fall short of the glory of God. So who gets to go to Heaven?"

"I don't know," Jennifer said with a shrug.

"God solved the problem through the person of Jesus Christ. So let me ask you, what is the greatest thing you ever heard about who Jesus is?"

"Well, I've heard He was the son of God."

"That's true, but I'm a son of God. Is Jesus different from me?"

"He did miracles and healed people."

"Those are things he did, but that isn't what I'm getting at." He rubbed his stubble-ridden chin; it made a scratching sound. "Have you ever heard that Jesus is God? The New Testament makes this claim in nearly every book. In *Colossians* it says that Jesus is the image of the invisible God, and God was pleased to have all his fullness dwell in him. *Romans* says that Christ is God over all and forever praised. *Philippians* says Jesus in his very nature is God. I could go on and on."

"I had no idea the Bible said all that."

"It's the best seller every year and almost no one reads it," he said. "Are you familiar with the story of doubting Thomas?"

"Isn't that where Thomas didn't believe Jesus had risen from the dead or something?"

"Exactly, and when Jesus appeared to the disciples a second time, Thomas called him, 'My Lord and my God!' And the significant thing is that Jesus accepted these titles. If Thomas shouldn't have called him God, Jesus would have corrected him. Jesus was quick to correct his disciples."

"You're right." She folded and unfolded her arms.

"Jesus is the infinite God-man, and He died on the cross to pay the penalty for our sins, and rose from the dead to purchase a place in Heaven for us which he offers to us as a gift."

Danial reached into his coat pocket and pulled out a Gideon's New Testament. He laid it flat on the palm of his left hand. "It works like this. Say my left hand represents me. I want to go to heaven, and God wants me to be in heaven as well. And say this Bible represents the record book of my life, and all the sins I have ever committed. As long as I have this sin in my life, I won't go to heaven. But here is the good news."

Danial held out his right hand parallel to his left, directly in front of Jennifer. Her eyes were glued to his hands.

"Say my right hand represents Jesus Christ. The Bible says, 'All we like sheep have gone astray. We have each turned to our own way, but the Lord laid on Him the iniquity of us all.'" As he spoke, he transferred the Bible from his left hand to his right by flipping his hands and sandwiching the Bible between them. He waited to speak until Jennifer stopped looking at his hands. They made eye contact, and Danial continued.

"This is what happened when Jesus died on the cross for us. God took all of our sins and the sins of all His chosen people who ever lived, and He placed them on Jesus. And just like I transferred the Bible from my left hand to the right, God transferred our sins and put them on Christ and then punished him in our place. Jesus died in our place; He paid the penalty for our sins. All we have to do is receive this precious gift through faith."

Jennifer began to cry. She pictured in her mind Jesus suffering and dying for her. She didn't know why, but she even imagined Jesus thought about her while He hung in agony on the cross. She pulled out the saturated handkerchief Danial had given her earlier and wiped her eyes. Mascara smeared across her face. She took a deep breath and asked, "Can you explain to me how I can have this faith?"

"I would be delighted to," Danial said, his voice filled with compassion. "Faith is the key to heaven. But just like there are different kinds of keys, there are different kinds of faith. It doesn't matter how sincere you are. If you believe in the wrong thing, you'll be sincerely wrong. First, I'll explain what saving faith is not, and then I'll explain what saving faith is. Sound good to you?"

Jennifer nodded as a single tear welled up in the corner of her eye. She patted the handkerchief against her face to dry it.

"What people usually mistake for saving faith is believing in God with their mind alone. Most people say they believe in God, but that doesn't mean anything. In fact, the Bible says, 'You believe there is one God, good! Even the demons believe that and tremble. The demons aren't going to heaven. Saving faith is more than merely believing with your mind. It takes trust."

Danial felt his face flush. Often when sharing this wonderful news he would get so excited he would nearly hyperventilate. He sat back, took a few deep breaths then continued.

"Saving faith is trusting in Jesus Christ alone for your eternal life. Notice I didn't say believing but *trusting*. Trusting is believing plus action. Let me give you an illustration. Many years ago, a man spread a tightrope across Niagara Falls. He walked across and to everyone's amazement he pushed a wheelbarrow full of bricks across the rope on his way back. When he arrived safely on land again, the crowd cheered him wildly. He motioned for the crowd to quiet down. When he had their attention, he asked, 'How many people believe I can push a person across the falls in this wheelbarrow?' The crowd cheered once again as everyone in the crowd raised their hand. Then he asked them a second question, 'Would anyone like to volunteer?' No one did."

Jennifer laughed. "I see the difference. The people believed he could do it, but didn't trust that he could do it."

"That's exactly right. We're called not only to believe in Jesus but also to trust in Him to get us to heaven. Does this make sense to you?"

"For the first time in my life, it makes perfect sense."

"Well, here is the big question. Would you like to receive the free gift of eternal life by trusting in Jesus Christ right now?"

12

8:15 P. M.

The last vestiges of sunlight glimmered over the western horizon, and life in Mt. Pleasant, Ohio settled in for the evening. The crickets chirped, the fireflies dotted the tree line with their yellow bulbs, and inside a brick Victorian century home, Marianne Lewis' heart broke in two.

After all, Erin certainly looked a lot like Lori Franks. What if there was some sort of mix-up at the hospital? What will happen to Erin? What if the court decides to give temporary custody to Lori Franks until this whole mess gets straightened out? How much should she tell Erin? At seven years of age, a traumatic experience like this could scar her emotional development forever.

* * * * * * *

8:17 P. M.

Danial prayed silently while he waited for Jennifer to answer the most eternally important question anyone ever has to face. But he couldn't understand why the hesitation. Tears streamed down her face, but she made no attempt to speak.

Jennifer couldn't believe she had lived her entire life without ever hearing this amazing news. Her emotions completely overwhelmed her to the point where she couldn't speak. She tried several times to open her mouth, but her lips refused to respond. Finally, she looked up; a strand of dirty-blond hair caught in her mouth.

"I would love to receive the gift of eternal life."

"That's wonderful, Jennifer," he fought the urge to shout. "Allow me to clarify the commitment you're about to make."

Jennifer smiled while she smeared her wet cheeks with the handkerchief.

"First of all, the commitment to Jesus Christ means transferring your trust to Him alone for your eternal life and believing he died for your sins, and that God has raised him from the dead. Do you believe that?"

Jennifer nodded.

"Good," Danial said. "You must receive Jesus not only as your Savior, but also as the Lord of your life. That means you live your life as Jesus directs. He directs you through the Bible and the Holy Spirit."

"I'm ready," she said.

"And finally, you must repent from the things you shouldn't be doing. A repentant heart is necessary for you to receive this wonderful gift."

"I've felt a war going on inside my heart." She blew her nose. "It amazed me today when you asked if you could share your faith with me, because I was about to ask you what made you so different. You're always smiling."

"The Holy Spirit is cool that way," Danial said with a toothy grin. No matter how many times he had shared the Gospel since becoming a Christian, it never ceased to amaze him how God worked all these things out in advance. He scootched closer to Jennifer and asked, "If you're ready to make this commitment, I can lead you in a prayer, and we can tell God what you just now told me?"

"I've never prayed out loud with anyone before – "

"I'll go slow, and I'll lead you all the way."

Danial reached out and took Jennifer's hands. They bowed their heads, and Danial began to pray.

"Dear Father God, we come to You in Jesus' precious name. I ask You to give Jennifer the strength to repent from the things she knows are wrong in her life. I also ask You to clear her heart and mind to understand fully the wonderful Gospel of Jesus Christ. I ask that You help her to believe.

"And now Jennifer, if you'd repeat after me. Dear Father God, I know that I'm a sinner."

"Father God, I know that I'm a sinner."

"I thank You for sending Jesus Christ to die on the cross for me."

She repeated.

"I ask you to come into my life as my Lord and Savior."

She echoed him word-for-word.

"I give you my life from this day forward to use as you see fit. In Jesus' name."

Jennifer again began to cry, however, she managed to repeat the words between heaving sobs.

"Dear Lord Jesus, I thank You for coming into Jennifer's life. I pray You'll anoint her with Your Holy Spirit so that she'll have full assurance she now has the gift of eternal life. Your Word says that Your gifts and call are irrevocable. We praise You for Your mercy and grace. In Jesus' mighty name. Amen."

By the time Danial finished praying, they both were in tears. They lifted their heads, and hugged, the embrace of a new brother and sister; they were now members of the same heavenly family.

They released their embrace, and Danial handed her the Gideon's New Testament. "I want you to have this. You should try to read the Bible everyday. I recommend you start reading the Gospel of John."

Danial helped her flip through the small pages to the Gospel of John. He slid a folded piece of paper between the pages to mark the spot.

"Try to read at least one or two chapters a day. And if you come across something you don't understand, underline it, and we can discuss it here in the mornings. Sound good to you?"

"I really appreciate this, Danial. I can't thank you enough for doing this for me."

"You don't need to thank me. I'm just one beggar telling another beggar where to find bread. It won't be long before you are doing the same for someone else."

"I hope so," she said.

"Aside from reading the Bible, if you want to grow spiritually you'll need to pray. Pray by yourself, pray at church, and pray with a friend. And don't think that you have to do all the talking when you pray. Spend some time listening to God. A lot of people complain they don't feel God is talking to them, but the truth of the matter is, they never give Him the chance to get a word in edgewise."

"I never thought of it like that."

"At some point you'll need a good church. I attend The Church on the Hill. If you'd like, I'll pick you up this Sunday, and we could go together."

"I'd like that very much." She folded the handkerchief and laid it on her lap. "I'm looking forward to it."

"Something else you need to do is tell someone else about the decision you just made today. I wouldn't be surprised if someone in your family has been praying for you for a long time now."

"As a matter of fact, my older sister is a Christian. She lives in Georgia, and I know she'll be thrilled to hear about this."

They spent the next two hours in good Christian fellowship. Danial shared how he had come to know Christ several years earlier. They laughed, cried, and prayed until they were both exhausted.

* * * * * * *

Thursday, August 17

Thursday afternoon just before quitting time, Danial received a certified letter from the Clerk of Courts notifying him that a trial date was set for Archie Kisner – September 7th – just three weeks away. Danial immediately called Judge William's bailiff and asked to have a hearing scheduled for Friday morning so that he could move for an extension.

* * * * * * *

Friday, August 18
7:45 A. M.

Danial walked into the courthouse preparing for what he thought would be a routine hearing. Surely some kind of mistake had been made; no judge in his right mind would schedule a capital murder trial to begin three weeks after the indictment came down.

Danial pushed open the huge oak door and found the courtroom nearly empty. Lori Franks sat behind the Prosecutor's table. A few lawyers milled around waiting for their hearings before the court. Danial took a seat at the defense table and opened his briefcase. A heavy-set Bailiff walked in from the Judge's chambers and shouted, "All Rise! Hear yea, hear yea, hear yea! This court is now in session. The Honorable Judge John Williams presiding."

The white-haired judge walked in, climbed the steps behind the bench, and rapped the gavel on the bench.

"You may be seated."

He sat down himself, put on the reading glasses that hung from a string around his neck and opened the file sitting on the bench in front of him. He flipped through the file, and removed his glasses.

"Let's begin. Why are we gathered here today, Mr. Solomon?"

"Your Honor, yesterday I received notice you set a trial date of September seventh for Archie Kisner, and I respectfully ask the court to grant a sixty-day extension so I can have adequate time to prepare."

"Your Honor." Lori Franks stood. "The State is ready to proceed now. Let's be honest here, the defendant was caught in the act. The evidence is cut and dry."

"With all due respect, Your Honor, a man's life is at stake. I don't see the need to rush — "

The judge held up his right hand, motioning for silence. "The request for a sixty-day extension has been denied. Trial will commence on September seventh with jury selection. Good day." He slammed the gavel down. "Next case."

Danial's jaw dropped open, dumbfounded. In all the years he practiced law, he never encountered such questionable events. An unsigned indictment mysteriously gets signed, a court date is set for a death penalty case for just a few weeks after the indictment, and now the judge completely disregards a valid motion, and doesn't even have the courtesy to act as if he considered it.

* * * * * * *

8:27 P. M.

Eugene Stedman eased his truck to a stop at the end of Fourth Street. He turned off the ignition; the truck shuddered and shimmied, then backfired. A large cloud of blue carbon billowed out of the exhaust. From his parking space, Stedman could see Grace Shower's apartment. She lived on the bottom floor of an over-and-under duplex. The siding, supposed to look like red brick and made of tarpaper, flaked off the building like old paint. A downspout slumped from the first corner.

He had spent the last four nights staking out her apartment and had her routine down pat. If his guess was right, Grace would be home by 9:00 P. M. He looked at his watch.

"It's about eight-thirty."

Stedman knew Showers wasn't going to sit down and spill her guts about Ralph Kisner if she had the kind of information he believed she had. A special ploy would be needed. His plan banked on the assumption those involved in the drug world were more afraid of those higher in the supply food chain than of the police. He only hoped he had the nerve to pull it off. Fifteen years ago this would have been a cakewalk, but things change in fifteen years.

He checked his watch again – 8:59 P. M. And as if on cue, Grace Showers turned the corner and headed for the front door of her apartment.

His heart pounded against the lining of his chest. A thin layer of sweat glistened on his wrinkled brow. He stepped out of his truck dressed in a black turtleneck, black fatigue pants and black, police issue, assault boots. He carried a crumpled paper bag under his arm. He looked around nervously, then slipped in the alley behind Shower's apartment. The moonlight fought through the valley of dilapidated buildings. Stedman felt more at ease as he crouched down near the back door to the apartment. Only a small cylinder of light shown off his face from the kitchen window where Shower's stood making a sandwich. He wiped his hand across his forehead; it felt dank and clammy.

His pulse accelerated, his mouth ran dry. He tore open the paper bag and fumbled with the black ski mask and service revolver. He jerked the mask over his head. With the gun in his right hand, he took a running start and burst through the back door.

Grace screamed.

"Hit the floor! Now!"

He jammed the gun in her face. "Shut up! I said get on the floor."

She dropped to the floor whimpering and waited for the sound of gunfire to snuff out her life. Stedman drove a knee into the small of her back.

"This ain't the cops, and I don't care if you live or die. I was hired to do a job, and I'll get paid no matter what. Do I make myself clear?"

Grace nodded.

He tucked the gun in the waist of his pants. He grabbed his trembling victim by the hair and pulled. She winced in pain.

"The people who sent me believe you and your boyfriend Kisner have been cutting the last few cocaine shipments."

"We didn't touch a thing. I swear! I haven't even seen Ralph in a month."

"Nice try, but I'm not buying it." He pulled tighter on the fistful of hair in his left hand. For some strange reason, he found himself enjoying his complete power over the frantic woman.

"Where's your boyfriend now, sweetheart?"

"I told you, I haven't seen him."

Stedman reached for the pistol. He pressed the gun against her cheek, and screeched directly into her ear. "That's not what I asked you! Where can I find him now?"

Grace blubbered out of control. She fought to get her halting words out. "I — heard — he — was — staying with his — uncle in Tiltonsville — but I can't — say — for sure."

"What's his uncle's name."

"Jim — Jim Morley."

He let go of her hair. Her forehead thumped on the floor. Stedman stood to make his escape, but realized he forgot something. He knelt back down, dug his knee into the small of her back again.

"Tell me about Gus Gram."

"What? What about Gus Gram?"

"Who is he dealing to?"

"I don't know."

Stedman yanked on her hair again.

She winced.

"I thought we got this straight before. We can do this the easy way or the hard way – "

"I don't know. I swear! All I know is he gets the stuff for some of his doctor buddies. That's all I know. Please . . . you're hurting me."

"If I find out you're lying, I'll be back. And I won't be so gentle next time. Do you understand me?"

Stedman bolted for the door before she could answer. He rushed out of the apartment and slipped into the dark alley. His heart thundered and pounded like a bass drum in his ears. He stashed the mask and gun in his pants before emerging from the end of the alley. He took a long walk around the block, and tracked back to the truck.

Stedman got the information he wanted and felt proud of himself, but the worst thing about it was he couldn't tell anyone how he got it. Now he'd sit back for a couple of days and follow the trail of activity. If his hunch was right, Showers would probably talk to Gus Gram, and with any luck she would also flush out Ralph Kisner. In the meantime, he intended to pay a little visit to the Jim Morley residence.

13

Tuesday, August 15
7:30 A. M.

Dr. Fritz stepped onto the pressure pad outside Operating Room 15 and the doors whooshed open. He walked into the sterile chamber, and the doors closed behind him. He stepped forward and the double doors in front of him slid open. The familiar scent of antiseptic tinged his nostrils. Dorothy Bernard lay underneath a blue surgical tent anesthetized; her baldhead elevated and pinned into a graphite head holder. Dr. Danville, Fritz's surgical resident, traced a purple surgical marker across the crown of her head in the shape of a large horseshoe. Two nurses dressed in pink scrubs attended to final preparations.

"We're just about ready to initiate the craniotomy," Danville said.

"You may proceed," Fritz said. "The ball is in your court for the next hour or so."

Danville took a deep breath.

"Scalpel."

The nurse standing to his right placed the blade into his rubber glove covered hand. He precisely traced the blade along the purple line, then handed it back to her. He attached a hook-like wire along the edge of the incision to retract the loose flap of scalp.

"Drill."

The nurse handed him the stainless steel instrument. He stepped on the foot-switch, and a high-pitched whine rang out. The instant he touched the bit to the skull it made the sound of a dentist's drill striking a molar, the smell of burning enamel filled the room. Bright red drops trickled into the irrigation bag attached to Dorothy's head.

For over an hour Dr. Danville drilled and sawed. He inserted an instrument into the seam and applied pressure, producing the sucking sound of a boot being pulled out of thick mud, and a fourth of Dorothy's skull popped loose. He picked up the bone with his thumb and middle finger and placed it on the tray.

"I'm ready to remove the dura matter," Danville said.

"You're doing fine, doctor," Fritz said with a nod. "Proceed."

"Scalpel."

The nurse placed the knife into the palm of his bloodstained glove. He tried to make the cut but struggled to get the blade through the leather-like protective lining. He pressed harder and the tip of the instrument punctured the membrane. A geyser of blood erupted into the air and sprayed across his glasses.

"Dr. Fritz – "

"Stay calm."

Blood continued to pulsate several inches into the air.

"I can't see."

"Don't panic, you must have struck a vessel stuck to the dura. I'll handle it." Fritz turned to the nurse to his left. "Bi-polar forceps, stat!"

She fumbled around for the instrument and handed it to him. He cauterized the vessel.

"Danville, go clean your glasses. Nurse, can we get this blood off the floor? I don't want to be three knuckles into this woman's brain and have someone slip and fall."

Danville moved away. Fritz, completely undaunted, continued to operate.

* * * * * * *

8:45 A. M.

A week passed since Marianne and Andy Lewis received notice of the child custody case pending against them. In spite of the added strain, things around their household returned to a semblance of normalcy, at least on the surface. Marianne mimicked the proper response to situations, but inside she waited for the dreaded knock on the door from the Children's Services agent who would come to tear their world apart.

Marianne took Erin by the hand and walked her to the wooded area behind their home. Erin climbed on the rope swing, which hung from an ancient willow tree. Erin's yellow sundress fluttered in the breeze as Marianne gently pushed her shoulders.

"Mommy, how come you watch me so much?"

"What do you mean, precious?"

"You look at me different now."

"I watch you all the time honey, because I love you."

"I know you love me, Mommy, but sometimes when I'm on the swing, I notice you come outside to push instead of watching me from the kitchen window."

From the mouths of babes . . . Marianne bent down on one knee and spoke to her daughter face-to-face.

"I've been so attentive lately because I realize in a whole new way what the Bible means when it says, 'Don't worry about tomorrow, for tomorrow, will worry about itself. Each day has enough of its own trouble. So every time I look at you, I thank God for entrusting you to me for another day."

Erin turned back to her swinging without giving the matter another thought. Marianne pondered the exchange. What Erin said was true. For seven days now, she had not let Erin out of her sight, afraid to look away for even a single instant. Marianne struggled with the Lord's will in this situation. Her prayers seemed to ricochet off the ceiling and land on the floor. Andy, on the other hand, appeared to be doing much better. He had the capacity to pray about a situation, put it in the Lord's hands, and then go about life with an unusual calm in the midst of the storm. Sometimes Marianne envied this child-like faith; sometimes she resented him for it; right now she was thankful her husband stood so firmly on his trust in God.

One of them needed to.

Andy Lewis had planned on spending the morning with Archie Kisner. With the trial only two weeks away, Andy knew he didn't have much time to reach this confused young man. Andy stopped by Archie's cell at least once every couple of days for a short word of encouragement or an invitation to prayer. But up to this point, he had received no response. At times Archie appeared to be nothing more than a brute beast, but at other times Andy believed he could see a little child behind those frightened eyes.

Andy Lewis strolled through the main entrance of the Jefferson County Courthouse. He stopped off at the snack counter and bought two Butterfinger candy bars, and stashed them in his shirt pocket. He hiked down the old marble steps and walked back to the range of jail cells. Much to his chagrin, he found Archie's cell empty. Andy backtracked to the front desk to inquire about the whereabouts of Mr. Kisner, only to find Danial Solomon had beaten him to the punch.

* * * * * * *

8:55 A. M.

Lori Franks tapped her French manicured fingernails on her daily planner; her eyes fastened on the clock above the door. In response to her Motion for Discovery, Judge Spitzer-Clark ordered the hospital to turn over every shred of documentation dealing with the case. Furthermore, the judge ordered the evidence sealed so it couldn't be reviewed until the hearing. In just a half-hour the moment of truth would arrive.

She watched the clock hands creep agonizingly toward the appointed time. She thought about drinking a shot of whiskey – just for luck – but decided against it. At 9:15 A. M. she grabbed her briefcase and headed for Spitzer-Clark's office.

* * * * * * *

9:20 A. M.

Since Danial had to be at the courthouse early Monday morning, he took the opportunity to stop and see his most infamous client. Danial waited in the attorney's conference room for the deputies to escort Archie in for the impromptu meeting. A few minutes later a young female deputy pulled open the door, and in walked a sleepy-looking Kisner. Some of his hair stood straight up and some was smashed to the side, a very bad case of pillow-head. His beard, matted and tangled, slanted to the side, and his eyes looked puffy and swollen. Even though he didn't say a word, Danial could tell Archie was not a morning person.

"Have a seat Archie. We need to discuss a few things."

Archie sat down.

"I don't expect you to say anything, so just nod if you understand. Okay?"

Archie nodded.

"Your trial will begin in two weeks, and you do realize the State is trying to execute you?" Danial waited for Archie to nod before continuing.

"We don't have much of a defense. They caught you in the act, so I intend to take a radically different approach. But even if it works, you're not going to walk away free. In fact, my main goal is to make sure you don't get executed. The first thing I want you to do is start shaving. You do know how to shave, don't you?"

Archie slowly bobbed his head up-and-down.

"I'm going to arrange to have a barber come in to cut your hair. But that isn't what I need to talk to you about." Danial leaned forward. "Archie, I need you to help me help you. I need some information."

Archie froze like a deer in headlights.

Danial stood up and paced around the small room. Archie followed him with his eyes.

"Where can I find your brother?"

No response.

"Archie, I'm not playing here. Where's your brother?"

No response.

"What can you tell me that I can use in your defense?"

Still no response.

Danial raised his voice to just under a shout. "You had better start talking to me, or in two weeks that jury is going to have you sizzling in the electric chair. Do you understand me?"

Archie dropped his eyes to the table in an almost catatonic fashion. Danial walked over to the door and shouted, "Officer, come get him. I can see I'm just wasting my time."

The female bailiff hustled in and removed Archie.

Danial checked his watch and started walking toward the elevator. He had just enough time to collect his thoughts and make it to Judge Spitzer-Clark's chambers for the discovery meeting.

* * * * * * *

9:45 A. M.

"How nice of you to join us, Mr. Solomon," Spitzer-Clark said. "We can get started now, if that's all right with you?"

"I'm sorry, Your Honor." Danial slithered to his chair and pulled a fresh legal pad out of his briefcase. He looked around the room. Inlaid oak panels covered the walls. Light from the early morning sun shone through the window and reflected off the brass lamps and fixtures throughout the room. He felt the plush, red carpet under his feet.

Spitzer-Clark sat at the head of the table; to her right sat Lori Franks and next to her sat John Simms, who represented University Hospital. Across the table, Danial sat by himself. At the far end of the conference table, directly across from the judge, a television and VCR were set up.

"Now that we're all here," Spitzer-Clark said, "we can begin the discovery. Ms. Franks has requested the hospital surrender any and all documents relating to her stay on June 6, 1990, any and all documents relating to Mrs. Lewis' stay on the same date, and any and all materials and documents generated by any medical or security personnel involved in either of these two cases. From what I understand, the hospital has supplied all such documents, which are now sitting on this table." She looked over at the hospital's representative. "Am I correct in saying that?"

"Yes, Your Honor."

The judge rummaged through the box and withdrew Lori's file. She scanned the first few pages, looked over at Lori, then said, "Ten minute recess."

"Recess?" Danial said. "But your Honor, we're just now getting started."

"What part of recess don't you understand, Mr. Solomon?"

* * * * * * *

9:45 A. M.

An elderly deputy escorted Archie Kisner directly from the attorney visiting room to the chaplain's office where Andy Lewis eagerly awaited him. Archie's hands were cuffed behind his back.

"You can remove his handcuffs while he's with me."

"Are you sure you want to do that, sir?" the guard asked. "He's a pretty violent man."

"I'm well aware of the charges pending against Mr. Kisner. Now, please remove the handcuffs and close the door behind you."

The guard shook his head, mumbled an obscenity under his breath, and unfastened the cuffs.

Archie sat down, rubbing his wrists. Andy placed the two candy bars on the table, and for a moment both men locked their eyes on the two chocolate treats like greedy pirates about to divide the plunder. While keeping his eyes focused on the candy, Andy began to speak.

"For the past few weeks I've stopped by to see you and offer you spiritual comfort. Up to this point you've been unresponsive, so I'll make you a deal. If you'll listen to what I have to say for just five minutes, and you allow me to pray with you, then I'll give you these two candy bars. Do we have a deal?"

Archie's face twisted into a boyish grin, and he rapidly shook his head up-and-down.

* * * * * * *

10:05 A. M.

The bailiff reassembled the groups of lawyers and ushered them back into Spitzer-Clark's chambers.

"I've reviewed the Franks' file, and I've decided to exclude it from discovery at this time."

Danial nearly jumped out of his seat. "Your Honor, with all due respect, how can you exempt one-half of the information available from discovery? We'll only see one side of the case."

"My decision is final."

"But your decision is patently unfair."

"That will be enough, Mr. Solomon." Spitzer-Clark slammed her open palm on the table. "I've reviewed the file, and my decision is final. We'll continue with the discovery. Unless, of course, Mr. Solomon wants to spend the night in jail for contempt of court."

"No, Your Honor."

"I saw some video tapes in the box. What are they?"

"They were in the archives from the day in question," John Simms said. "I don't know what's on them. You sealed the evidence before I could review them."

The bailiff sifted through the box and pulled out the first tape. The group reviewed forty-five minutes of an exceptionally boring videotape of people walking in and out of the main entrance to University Hospital. It was so agonizing that only with great trepidation did the judge order the second tape be placed into the machine. Before the images began filling the screen, a typed message popped up.

"Video Footage From Fire Alarm."

The television showed a split screen of three separate cameras simultaneously activated by the fire alarm: one showed Lori Franks unconscious on the birthing table in room one; the second camera covered the main hall and revealed Dr. Merashoff pulling the alarm; and the third showed Marianne Lewis in room three.

The entire group watched the scenes flash by in utter disbelief as Merashoff ran back and forth orchestrating the masterful switch.

The last scene showed the aged doctor pushing Franks' baby down the hallway. He made it about thirty feet before he collapsed and died.

"No way did that just happen," Danial said, his mouth still hanging open.

* * * * * * *

11:10 A. M.

Danial staggered out of the meeting, dazed and rattled and feeling like he just learned his entire family had been slaughtered. No doubt Merashoff switched the babies; he was good enough to do it on camera – case closed. Only two questions remained: How much would the hospital pay? And who gets custody of Erin?

"What am I going to tell Marianne and Andy? This is going to crush them."

Danial walked lackadaisically toward the fire escape stairway. "How can I possibly tell them Erin isn't their daughter? Worse yet, how can I tell them there stands a good chance they will lose her forever?"

He didn't dare take the elevator and run the risk of bumping into Andy someplace in the building. Danial needed time to get away and think. He pulled open the door to the stairwell, and some odd feeling made him look back over his shoulder. Gus Gram and Judge Williams walked into Judge William's chambers.

That's odd for those two to be meeting together.

Danial didn't ponder it long; he had more important things to dwell on. Lori Franks would doubtlessly exploit this discovery and push the court to move forward quickly.

Danial stumbled at the bottom of the stairwell as he unexpectedly ran out of steps, lost in his thoughts. He made it to the attorney's parking lot without being detected. He ducked in his Dodge Intrepid and sped off. He had no place to go, but at least no one would find him before he had a chance to sort out some of this madness. He pointed his car toward Route 7. Driving by the Ohio River always relaxed him.

* * * * * * *

11:14 A. M.

Lori Franks reveled in complete ecstasy as she sashayed out of the judge's chambers. She took the elevator back to her office, closed the blinds and decided to celebrate. She reached into her bottom drawer and pulled out her trusty flask. Thoughts of money, lots of money, raced through her head.

"This must be worth millions! With this kind of money I could be Attorney General! I could quit all together and travel! I can have anything I want!"

She danced around the office with an invisible partner.

"I could move to California and break into the movies. As pretty as I am, it should be no trouble at all. In a few months I'll have the world by the tail."

The celebration crashed to the floor along with her stomach by a thought that popped out of nowhere. She plopped down in her chair as if kicked in the stomach by an invisible foot.

"This means I am a mother!" She slapped herself on the forehead. "I guess being a mother wouldn't be too bad. I'm sure we could get used to one another. We'll go shopping together, and travel in the summer. I'll just send her away to boarding school during the winter months so she won't cramp my style. Yeah, it will work out just fine."

* * * * * * *

11:35 A. M.

Danial drove by University Hospital and tramped on the breaks. His car skid to a stop. "Judge Spitzer-Clark didn't want me to see what was in the Franks' file. I would imagine someone in the hospital could tell me what's in that file without breaking doctor-client privilege."

He pulled his car into the parking lot. He needed a break – any break. He walked into the busy reception area. A lengthy line of people waited in front of the receptionist's desk. Instead of waiting, Danial walked over to the wall directory, and looked for John Simms. Surely he would be more than willing to help; Simms saw the tape. How could he not want to mitigate the hospital's damages?

Danial made his way through the labyrinth of halls and floors. He found the door labeled John Simms – Chief Legal Advisor, and walked in.

"May I help you?" the pretty secretary asked without looking up from her computer.

"I'm her to see Mr. Simms."

"Do you have an appointment, sir?"

"No I don't." He leaned over a little closer to her face. She looked up to see Danial's deep blue eyes twinkling at her. He flashed a disarming smile and said, "But if you tell him Danial Solomon would like to discuss this morning's meeting with him, I'm sure he'll be delighted to fit me in."

She returned his smile and fumbled with the phone.

"Mr. Simms, a Danial Solomon is here to see you. Something about a meeting the two of you were in this morning?"

She hung up the phone and stood up. "Right this way Mr. Solomon. By the way, my name is Francine Amberg."

"Nice to meet you Francine. I appreciate all the help."

They shook hands; she held the grip a little too long.

Danial had been unattached for a long time, and single women seemed to have a sixth sense alerting them to his availability. His striking good looks attracted more than his share of would-be mates; he simply lacked the skill to pick the right one. Relationships turned into disaster with predictable regularity. Danial trusted too much or gave too much and ended up being taken for granted. He cynically concluded God intended him to remain single.

Danial walked into the posh office; John Simms still looked stunned. The two men shook hands, and Danial got right to the point.

"I'm guessing everything that happened this morning was as big a surprise to you as it was to me."

"That's an understatement," Simms said. "Believe me, if I would have known what was on those tapes, I would have erased them or at least buried them so deep in the hospital archives they would never again have seen the light of day."

"The damage is done," Danial said. "I came to talk to you about Lori Franks' file. For whatever reason, Spitzer-Clark didn't want us to see the contents."

"I thought that was a bit odd myself." Simms took a seat behind his desk. He motioned for Danial to sit as well.

"I can't stay long," Danial said.

"I have a buddy who works in the records office down at the courthouse," Simms said. "He owes me a favor. I can have a duplicate of her file on my desk in two days."

"I wouldn't feel comfortable being a part of that. She has a right to confidentiality."

"Confidentiality! Are you crazy? She's about to become the Ohio Valley's richest woman at this hospital's expense, and you're worried about confidentiality."

"That's not the way I work. Besides, anything we could learn from that file wouldn't be admissible. I need something I can walk in and slap Spitzer-Clark in the face with, and I don't want to lose my license in the process."

Simms swiveled in his chair, and ran his fingers through his thick black hair. "This is going to take some doing." He looked out of his window. "Let me work on it. I'll give you a call as soon as I get my hands on something we can use. Do you have a business card on you?"

Danial reached for his wallet. The two men exchanged cards. Simms examined Danial's card and said, "I've never seen your first name spelled like that before."

"Actually, my parents spelled it D-A-N-I-E-L. But when I became a Christian I did a study on the names of God, and I discovered that in the Hebrew language *El* is one of the names for God. I really didn't feel worthy having my name end with the name of God, so I changed the spelling to D-A-N-I-A-L."

"Apparently, you have grossly overestimated my interest in your name."

He walked Danial to the door. Francine Amberg waited eagerly to show Danial out of the suite. She had obviously put on fresh make-up, and tried to make small talk on the way to the door.

* * * * * * *

3:55 P. M.

Andy Lewis strolled out of the courthouse feeling like a million bucks. He spent nearly the entire day with Archie Kisner, and even though Archie didn't say a word, the two men somehow managed to bond. Andy spent most of the morning reading from a children's version of the Gospel of John. Archie paid close attention and enjoyed the pictures. At the end of the day, Archie looked noticeably sad to have to return to his cell for the afternoon count.

Andy knew he had made a strong connection. Archie may not have been very bright, but at least he could understand some fundamental things. He must have known that Andy cared about him, and he had heard for the first time in his life that a man named Jesus cared about him too.

Andy was so excited he didn't know whom to tell first. He decided to call Marianne and tell her the news, and then stop by Danial's office. He knew Danial would be thrilled about the breakthrough. He called his wife from the phone booth outside the courthouse, and after a pleasant conversation, he drove over to Danial's office. Since Danial wasn't in, he decided to wait. Jennifer poured him a cup of coffee. Her smile beamed so brightly Andy just had to ask, "What are you so happy about?"

"I'm surprised Danial didn't tell you."

"Tell me what?"

"I asked Jesus to come into my life."

14

4:55 P. M.

Eugene Stedman fought to keep his dilapidated truck in the right-hand lane as it rattled and bucked along Route 7. He thought back over his wasted day sitting in the Co-op parking lot staking out the Morley residence. He blurted out a storm of obscenities that would have made a rap-star shudder.

Stedman pulled the truck into the first open space along side Danial's office. He stepped out of the truck, took one last drag off his cigarette, and flicked it to the ground in a shower of red ashes. He doubled-over coughing.

"I really need to quit."

He yanked open the front door and saw Jennifer and some man with their heads bowed, holding hands.

"What kind of craziness is going on here?"

Andy and Jennifer lifted their heads and released one another's hands. Jennifer looked at Stedman, feeling a little embarrassed, and said, "Danial's not in yet, but I expect him at anytime. Would you like a cup of coffee while you wait?"

"Yeah, I sure could use a cup of coffee right about now."

Stedman stared at Andy while the middle-aged secretary scurried over to the coffeepot.

"What was all that about?"

"We were having a quick prayer," Andy said. "I'm sorry if we made you uncomfortable." His face and baldhead flushed with embarrassment. "We didn't think anyone but Danial would be walking in. Please accept my apology."

"Apology accepted," Stedman said dismissively. "Don't get me wrong. I've got nothing against religious people, I'm just not used to seeing people pray anywhere but in church."

* * * * * * *

University Hospital
5:05 P. M.

Dorothy Bernhart's condition continued to deteriorate. During this slide Grandma Bonfini kept up a prayer vigil almost around the clock. And the more she prayed, the worse things got.

Grandma stroked Dorothy's hand and whispered something in her ear. An alarm blared.

"Nurse! Nurse!" Grandma shouted. "Somebody help!"

The shift nurse rushed into the room. "What happened?"

"It's that," Grandma said pointing to the monitor.

"She's in cardiac arrest!" The nurse pressed the emergency intercom button on the wall behind Dorothy's head and yelled, "Code Blue, Room 316! Code Blue, Room 316!"

She spun back around and shouted at Grandma Bonfini, "You've got to leave now."

"But I was just standing over – "

"Get out now!"

The old woman barely got out of the way when the emergency response team flew into the room. They whisked Dorothy's failing body to the Intensive Care Unit.

Grandma Bonfini anxiously tried to get answers from everyone and anyone she managed to stop. After about a half-hour of fruitless attempts, the shift nurse returned to her station.

"Excuse me, young lady," Grandma said to the fiftyish nurse behind the desk. "Could you please tell me what has happened to Dorothy Bernhart?"

"Are you related to the patient?"

"No Ma'am. But I've been to see her everyday since she arrived here."

"I'm not supposed to give out information on any patient to anyone but family, but I really can't see the harm telling you. Mrs. Bernhart has suffered a heart attack. She has been taken to Intensive Care."

"What will happen now?"

"They'll try to stabilize her heart. All coma patients are different; we don't know how she'll respond. I've been instructed to notify her family that she may not make it through the night."

* * * * * * *

5:35 P. M.

Danial pulled his Dodge Intrepid into his reserved space. He noticed Andy Lewis' car parked a few spaces down, as well as that eyesore Eugene Stedman called a truck. He climbed the steps to his office.

"Lord, give me the strength and the compassion to break the news to Andy." He pushed open the door.

"Boy, do I have news for you, Danny boy," Andy said. His face beamed with excitement.

"I've got news for you too," Danial said without his customary smile. "But since we may be awhile, how about letting me see Mr. Stedman first."

"Fine with me," Andy said. "Jennifer and I were kind of in the middle of something anyway. Let me know when you're ready."

"Is it all right if I use your phone?" Andy asked Jennifer. I want to let Marianne know I'm going to be a little late. I don't want her to worry."

"Sure."

Danial escorted Stedman into his office and closed the door behind them. He took his seat behind his desk; Stedman sat in the chair across from him.

"What do you have for me this week?" Danial asked.

"I've got good news and bad news. Which do you want first?"

"Give me the good news. I've had about as much bad news as one man can stand in a day's time."

"The good news is, I was able to track down Ralph Kisner's girlfriend, Grace Showers, and she was quite helpful. She confirmed Ralph's drug connections with some bigwigs. In fact, are you ready for this?" Stedman leaned forward and put his hand up in front of his mouth as if to shield his lips from some unseen observer. "Both of my sources say Ralph delivers drugs to Gus Gram."

"Gus Gram!! You mean County Coroner, Gus Gram!"

"That's the guy."

"How reliable are these sources?"

"I'd stake my life on the information I've just given you. Of course, these aren't the kind of people you can put on the stand. But they had no reason to lie to me."

Danial leaned forward in his chair intently focusing on every word that came out of Stedman's mouth. He took a few notes and asked the haggard-looking private detective to continue.

"Here's how I see the pieces fitting together. Ralph Kisner is some kind of drug runner for a dope man out of Pittsburgh and brings the stuff to Gus Gram in Steubenville. Gram turns around and sells the dope to some of his doctor buddies at University Hospital."

"Can you prove any of this?" Danial asked.

"Absolutely not."

"What good is it then?"

"It's reliable information, and it's a start."

"Where's Ralph Kisner now?"

"That's where the bad news comes in. Showers told me she thought he was staying with an uncle in Tiltonsville. I had a serious talk with the uncle this afternoon, and I'm convinced he told me the truth; he said he hadn't seen Ralph in weeks."

"How can you be so sure he wasn't trying to protect Ralph?"

"Believe me, I have my ways of knowing. And you can be certain Ralph hasn't been there."

Danial leaned back in his chair, a stern expression draped across his face. "The trial starts in two weeks. You'd better move heaven and earth to find Ralph Kisner. I'm not sure if or what he can tell us, but I do know this – without him, Archie doesn't stand a chance."

"What do you want me to do about this Gus Gram thing?"

"Keep digging. If we can set that rat's nest on fire, who knows what will come crawling out."

"Very good, sir," Stedman stood up and stretched out his hand. "I'll do whatever it takes to find Ralph Kisner. You can count on it. And by the way, I've brought in my expense sheet for these first two weeks. I really could use the money."

"Drop it off with Jennifer on your way out. I'll have her cut you a check in the morning."

"Very good, sir. As always, it's a pleasure doing business with you."

* * * * * * *

University Hospital
5:45 P. M.

"Her heart stopped again, doctor!" screamed the frantic nurse.

"Hand me the defibrillator paddles!" Dr. Davies shouted.

The nurse standing to his right tossed him the paddles.

"Charge paddled! Clear!"

Everyone scattered from the table. Davies sent a surge of electricity through Dorothy Bernhart's body; it lurched into the air.

"No pulse, doctor!"

"Charge! Clear!"

Davies hit her again with the paddles. Her lifeless body leapt into the air a second time.

"We've got a pulse. It's weak, but we have a pulse."

"Adrenaline! Stat!"

Davies forced the harpoon-sized needle through Dorothy's chest cavity and into the heart. Her pulse quickened. By six o'clock Dorothy Bernhart's brush with death was over. The respirator kept her breathing slow and constant. Grandma Bonfini made her way to the Intensive Care Unit, but she was denied visitation. She got up on her toes, and stretched her four foot ten inch frame just high enough to peer through the large window separating the Intensive Care Unit from the rest of the hospital. And in that position the eighty-five year old woman prayed like never before.

* * * * * * *

Jefferson County Jail
6:10 P. M.

Deep in the stifling and sweltering bowels of the Jefferson County Jail, Archie Kisner lay sweating on his bunk trying to comprehend the events of the day. A single bulb hung by a wire over the catwalk outside his cell; its dull illumination spilled in through the bars. Archie could stand in the middle of the cell and touch both walls by spreading out his arms. The two sidewalls were sheets of steel covered by two hundred years of battleship-gray paint. A cockroach meandered through the large paint chips lining the floor like fresh snowflakes. A narrow, wrought iron door slid open on rollers.

The meager cell contained a steel toilet with no seat and an old steel sink with only one faucet. A thin, urine-stained mattress covered by a threadbare, wool blanket laid on top of a slab of steel, and comprised the bed. A strong, sour smell of sweat choked the air.

In this stronghold of Satan, in this very cell where the most wretched humanity Jefferson County ever produced had once lain, a confused young man tried to sort through some of the things he remembered from his visit with the chaplain.

I don't know why but that tall guy is nice to me. And he says this Jesus feller likes me too. I can't figure out why though. That feller talked about goin' to heaven or hell too, I do recall. I wonder what that was all about. These are hard things.

* * * * * * *

6:15 P. M.

As soon as the old private detective stepped out of the office, Andy marched in. He could hardly restrain his excitement. Meanwhile, Danial felt like the executioner waiting to drop the axe on a life-long friend.

"Boy, do I have some news for you!"

"Well Andy, I have some news for you too. But why don't you go first, I think mine may take awhile."

"Sounds good to me." Andy's enthusiasm diminished; he wondered why Danial looked so glum. "Well, I spent pretty much the entire day with your boy Archie, and I think we had a breakthrough. He allowed me to read portions of the Scriptures to him, and we even prayed together."

"That's great Andy," Danial said, his voice emotionless.

"Well, don't hurt yourself with all the exuberance."

"I'm sorry Andy. I'm really happy about your news. Really I am, but I've got to be honest with you, what I'm about to say will probably be the most difficult words you have ever heard."

"What is it?"

"It's on tape. They got the whole thing on tape."

"What are you talking about?"

"The hospital has video tape footage of the babies being switched at birth."

"They what!?"

"A doctor named Merashoff . . . he did it intentionally."

"He was like family to us – "

"I really don't know what to say."

"If the babies were switched at birth, then where is our baby?"

"I'm sorry Andy, but your baby was a still-born."

Andy dropped his head into his hands. He felt as if a hand of ice had been laid on his heart. "What am I going to tell Marianne?"

Danial tried to think of something encouraging to say, but his mind went blank. Just at that moment, Jennifer walked through the door.

"I came to say . . ." She saw the look on the two men's faces. She didn't know much theology, but what she had learned after her first week of following Christ she now offered.

"Whatever it is, God is in control." She left to make a fresh pot of her trademark coffee.

Danial looked at Andy and said, "From the mouths of babes, huh, my friend."

Andy nodded his head.

"She's right, God definitely knows what He's doing even when we don't. 'For I know the plans that I have for you, declares the Lord, plans to prosper you and not to harm you, plans to give you hope and a future.'"

"That's all well and good, but I still have to go home and look at the person I love most in this world and tell her Erin is not our child. I would rather die first."

"I'm sorry." Danial's eyes misted up. "I know this isn't the best time to ask you to focus, but I need to prepare you for what most likely will happen next."

"Go ahead Buddy, I've got to hear it sooner or later."

"Most likely, Lori Franks will file a Motion requesting visitation rights, and considering the judge we have, I can guarantee she'll get at least some visitation. Also, the Children's Services Board will be involved. They'll supervise the visits at first. They'll probably interview you and Marianne, and observe your interaction with Erin as well. Ultimately, they will make a recommendation to the Court."

"The best possible home for Erin is the one she lives in."

"I know it is, but these are the things you need to be prepared for. If you'd like, I could come up to your house in a few days and explain all this to Marianne once she's had the chance to take it all in. She may take it better coming from me. After all . . ." Danial said with the first smile of the afternoon, "you're not just a friend, you're also a client."

* * * * * * *

The remainder of the week blurred by for Danial. He met several times with Eugene Stedman. Although Stedman confirmed the connection between Ralph Kisner and Gus Gram, he had no luck finding Ralph. A long-time source at the phone company produced documentation verifying several calls had been made between Grace Showers and Gus Gram following Stedman's impromptu visit.

Danial also made another trip out to the Ohio Valley Right to Life Society for a meeting with Reverend Stone. And as he had promised, Danial made a trip out to the Lewis household. Trying to explain the legalities to a woman losing her daughter was like rubbing sandpaper across an open wound.

For the first time since becoming a Christian, Danial had the overwhelming desire to go out and get drunk; the devil waited for the most opportune time to bring back the old temptation.

During this same week, Lori Franks felt on top of the world. She met with Judge Spitzer-Clark, and in violation of the code of ethics, the judge advised Lori on how to proceed in the very custody case she would ultimately decide. The judge also advised her on how to prepare for prosecuting a death penalty case. By the end of the week, Lori had interviewed all her prospective witnesses and had their testimonies neatly rehearsed and polished. In her mind, the State's case was completely solid; the clearest open-and-shut case she had ever prosecuted. In order to keep her own mind clear, Lori decided to wait until the prosecution had rested before filing for visitation rights. This also would put the emotional burden on Danial Solomon just as he would need to focus on his most critical part of the trial. Yes, at this point, Lori Franks was riding very high.

****

In the days following her traumatic encounter with Eugene Stedman, Grace Showers barricaded herself inside the run-down apartment she called home. Seized with fear, she refused to go outside for any reason whatsoever; she wouldn't even leave the apartment to get her daily fix of heroin.

At first she felt like she caught the flu. Her stomach felt nauseated, and her body ached all over. A few hours later her nose started running, and diarrhea set it. The next day the erector muscles in her back betrayed her, leaving her hunched over without the strength to straighten up. She became so nauseated, water would no longer stay down. The very thought of food induced dry-heaves. Her body temperature dropped. She wrapped herself in an old afghan in a futile attempt to get warm. At the same time her forehead burned with fever; her face covered in a cold sweat, and her body wracked with pain.

Midway through the third day Grace reached the end of her endurance.

"If leaving the house means gettin' killed, then so be it. Death would be a welcome change to this hell."

She mustered the strength to lift her purse from the kitchen table, and still wrapped in the sweat-saturated afghan she limped to the back door. She no sooner stepped out the back door than two men in dark suits met her.

"Ms. Showers, my name is Detective Arkush and this is my partner Detective Lindsel. We're here to ask you a few questions. Would you step back into the house please?"

Grace tripped on the afghan wrapped around her feet as she attempted to turn around. Detective Lindsel caught her before she fell. The jolt caused a bolt of pain to shoot through her head.

"Looks like we got here just in time," Lindsel said to his partner as he helped the obviously drug-addicted woman back into the house. "I'd bet my last dollar Ms. Showers was on her way to get a fix."

It took every ounce of energy Grace had to merely put a few coherent thoughts together.

"At least going to jail is better than death. Maybe they'll give me the help I need."

15

Tuesday, September 8
7:10 A. M.

Danial Solomon pulled into the courthouse parking lot and almost ran over a crowd of reporters who swarmed his car. He nudged the car through the mob and parked the best he could. He struggled to open the door against the pressing throng. He stepped out and was greeted by several microphones thrust in his face.

"Mr. Solomon, why were you at the courthouse so late last night?"

"Jury selection took longer than usual."

"Why's that?" Another reporter asked

"Let's just say Ms. Franks and I had a few differences of opinion."

"How does it feel defending a cold-blooded killer?"

"I'm not going to dignify that with a remark." He pushed through the crowd.

"Is there a conspiracy, Mr. Solomon?"

"I didn't say that."

"Is your client a Mafia hit man?"

"That's absurd. Now if you'll excuse me."

"We understand you're being paid an extraordinary amount of money for this case?"

Danial rolled his eyes.

He pushed and shoved his way to the courthouse steps where a line of black uniformed deputies waited to stave off the crowd of vipers. Once inside he headed for the attorney visiting room. When Archie walked in fifteen minutes later, Danial could not believe his eyes. Archie was clean-shaven with clean hair combed straight back. He wore a navy blue pair of pants and a white sweater, donated by the Salvation Army. With the exception of his head being a bit lopsided, and the scar protruding from under his hairline, Archie looked like an average young man.

"You cleaned up real good," Danial said with a smile.

Archie didn't say a word, but he grinned.

"You know what today is?"

Archie nodded.

"I'm going to do the very best I can for you. But I want you to know up front, things aren't looking too good. I intend to use an extremely unique trial tactic today. I'm not even sure the judge will allow me to present everything I've planned."

Danial opened his briefcase and removed a manila folder. "I'm going to go over this with you; it's the State's witness list. I don't want you to be surprised. And no matter what they say, try and stay calm. We don't want the jury thinking you're some kind of lunatic."

For the next hour Danial reviewed the State's witness list and police reports with Archie. At 8:45 A. M. a deputy knocked on the door and shouted, "Fifteen minutes counselor."

"Thank you," Danial said.

He jammed the paperwork back into the folder and stuffed the hefty wad into his brown leather briefcase.

"I understand you've been spending some time with Chaplain Andy over the past two weeks."

Archie nodded his head.

"He tells me you let him pray with you. Is that correct?"

Again Archie nodded his head.

"Well, considering your life is literally on the line here, I'd like to pray for the both of us right now. Is that all right with you?"

Archie bowed his head.

Danial fervently cried out to the Lord. For about five minutes he asked for strength and wisdom, and the guidance of the Holy Spirit. He finished praying and said, "Let's go get em' champ."

* * * * * * *

9:00 A. M.

Danial took his seat and looked around. The courtroom buzzed with excitement. Gawking spectators packed the gallery to overflowing. Media personnel lined the walls and exchanged notes and rumors. Bailiffs turned away-disappointed citizens at the doors.

County Prosecutor Anthony DiAngello, dressed in a double-breasted Armani suit, stood calmly behind the State's table. Lori Franks sat next to him twirling a gold pen through her fingers. Her black hair, pulled back in a braided ponytail, shimmered in the incandescent light. She wore a fitted blue skirt with a matching blue blazer. In spite of his personal feeling about the woman, Danial had to admit she looked absolutely beautiful.

The gallery burst into a chorus of boos and hissing when the handcuffed defendant made his much anticipated arrival. Two deputies, one in front and the other in back, escorted Archie through the jeering crowd. They led him to the seat next to Danial, unfastened the handcuffs, and then sat on the wooden bench behind the defense table.

A few moments later the bailiff stepped through the large oak door to the left of the bench. He surveyed the room then shouted, "All rise! Hear yea, hear yea, hear yea! This court is now in session. The Honorable Judge John Williams presiding."

The old white-haired judge strolled into the courtroom and ascended the three steps to the bench. In one methodical motion he struck the gavel to the top of the bench and dropped his girth down in his chair.

"You may be seated," Williams said. "Bailiff, escort the jury to their seats, and we'll begin."

The bailiff walked over to the door adjacent to the jury box and disappeared inside. The jurors filed out and took their places.

Judge Williams nodded to the jury foreman to make sure everyone was ready.

"We'll begin with opening statements. The prosecution will go first." Williams looking over at Lori Franks and said, "You may begin."

"Thank you, Your Honor."

Lori sauntered toward the jury box, her hells clicking on the hardwood floor. She slid her hands along the thick mahogany rail lining the jury box.

"Ladies and gentlemen of the jury, my name is Lori Franks, and I'll be representing the citizens of this great State of Ohio." She paced slowly from one end of the jury box to the other, being careful to make eye contact with each individual.

"In a perfect society we wouldn't be here today; there'd be no crime. We'd be out barbecuing with our families, boating with our friends or maybe swinging in a hammock reading a good book. But we don't live in a perfect society. The reason we don't is because predators like Archie Kisner are out there stalking our streets and breaking into our houses.

"But Archie doesn't break into any old house. No, he goes through the obituary and preys on the families of the dead like some sadistic vulture. Can you imagine coming home from burying your mother or husband only to find your sanctuary violated, and your valuables gone.

"The State will show Mr. Kisner chose his victim in this case by going through the obituaries of the local newspaper. He selected a woman who lost her husband in a tragic automobile accident, and broke into her home. That woman is Dorothy Bernhart. But Ms. Bernhart won't be appearing before you." Lori stopped and leaned into the center of the jury box.

"The reason Dorothy Bernhart won't be appearing at this trial is because as we speak, she clings to life at University Hospital in a catatonic coma, the result of Archie Kisner's handiwork." She stood perfectly still. "The tragedy doesn't stop there. At the time of her savage attack, Dorothy Bernhart was about to give birth to her first child; the only part of her deceased husband she could have held onto in the midst of this horrible ordeal. But, this flicker of light, this tender reed fell into Archie Kisner's hands, and he ripped it from her belly – " She slammed her tiny hand down on top of the railing. The thud echoed through the deadly silent courtroom.

"The State will show beyond a reasonable doubt, the defendant, Archie Kisner, on the night of August fourth, broke into the Bernhart residence at three-oh-three Lovers Lane and brutally assaulted Dorothy Bernhart and in the process killed her unborn child.

"This isn't going to be a long, drawn-out trial. It's open and shut, not complicated at all. The State will offer the testimony of a veteran police officer who will testify he caught Mr. Kisner in the act of attacking and beating Dorothy Bernhart. That officer will testify he had to physically wrestle Mr. Kisner off of the unconscious Dorothy Bernhart to stop the attack.

"The State will also call the physician who delivered and attempted to resuscitate the unborn child. He will testify the baby died before she drew her first breath, and he'll describe in gruesome detail the injuries Dorothy Bernhart and her unborn baby sustained in the defendant's onslaught.

"Lastly, the State will call the County Coroner who will testify the baby in question died as a direct result of the defendant's murderous attack. The State will enter the photographs of both Dorothy Bernhart and the deceased, so you'll have the opportunity to see first hand the truly sinister nature of this crime." She started pacing again.

"This is a case about death. Not only the death of baby Jane Doe Bernhart, but also the death of Archie Kisner. You will be asked to send a strong message to the Archie Kisners of the world, and that message is: If you attack and kill our wives and children here in Jefferson County we will put you to death. That message will make our peaceful community a safer place to live. Thank you for your attention."

Lori Franks slowly returned to her seat in complete silence.

* * * * * * *

9:15 A. M.

Eugene Stedman slept peacefully in a doublewide trailer on a little plot of land next to the Ohio River in the industrial town of Mingo Junction. Empty beer cans and crushed cigarette packs littered the floor along with dirty clothes piled in heaps and strewn over furniture, and a stench of sour milk and WD-40 permeated the dwelling.

The phone on the nightstand startled Stedman awake. He picked up the receiver and instinctively reached for his pack of cigarettes.

"Who is this?" Stedman demanded; he place the phone on his shoulder and attempted to light the cigarette with a nearly exhausted lighter.

"I understand you've been looking for me."

"I've been looking for a lot of people." He shook the lighter and managed to get a flame. "Which one of those people might you be?"

"I'm not going to give you my name over the phone, but I'll give you a hint; my brother went on trial today for murder – do you know who I am?"

"Yep, I sure do – "

"Good, I've got some information I believe your employer will find helpful, but I can't give it to you over the phone. Can we meet someplace?"

"We can meet anywhere you want."

"Someplace public . . . how about the fountain in the middle of the Fort Steuben mall at noon. And don't even think about notifying the police. If I get the feeling you're being followed, I'll go so deep in hiding no one will ever hear from me again. Do I make myself clear?"

"Perfectly clear. But how do I know you aren't some nut trying to set me up?"

"You want something, huh? Well, how's this? What me and my brother were looking for up on Lovers Lane is still there, and certain people are willing to kill to get it – "

"Don't say another word. I'll see you at noon."

The phone went dead.

* * * * * * *

9:19 A. M.

"Mr. Solomon, you may proceed," Judge Williams said as all eyes turned to the defense table.

Danial stood, nodded to the judge, and then slowly made his way to the jury box. He placed both hands on the wooden rail and swayed back-and-forth.

"Ladies and gentlemen, I'm Danial Solomon; I'll be defending Archie Kisner. And I'm going to tell you right off the top, my client is accused of some pretty heinous crimes. The evidence you'll hear and see will literally make your skin crawl. I know, because mine did when I first learned of the facts involved in this case.

"The State feels they have the proverbial smoking gun. And you know what? They're right. Later on this morning, a veteran police officer will be sitting on that chair right there." Danial turned and pointed to the empty witness stand. "He'll tell you he saw my client beating Mrs. Dorothy Bernhart. And I'm not going to deny it."

Hushed whispers fluttered through the gallery.

"I may ask the officer some questions as to his procedures, or maybe some questions concerning a few possible scenarios, but I'm not going to deny my client was found pounding on the chest of the pregnant Dorothy Bernhart.

"Let me tell you something else I'm not going to deny. I'm not going to deny my client was illegally in the Bernhart's residence on the night in question. He was there and he shouldn't have been. He is without excuse. But allow me to give you this to think about. Things are not always as they seem."

Danial paced in front of the jury box, his shoe leather squeaking with each step.

"Ms. Franks said your job is elementary. You must simply determine whether or not Archie Kisner murdered baby Jane Doe Bernhart. And she says if you find him guilty, you must then put him to death. This is where the State and I differ. The question is not <u>if</u> Archie Kisner is guilty of murder, but whether or not any murder occurred at all."

The gallery murmured, some shouted derogatory remarks at Danial.

"Order!" Williams slammed his gavel to the bench. "Order in the court."

The crowd quieted down. Danial continued. "Please allow me to explain my last statement. Obviously, I'm not trying to say beating an unborn baby to death is a moral or ethical thing to do. I'm simply pointing out an unfortunate point of law – in the State of Ohio it is legal to kill unborn children. Some choose to call it abortion, personally, I call it murder. But the fact remains, in Ohio it's lawful to kill unborn children. I, as a defense attorney, have taken an oath to zealously defend my client within the fullest extent of the law, and I intend to do that.

"This case is not about personal opinions, it's about the law. I personally believe no baby should be murdered whether it be eight months old, eight weeks old, or eight days old. However, my opinion doesn't count here. My job is to present you the law, and allow you to determine if the facts of the case violate the law."

"The Supreme Court in this State has determined a life does not officially begin until the baby takes its first breath. It uses this ruling to uphold all manners of abortion; including abortions that take place in the eighth or even ninth month of pregnancy. The Constitution of this country, as well as the Constitution of this State, boldly proclaim equal protection for all citizens under the law. If one class of citizens are permitted to kill unborn babies, then all classes of citizens are permitted the same rights.

"So, ladies and gentlemen, your job is much more complicated than Ms. Franks would have you believe. The ultimate verdict you reach will have an impact far beyond Archie Kisner. In fact, it could impact this country in ways none of us fully understand." Danial surveyed the faces of each jury member before concluding.

"Beyond a reasonable doubt . . . I'm sure you've heard that concept somewhere before, if not in you high school Civics class, then on *L.A. Law* or some other television show. But allow me to take just a few seconds to explain the true meaning of the phrase. Reasonable doubt is the amount of doubt it takes to keep you from staking your life on a decision. For instance, in the days of old when Christians were being thrown to the lions, each condemned prisoner was given the chance to renounce his or her faith and be spared from death. To be sure, some indeed renounced their faith. They had a *reasonable doubt* Jesus wasn't who he said he was. Those who chose to jump into the lion's den and face certain death had faith *beyond a reasonable doubt*. Do you see the difference?"

A few heads bobbed up and down.

"So whatever conclusions you come to, you must be certain enough to stake your life on it. Thank you."

Danial pivoted to return to his seat.

"Mr. Solomon, approach the bench," Williams said.

The judge turned off his microphone and leaned over so he was nose-to-nose with Danial. The old white-haired judge spoke slowly and deliberately.

"Mr. Solomon, I don't know what kind of mockery you're trying to make out of my courtroom, but I'm telling you right now, I'm not going to have it. If it weren't against local procedure to interrupt opening remarks, I would have found you in contempt. I'm going to allow you to continue with this line of defense . . . for now, only because I really don't think it's going to work. But consider this your warning. If you so much as smirk wrong in my court, I'll declare a mistrial and have you thrown in jail. Do I make myself clear, Mr. Solomon?"

"Yes sir, Your Honor."

"Good, you may return to your seat."

Danial returned to his seat fighting to keep a straight face. He had a bad habit of making himself laugh at the most inopportune times. A little voice in the back of his head would crack a little joke, and that voice had just said, "Your Honor, if you are going to talk directly into someone's face, then I would advise you to hit those dentures with a little mouth wash."

Judge Williams turned his microphone back on. "Is the State ready to call its first witness?"

"Your Honor, could we have a ten minute recess?" Lori asked.

"We've just begun."

"I realize that, You Honor, but ten minutes is definitely needed after such off-the-wall opening remarks offered by the defense."

"Ten minute recess. Bailiff, please show the jury to the waiting room." He rapped the gavel and everyone scurried around the courtroom.

Lori dropped her head into her hands and bent over the table.

He must have gotten into my medical files somehow. He's doing this to embarrass and hurt me. Well, I've got something up my sleeve for Mr. Danial Solomon. If he wants to play hardball, so will

I. If I can't get him here, I'll hit him where it really hurts — I'll squeeze the Lewis'.

16

8:19 A. M.

Ralph Kisner's hands shook so frantically he couldn't place the receiver back on the phone. After three attempts, he pulled the phone off the wall and slammed it to the floor. He launched a blistering string of expletives and stomped the broken mess of electronics as if they were to blame for the cesspool his life had become.

Weeks of being on the run exacted a high toll on the thirty-year old man. The puffy bags under his brown eyes looked as though they were filled with used coffee grounds. Sleep was a luxury Ralph Kisner couldn't afford. The police were looking for him; Eugene Stedman was looking for him; Gus Gram was looking for him; and a few boys out of Pittsburgh were looking for him. It felt like four, vicious, claustrophobic walls were collapsing in, and three of them would gladly put a bullet in his head.

Ralph looked nothing like his younger brother Archie. Ralph was tall and lanky and slouched at the shoulders. He had long brown hair he usually wore hanging loosely around his shoulders. However, on days like today he pulled it back in a ponytail, clutched with a rubber band.

Ralph's unusually deep-set eyes were protected by a ridged and pronounced brow-line. His skin was pocked and scarred from years of acne. His mouth turned down at the corners, and his usually clean-shaven face was covered with two weeks of growth.

His clothes were dirty and smelled like sweat. He'd managed only two showers since all this madness began over a month ago, and then only when he broke into a house to eat, rest and make a few phone calls. As the ordeal stretched on and paranoia set in, Ralph called no one. In his mind, every phone was tapped and every old friend a snitch waiting to get paid.

The unbearable weight of the world crushed down upon him, and out of this desperation Ralph Kisner called Eugene Stedman. This small, simple step seemed to restore a little sanity to his confused existence. He figured the old man could quietly get him in to see Danial Solomon.

Ralph rummaged through the nicely appointed Tudor home, tucked away on a secluded cul-de-sac near the Steubenville city limits. The owner had made the mistake of leaving the back door unlocked, which to Ralph meant a welcome change in luck. He found a spare set of keys to the Ford Tempo parked around back.

"Things are looking up."

An old Pittsburgh Pirates baseball cap sat on the counter near the door. He grabbed it and pulled it down to his eyes. He put on his mirrored sunglasses and hustled out the door.

He walked boldly to the car parked in the driveway as if he owned it. *If I can get to Solomon, he might be able to work a deal with the Feds to get me immunity, or maybe into the witness protection program. That would suck, but at least I'd be alive.*

The engine started on the first turn; Ralph adjusted the seat.

"Whoever owned this car has got some short legs."

He checked his makeshift disguise in the rearview mirror and cautiously pulled out onto Wellsley Avenue. He navigated the winding side streets, and took a deep breath before speeding down Sunset Boulevard heading south toward the mall.

"I need to make it to the mall without being caught." He slouched lower in the seat. "I can blend in down there like a maggot in rice."

He took the long way around to avoid traffic. The rear entrance was usually less crowded at this time of the morning. Ralph pressed the break at the intersection outside the mall parking lot and waited for the light to change. He rehearsed in his mind what he would say to Eugene Stedman once they met at the fountain.

He pulled into the parking lot, lost in his thoughts. The car drove on autopilot as it wove its way through the maze of parked cars.

A black sedan with black-wall tires followed closely behind. A red light flashed from the dashboard. Ralph didn't see it. A siren squawked, and Ralph pulled into the closest vacant spot. His stomach twisted into knots as the plain clothed detective paced along the side of the car. His mouth ran dry, his hands trembled, and a thin layer of sweat covered his forehead.

Stay calm, Ralphy boy. Don't panic. This could be mall security doing a random check. There is no way this car could have been reported stolen that fast.

The officer tapped on the driver's side window and motioned for Ralph to roll it down.

"Good morning, detective . . . Arkush," Ralph said, staring at the identification the detective thrust through the window. "What seems to be the problem?"

"I'll get to that in a moment. Could I see your driver's license and registration please?"

Ralph instinctively reached for his wallet; his arm froze in mid-air.

"I'm sorry, sir. I must have left it at home."

The detective seemed to be buying it so Ralph laid it on thicker. "I'm supposed to pick my wife up at eleven, and I didn't want to be late. You know how that goes. I must have left it sitting on my night stand."

The detective motioned for his partner to approach the car. The two men conferred near the trunk; Ralph froze in his seat on the verge of panic. Arkush returned to the driver's side window.

"Sir, place you hands on the steering wheel and sit absolutely still. My partner is going to search your car."

Ralph placed his hands on the wheel.

"But what's the problem, officer? Did I run the red light or something?" A mixture of desperation and terror filled his voice.

"Shut up and sit still." The edgy detective placed his right hand on the butt of his shoulder-holstered pistol. "If you don't create a problem, there won't be a problem."

The second detective opened the rear door and climbed in the back seat. Ralph's head snapped back, pinned to the headrest. He glanced up at the rear-view mirror. He could see the plain clothed detective with his arm stretched forward clenching his ponytail. The officer leaned forward and spoke directly into Ralph's ear.

"We've been looking all over for you, Kisner."

* * * * * * *

8:39 A. M.

"Is the State ready to proceed?" Judge Williams asked as he peered over his round spectacles.

"We are Your Honor," Lori said.

"You may call your first witness."

"The State calls Sergeant Peter Gates."

At the announcement of his name, the middle-aged officer stood on his feet at the back of the courtroom and walked down the center aisle. Immaculately dressed with his chest full of citations and medals from twenty years of service, Gates walked through the swinging, waist-high partition, and made his way to the stand. The bailiff carried a Bible over to the witness and said, "Place your left hand on top of the Bible and raise your right hand."

Gates complied.

"Do you swear to tell the truth, the whole truth and nothing but the truth, so help you God?"

"I do."

"You may be seated."

The bailiff returned to his post in front of the chamber door.

"Ms. Franks, the witness is yours."

"Thank you, Your Honor." Lori approached the witness stand.

"Would you please state your name for the record?"

"Peter Gates. G-A-T-E-S."

"And would you state for the record your occupation and the number of years you have worked in that capacity?"

"I'm a police officer with the city of Steubenville, and I've been on the force for twenty-one years."

"In your own words, would you please recount for the jury the events of August fourth." Lori walked over to the jury box and leaned on the railing. She positioned herself so the witness would appear to be looking directly at the jury as he answered her questions.

"I'm guessing you want me to begin at about twenty-hundred hours?"

"That's correct, eight o'clock in the evening."

"Well, my partner and I were out patrolling the neighborhood when a call came in from the dispatcher saying a silent alarm was going off at three-oh-three Lovers Lane."

"And for the record, what is your partner's name?"

"Officer Sharps."

"What happened next?"

"We answered the call. As I recollect we arrived on the scene a few minutes later. Immediately, I suspected something wrong."

"Why was that?"

"Ordinarily, when a false alarm goes off in such an exclusive neighborhood and the patron is home, they'll meet us at the front door to explain what had caused the false alarm. When we arrived at the Bernhart residence a car sat in the drive but no one met us at the door."

"Then what did you do?"

"I told my partner to call for back-up and to watch the front of the house while I went around back."

"Is this standard procedure?"

"Yes, it is."

"Continue."

"Like I said, I told Sharps to call for back-up, and I went around the back of the house. I saw no signs of forced entry on any of the side windows, but when I got to the back door I noticed the glass near the door knob busted in."

"Then what did you do?"

"I radioed Sharps to report what I had found, then I drew my weapon and entered the house. The rear entrance led into the kitchen. Once inside I heard what sounded to be footsteps coming from upstairs. So I found my way to the steps and followed the noise to the master bedroom where I discovered a man straddling Mrs. Bernhart's torso."

"What was the man doing when you entered the room?"

"Pounding on her chest."

Mumbling rippled through the gallery.

"Is that man in the courtroom today?"

"Yes, he is. Although, he didn't look so clean-cut then."

"Would you please point to the man?"

The witness stood and pointed at Archie Kisner.

"Let the record show the witness has identified the defendant," Judge Williams said looking at the court stenographer.

"What happened next?" Lori asked.

"I ordered the defendant to lay face down on the floor. He complied and I arrested him. Just about that time, the back-up officers arrived and attended to Mrs. Bernhart. I took the defendant down to my squad car where Officer Sharps read the defendant his rights."

"Did you search the defendant?"

"Sharps did."

"Did Officer Sharps find anything?"

"He found a wad of paper in the defendant's back pocket. One of the pages turned out to be the obituary of Dr. John Bernhart taken from the Herald Star. The second was a page torn from a phone book with Dr. and Mrs. Bernharts' address circled in red."

"Your Honor, the State would like to enter these pages as State's exhibits A and B." Lori walked over to the prosecutor's table and picked up a plastic bag with the two pages mounted on cardboard backing. She handed them to the jury to review, then returned to the witness stand.

"So, you mean to tell me the defendant chose his victim by rummaging through the obituaries like some kind of perverted zombie?"

"Objection," Danial said. "Conjecture."

"Sustained," Williams said. "The jury will disregard the last statement of the prosecutor."

"The State has no further questions for this witness." Lori promenaded back to her seat. She could see by the look on the jurors faces her comment hit home. Lori knew well that an instruction to disregard a statement sounded good in theory, but was impossible to practice in real life. Once words are spoken, they remain in the memory for later recall.

"Mr. Solomon, would you like to cross-examine the witness?" Williams asked.

"Yes I do, Your Honor."

"The witness is yours."

Danial got up and walked up to the witness stand and greeted Officer Gates. He then shuffled over to the jury box and stood with his back to the witness.

"Officer Gates, I have carefully read the police reports you and your partner submitted. I have also read the report submitted by the forensic team who went over the house with a fine-tooth comb. And I have reviewed the dispatcher log. So, knowing I've sifted through all this documentation, would it be fair to say your testimony so far is incomplete?"

"Objection, Your Honor!" Lori shouted as she sprang to her feet. "The question is vague."

"Sustained. Mr. Solomon, please be more specific."

"Certainly, Your Honor." He turned to face the witness who had folded his arms across his chest and leaned back, and to the left, in the witness chair.

"Officer Gates, you said you responded immediately after the call came in on the radio. However, the dispatcher's log shows you were only one block away from the Bernhart's address when the radio transmission was made, yet it took you over twelve minutes to respond. Where did you go before responding to the alarm?"

"I didn't go anywhere. I answered the call as soon as it came in."

"Then why did it take you twelve minutes to drive about three-hundred yards?"

"I don't know. Maybe the dispatcher made a mistake."

"I don't believe the three million dollar computerized dispatching system is capable of making a clerical mistake. In fact, I have a transcript of the radio transmission from the night in question, which perfectly records the time of each radio transmission. If you'd like, I can get those records brought in."

"That won't be necessary," Gates answered. "If the log says it took twelve minutes, it took twelve minutes. We may have stopped for coffee, but I don't recollect."

"A convenient lapse of memory," Danial said with a smirk. "You said you entered the house, heard footsteps and then ran up the steps and discovered the defendant beating Mrs. Bernhart. Is that correct?"

"That's what I said, ain't it?"

"Indeed, Officer Gates that's what you said. Then would you explain to the jury why the radio log has a gap of almost five minutes from the time you entered the house until the time you radioed arresting Mr. Kisner?"

"You can't expect me to remember all the details. Everything happened so fast."

"Maybe this will refresh your memory," Danial walked over to his table and picked up a stapled packet of papers. "This is the forensic report which states the investigating officers found two bullets, fired from your service revolver, embedded in the wall. Would you please explain to the jury who or what you were shooting at?"

Gates sat with his head down, his thumb and forefinger against the bridge of his nose. "That's right, I do remember now. Once inside the house, I switched off my flashlight to allow my eyes to get accustomed to the dark. I crouched by the door leading to the living room. I drew my weapon and sprang into the opening. I saw the outline of a man and ducked back inside the kitchen. I identified myself as a police officer and sprang back into the doorway with my weapon pointed out in front of me like this." He pantomimed with his hands. "I saw an assailant bearing down on me. I ordered him to drop his weapon. He refused. I made a move, he flinched so I fired a couple of warning shots."

"Warning shots, huh? The bullets entered the wall four feet ten inches from the floor. That's about chest high. Is that where you normally fire warning shots?"

"It was dark – "

"Did you hit anyone?"

"No."

"What did this alleged assailant do after you shot at him?"

"I . . . uh . . ."

"Sergeant Gates, there was no assailant. Your shots hit a mirror. You were held at bay for five minutes by your own reflection."

"I . . .um . . ."

"Have you killed many wall hangings in your career?"

A spattering of snickers trickled from the gallery.

"Objection! Badgering the witness."

"Sustained. Mr. Solomon, consider this your final warning. I'll not tolerate such antics."

Danial nodded and then walked over to the jury box with his back to the witness again. He riveted his eyes on the larger-than-life portrait of Baron von Steuben. He lingered in that position for an uncomfortable period of time, as if pondering his next question. He meant to unsettle the witness. Danial waited until he heard Gates squirming in the chair.

"So, you admit being delayed inside the house?"

"Yeah, I was delayed, what's the big deal?"

"I'll tell you what the big deal is." Danial spun around to face the officer with anger flaring in his eyes. "If you'd have done your job instead of wasting twelve precious minutes going for coffee, and another five minutes playing with the mirror, we probably wouldn't be here right now. Cause and effect, Sergeant. Had you arrived on the scene a minute or two earlier neither the assault nor the alleged murder would have taken place." Danial held his right hand up toward Lori Franks. "But before the State objects once again, allow me to ask you another question. Was it hot the night in question?"

"It was warm."

"Just warm? In early August?"

"It was muggy."

"Was it uncomfortably warm inside the house?"

"No, it was cool as I recall."

"No doubt, the air conditioner was on."

"Yeah, I would guess the air conditioner was on."

"Yet the forensic report said the bedroom window was open."

"I really didn't pay much attention to the window, but if the reports say it was open it must have been open."

"You testified earlier you've been on the police force for over twenty years, so as a professional law enforcement officer why do you think a second story window would be open on such a warm summer night?"

"I really don't know, maybe for an escape route."

"That would be my guess, but since the defendant was caught in the act so to speak, he wouldn't have had a chance to open the window. So who opened the window?"

"I don't know. Maybe he opened it before the attack."

"Is it possible a second intruder escaped out the window before you arrived on the scene?"

"Anything is possible, but I'd say unlikely."

"Unlikely, but possible?"

"Yeah."

"Would it be fair to say a second intruder could have also been involved in the attack on Mrs. Bernhart?"

"I guess it's possible, but as I said it's highly unlikely. I didn't see any evidence of a second intruder."

"Why do you suppose the defendant was in the house?"

"To rob it."

"Did you find any of the victim's possessions on Archie Kisner when you arrested him?"

"No, we didn't."

"Nothing at all, huh? Didn't you think that was odd? I mean, if this was a robbery, wouldn't he have stolen something?"

"I . . .uh . . . no, I didn't think it was odd. Mrs. Bernhart probably surprised him before he had the chance to steal anything."

"That's a plausible explanation." Danial drifted toward the defense table.

"But is it also possible a second intruder assaulted Dorothy Bernhart and escaped out of the bedroom window with the valuables before you entered the room?"

"That's a reach, isn't it counselor?" Gates said.

"It may be a reach, but is it possible?"

"Possible, but not probable."

"But possible, nevertheless?"

"I guess anything is possible."

"No further questions, Your Honor."

17

9:50 A. M.

"Are you sure you want to go down there, Andy?" Marianne asked as he fumbled with his tie in front of the small mirror on top of the dresser.

"I feel I need to be there for Danial. He's going to be all alone like a sheep in the middle of a pack of wild dogs."

"But how can you stand to look at that woman? She's tearing our life apart."

"It won't be easy."

"I know it's not Christian-like, but I'd love to spit in her face."

"Honey, it's all right to be angry. Anger is neither good nor bad. It's what we do with the anger that makes it right or wrong."

"I know, but I can't help myself."

"I don't think hacking a loogie in her face is a positive expression of Christian love."

They both got a laugh. It seemed like forever since they laughed together. They still hadn't mustered up the courage to tell Erin the news. In the back of their minds they hoped God would make all of this go away. In fact, they had prayed every night that somehow, some way, they would never have to tell Erin. And they earnestly prayed Erin would never spend one night with Lori Franks. In their eyes, she was the devil incarnate; Danial agreed with them.

"What are you going to do when you see her?" Marianne asked.

"I really don't know. I hope I'm able to keep my mouth shut." He finished knotting his tie. "I won't be able to sit too close to the front. The trial started forty minutes ago, and I'll be lucky to stand on the back wall." He took a couple of deep breaths. "I hope seeing me will prick her conscience enough to make her stop this madness."

Marianne shook her head. "Andy, I don't think she has a conscience."

* * * * * * *

10:45 A. M.

"The State calls Dr. Mark Davies," Lori shouted.

The witness made his way to the stand and the old judge administered the oath.

"Mr. Davies, would you please state for the record your occupation and the amount of time you have held your present position."

"I'm a medical doctor specializing in obstetrics, gynecology, and emergency neo-natal procedures. I've held my present position at University Hospital for seven years."

"Were you on duty the night Dorothy Bernhart was rushed into the emergency room; the night of the savage attack?"

"Yes, I was."

"Would you please describe for the jury in your own words what exactly took place that night." Lori walked over to the jury box and leaned against her familiar spot on the railing.

"I arrived in the ER shortly after Mrs. Bernhart was brought in. As I recall, she was unconscious. I discussed our options with the Chief of Staff, and we agreed an emergency C-Section provided the best chance of survival for both mother and child."

"Did you perform the operation?"

"Yes, I did."

"Before you explain what happened during the operation, would you please describe Dorothy Bernhart's injuries for the jury?"

"Mrs. Bernhart had been savagely beaten, her face swollen and bloody. X-rays showed a cracked jaw and multiple fractures around the eye orbitals from blunt force trauma. I believe two ribs were cracked, and her torso was riddled with fist-sized bruises. A ring of discoloration surrounded the base of her distended abdomen."

"What happened next?"

"We rushed her to surgery. As soon as I made the incision I knew the situation was bad. The placenta was ruptured – "

"Excuse me for interrupting doctor," Lori said. "But could you put that in layman's terms for us?"

"Certainly. The placenta is a vascular organ housing the developing fetus. It's connected to the fetus by the umbilical cord, and it serves as the structure through which nourishment for the fetus is received from, and wastes of the fetus are eliminated into."

"Could you try one more time," Lori said with a cute smile. "I don't know about the jury, but I'm still lost."

"Sorry about that. Basically, the placenta is the water balloon inside the mother where the baby lives."

"That's better. And you said this water balloon was ruptured. How much force does it take to cause such a rupture?"

"A great deal of force would be necessary. The placenta is remarkably flexible. A baby in the breach position can actually be rotated within the mother by applying deep pressure to the appropriate spots on the placenta."

"Would you say the weight of a two-hundred and thirty pound man sitting on top of the placenta would be enough force to rupture it?"

"Objection! Your Honor!" Danial shouted as he leapt from his seat. "The question is leading."

"Overruled!" Judge Williams shouted back. "The witness will answer the question."

Danial sat down and shook his head.

"Yes, I'd say a large man sitting directly on top of a pregnant woman would provide enough force to rupture the organ."

"What about the baby?"

"The infant sustained a great deal of trauma to the head and torso. You'd have to check with the post-mortem, but I believe a rib splintered and pierced the heart and lung. It looked as if the baby had been thrown down a flight of steps."

Gasps rippled through the gallery. Danial noticed a few jurors shaking their heads and looking disgusted. *She's got them right where she wants them.*

"I have one final question," Lori said. "In your professional opinion, was the baby alive or dead when you delivered it?"

"The baby was dead."

"Are you absolutely certain?" Lori asked.

"Without a doubt."

"Thank you very much, Dr. Davies. I have no further questions, Your Honor."

"Mr. Solomon, would you like to cross-examine the witness?" Williams asked as he looked at his watch.

"Yes, I would."

"It's just about eleven-thirty right now. This looks like a good spot to break for lunch. We'll begin again at twelve-thirty. Court stands in recess." He thwacked the gavel then rambled into his chambers.

Barely controlled chaos ensued. The bailiff escorted the jury into the deliberation room. Two deputies slapped the cuffs on Archie and whisked him away. Reporters fought to get to the phones, and in the midst of the confusion, Danial felt a hand on his shoulder.

"Hey buddy," Andy said. "Would you like to get some lunch? It looks like you could use a break."

"Boy, am I glad to see you. I was beginning to feel like the main course at a cannibal luncheon."

"I was standing in the back. I didn't want to get too close to you know who."

"I don't blame you. I don't like getting too close to her myself."

* * * * * * *

11:25 A. M.

Having tried unsuccessfully to get a message to Danial Solomon through the crowd at the courthouse, Eugene Stedman drove to his meeting at the mall. He paced around the fountain tapping his watch. No sign of Ralph Kisner, but then again how do you spot someone you've never seen before.

Maybe this was a set-up. With my luck, Ralph is probably at my house tearing the place up to see what I've got on him. Or maybe his buddy Gus Gram is involved here. I'll give him another ten minutes.

Ten minutes came and went, and Stedman stormed out of the main entrance feeling like a sucker. He lit up a cigarette and looked around for his truck. A crowd surrounded an ambulance and several police cars in the lot in front of J. C. Penney's. Stedman hiked over to see what was going on. He pushed through the mob and recognized one of the detectives.

"What's going on Pete?" Stedman asked. "Heart attack or something."

"Looks like a dope deal gone bad. The car is filled with residue. We found the driver slumped over the wheel with his throat cut. His body was still warm when we got here; he couldn't have been dead long."

"Who is he?"

The detective yelled over to his partner. "Hey, what's the name on the driver's license?"

"Let me see, here it is – Ralph Kisner."

* * * * * * *

12:30 P. M.

"Is the defense ready to proceed with cross-examination?" Judge Williams asked as he settled back into his high-backed leather chair.

"We are," Danial answered.

"Very good, you may proceed." The judge looked over at Dr. Davies and said, "Remember, you're still under oath."

He nodded.

Danial stood at his table for a few moments and then walked over to the witness stand.

"Dr. Davies, your name sounds familiar to me. Are you the same Dr. Davies who was a resident under Doctor Merashoff a number of years ago?"

"One and the same."

"Do you recall assisting Dr. Merashoff about seven years ago when a fire alarm went off – "

"Objection!" Loir screamed, her voice sounded like she had just stepped in a bear trap. "May we approach the bench, Your Honor?"

"Approach."

The two adversaries walked up to the edge of the bench. Lori's violet blue eyes, filled with hatred, locked onto Danial's. Judge Williams leaned forward.

"Your Honor, Mr. Solomon is questioning the witness as to matters not relative to this case. In fact, that last question has to do with a domestic case Mr. Solomon and I are disputing. And to make things worse, I believe the question stems from a confidential medical file Judge Spitzer-Clark has sealed – "

"I beg to differ, Your Honor," Danial said. "The Lewis medical file has been surrendered to me by the Lewis family. Andy Lewis is in the courtroom this afternoon. He could confirm – "

"That won't be necessary," Williams said. "But what's the relevance of your question?"

"Allow me to explain. I have videotape evidence that shows Dr. Davies has in the past mis-diagnosed the condition of a newborn baby. My question merely demonstrates to the jury the witness may not be reliable."

"Mr. Solomon, are you trying to say the witness was mistaken when he said Dorothy Bernhart is in a coma?"

"No, Your Honor."

"Was he mistaken when he said her baby is dead?"

"Well, no – "

"Step back to your places."

Lori and Danial shuffled backwards toward their respective tables.

"The objection is sustained. The defense will ask another question."

"Dr. Davies, in all of the years you've practiced medicine, have you ever performed a partial-birth abortion?"

"We prefer to call it a late-term abortion, and yes, I have performed such procedures."

"Would you please describe for the jury exactly how that procedure works?"

"Objection!" Lori yelled once again. "What does that have to do with this case?"

"Your Honor, I'm trying to establish for the jury the kinds of violent acts legally permitted to take place upon an unborn child. This question strikes at the very heart of my defense."

"Objection, overruled. You may proceed, Mr. Solomon . . . cautiously."

"A late-term abortion is a rather simple procedure. Labor is induced and forceps are used to reach in and grasp the fetus by the legs." Davies pantomimed the procedure with his hands as he explained. "The fetus is delivered to the neck. At that point a sharp instrument is inserted in the skull – usually a pair of surgical scissors – and a suction device is used to extract the brains."

A few wincing moans fluttered through the air.

"Did you say scissors?"

"That's correct."

"So stabbing an eight month old baby in the back of the head and then sucking out his brains is legal in this State?"

"Yes, it is."

"Are these babies viable? That is, would they be normal, healthy babies if you delivered them all the way?"

"For the most part, I'd say the majority are viable."

"So let me get this straight. What you are telling me is that if you would pull the baby out another six inches it would be a living person?"

"That's correct."

"So what happens if you are in the middle of one of these partial birth abortions, and the baby is accidentally delivered completely? Are you permitted at that point to insert the scissors into the baby's skull and suck out the brains?"

"Of course not. A doctor is required by law to go to whatever lengths necessary to care for a post-abortive infant."

"You answered correctly, doctor," Danial said as he stepped back from the witness stand. "The Ohio Revised Code says a doctor can be charged with manslaughter if he allows a baby to die following a botched abortion. So to clarify, it is legal for a doctor to take the life of a perfectly healthy baby, just so long as the head isn't completely delivered."

"That's correct."

"And in your professional opinion was Dorothy Bernhart's baby's head still in her womb when she was assaulted?"

"Objection!"

"Withdrawn. I have no further questions."

"The witness may step down." Judge Williams once again looked at his watch. "Court's adjourned for the day."

He looked over at the jury and sternly warned, "The jury may not discuss this case with one another or anyone else. Furthermore, you may not watch the news or read any newspapers until the trial is over. Do I make myself clear?"

The jury shook their heads in affirmation. In reality, they unanimously couldn't wait to disregard the instructions.

18

5:10 P. M.

Danial drove back to his office following the first day of the trial and carefully played back the day's testimony in his mind. He thought of a million other questions he should have asked, and as far as he could tell, things hadn't gone well. The jury didn't seem to be following his logic during cross-examination. If he continued his present course, he ran the risk of talking over the jury's head, in which case Archie was a dead man.

"At this rate," Danial said, "she could rest tomorrow afternoon, and I don't have a single witness to refute anything she's saying. This is bad, really bad."

Danial's train of thought snapped at the sight of Stedman's jalopy parked on the street in front of his office.

"Maybe he'll have some good news for me."

Danial stepped out of his car. A gust of wind blew a cloud of dust across the parking lot. The placard above the door swayed with a rusted squeak. He pulled open the door to the pungent scent of thick, black coffee. Something must be wrong.

"Mr. Solomon, I need to talk to you in your office," Stedman said.

"Step right in, I hope you've got some good news for me. We certainly need some."

The two men walked into the comfortably furnished office and took their normal seats. Stedman's eyes looked distant and shaken. The expression on his face made Danial feel uneasy. This wasn't going to be good news.

"Well, what do you have?"

"I almost hate to answer, because it's definitely cliche, but, I've got good news and bad news." He cleared his throat. "Which do you want to hear first?"

"Give me the good news."

"The good news is, I received a telephone call from Ralph Kisner, and he wanted to talk."

Danial nearly leapt out of his seat. His heart raced. "What did he say? What did he say?"

"He said he was with Archie up on Lovers Lane the night of the crime. They were on a mission for someone, and they weren't robbing the joint."

"What else did he say?"

"He said he wanted to meet me at the mall today at noon to talk in person."

"What?! Are you serious?" Danial's voice cracked. "Did you meet him? What did he say?"

"Well, that's where the bad news comes in." Stedman forced a grin. "The bad news is, old Ralphy got himself killed in the parking lot before we could get together."

Danial exhaled and slouched back in his chair like someone had kicked him in the chest. Despair raced through his mind. Ralph Kisner was the missing link.

"Now what am I going to do?"

Danial took a couple of deep breaths and attempted to clear his mind. He pressed down on the intercom and said, "Jennifer, please bring in a pot of coffee. Mr. Stedman and I are probably going to be a while."

* * * * * * *

5:22 P. M.

Lori Franks didn't exactly know how to feel. From a legal standpoint, things must have gone well. But, how could it not go well. The defendant was caught in the act, and wouldn't even speak in his own defense. Anthony DiAngello seemed pleased and couldn't say enough about how proud he was of the way she handled herself with Solomon. But yet a burning rage consumed her soul. She felt like smashing something. She stormed around her office talking to herself.

"I know that no-good, Bible-thumping hypocrite went through my files. His entire defense is nothing but a sham, a personal attack on me. He knows he can't win, so he's trying to play mind games with me. Well, two can play that game. I'll file my Motion for Custody tomorrow morning, and we'll see how he likes being caught off guard."

A sinister smile formed on her lips. "If I knew I could get away with it, I'd plant ten kilos of cocaine in the trunk of his car and call the sheriff myself."

Lori fought off the urge to get drunk. She knew better than to argue a case with a hangover. She'd tried that before. No, tomorrow she would need to be at her best.

* * * * * * *

5:28 P. M.

"Let's go over this again," Danial said. "Someone had to know you were meeting Ralph at the mall; they were waiting for him. Did he say where he called from?"

"No, he didn't," Stedman coughed, then cleared his throat. "As paranoid as he sounded on the phone, I'd imagine he was careful enough to call from a pay phone."

"If he did then that leaves two possibilities. Either your phone is tapped, or every pay phone in the city is tapped. Is there anyway you can have your phone checked?"

"I guess my phone could be tapped. But I'm sure whoever it was covered all his tracks."

"Is there any doubt in your mind who's responsible here?"

Stedman shook his head. "It's got to be Gram. He's the only one who has enough to lose to murder to protect himself."

"You're probably right, but there's no way to prove it . . ." Danial's mind had clicked on to something.

"What is it?" Stedman asked.

"I was just thinking. You said Ralph and Archie weren't up at the Bernhart's residence looking to rob it. So what were they looking for?"

"Got me."

"What if Gus Gram sent them up there to retrieve something he didn't want Dorothy Bernhart to find when she went through her husband's effects?"

"I guess that's possible. Ralph said they didn't find it."

"So whatever it was, it must still be there."

"Gram could have sent someone else to get it. He's got all kinds of connections. And as far as that goes, he could have looked for the stuff himself. He had access to the crime scene shortly after the assault."

"Well, let's think this through," Danial loosened his tie. "We know Gram is supplying drugs to some doctors at University Hospital. He might be running the entire drug trade in the area for all we know. We also know that John Bernhart was a doctor at University Hospital, and three days after his death his house gets broken into. We're assuming Gus Gram is the key player behind all of this. So the only conclusion I can see is that John Bernhart and Gram were in business together."

"Makes sense to me," Stedman said. "But, if Bernhart was on drugs, wouldn't the autopsy show narcotics in his system?"

"Think about it for a moment. Who does the autopsy?"

"The Coroner."

"I'm sure the autopsy said exactly what Gus Gram wanted it to say. Besides, people who sell drugs don't always use drugs."

"What do we do now?" Stedman asked, itching for adventure.

"How would you feel about taking a ride up to Lovers Lane with me later this evening?" Danial said. I've got to know what Gram is so afraid of."

"The police have the place lit up like a Christmas tree. How do you intend to get in there undetected?"

"That's why I pay you the big bucks."

* * * * * * *

6:05 P. M.

Andy Lewis turned off his television after the six o'clock news ran the lead story of Ralph Kisner's murder.

"When it rains it pours," Andy said. "I guess I'd better get down to the jail and break the news to Archie. I bet he thinks the whole world has gone crazy."

He looked over at Marianne. She held Erin tenderly on her lap, and the two were slowly rocking in the recliner. Marianne looked defeated.

"It has been a few weeks since all of this hit us, and I've just realized we haven't prayed together since then."

Erin stood and ran over to hug her father, Marianne right behind her. Andy pulled both of them close and began to pray.

"Our most gracious and heavenly Father, we come to You today in the name of our Lord and Savior Jesus Christ. I want to confess our sins of worry to You, and we once again place this entire situation into Your loving hands."

"Dear Lord, we know we're in the midst of a spiritual battle here, and it looks like we're losing. But, You told us in Your Holy Word that in this world we would have troubles, but we should take heart because You have overcome the world."

"Father, we ask You to watch over Danial as he prepares for trial tomorrow. We also ask that You give him great wisdom in dealing with our case as well. I also pray for Archie Kisner. I pray You'll comfort him as he hears the news of his brother's death. Draw him to You. We ask You these things in Jesus' name – Amen."

* * * * * * *

6:35 P. M.

Danial waited in the Kroger's parking lot tapping his foot and watching his watch. Stedman pulled in the space right next to him; his truck shuddered and backfired before coming to a stop. He climbed out of the rust-bucket and crushed out his cigarette.

"We had better take your car. My truck would stick out like a sore thumb up in the high rent district."

"Do you really think so?"

"Hey, it gets me around."

"So what's the game plan?" Danial asked. "I brought my golf clubs like you said."

"The way I see it, we can't just waltz up there and knock on the front door. More than likely the house is under twenty-four hour surveillance. We'll need to come in from behind."

"How do you propose we do that?"

"I was looking at a map of Steubenville, hold on, I'll get it." He reached in his truck and grabbed the map and spread it out on the hood of Danial's car.

"Here's Lovers Lane." Stedman traced his crooked index finger across the map. "The back nine holes at the Country Club run parallel to these woods here that extend all the way up to the rear of the Bernhart property."

"Uh, huh."

"Don't you see? We go golfing. If we time it right, we'll reach the back nine just as it's getting dark. We slip in the woods and make our way to the Bernhart house." Stedman looked up from the map. "What do you think?"

"I think you've been watching too much television."

"Have any better ideas?"

"No."

"Then let's get goin. "

Stedman grabbed the clubs from the back of his truck and threw them in the back seat of Danial's car. The two men drove to the Steubenville Country Club. Danial signed them in, and they began a wretched round of golf. The sun dropped below the horizon as they reached the tenth tee. The sky turned apple-green.

"Hit your ball in the woods over there." Stedman said pointing to the trees lining the right side of the fairway.

"Why don't you hit your ball in the woods? You've been in them all day."

"If I tried to hit the ball in the woods I'd probably end up right in the middle of the fairway."

"You're probably right about that."

Danial stepped up to the tee and sliced the ball into the woods. They pretended to search for the ball until they were deep enough into the woods to be completely unseen.

Stedman unzipped the side compartment on his bright red golf bag and pulled out two black jumpsuits.

"Here, put this on, then hide your bag in those bushes over there."

"Is this really necessary?" Danial asked.

"In the courtroom you run the show, out here I call the shots."

Danial obeyed. A few minutes later the black-clad duo trudged through the dense underbrush toward Lovers Lane. Crickets chirped to mask the sound of their footsteps.

303 Lovers Lane was a large, two-story, brick Colonial with six tall white pillars in front. Black shutters framed each of the eight

front windows. The bottom four had flower boxes filled with pink and white geraniums. Floodlights hidden behind the well-manicured shrubs lit up the front of the house. The lawn was meticulously cut. The rear of the house was forty yards from the tree line. The moon reflecting off the pool provided the only illumination.

Stedman and Danial squatted down on the edge of the woods and looked across the clearing behind the Bernhart property. Danial swatted a mosquito on his cheek.

"I'll go first," Stedman said. "Since there's no cover it's important you copy my moves precisely to avoid detection."

Stedman bolted out of the woods like an ostrich on Valium. He got halfway across the expanse and dropped to his belly. He executed a series of rolls and combat maneuvers with such effort and slowness Danial actually started to laugh.

"Yeah, right. All I need is for you to goof around and break a hip trying to live out your Rambo fantasies."

Danial crept across the yard the best he could and met Stedman at the back of the house. Yellow police tape stretched across the door and fluttered in the steadily increasing breeze. The windowpane nearest the doorknob was broken just as Gates had described.

"What do we do now?" Danial asked.

"We go in."

Stedman quietly removed the tape. He reached his hand in through the missing glass and pushed the door open. He pulled a small flashlight from one of the zippered compartments on his jumpsuit.

"Give me that," Danial whispered. "I've read the description of the house in the police reports. I can lead us straight to the master bedroom."

Stedman handed Danial the flashlight like a child who had been scolded. Danial's heart pounded as they tiptoed through the strange house. A crunching sound froze them in their tracks. Danial darted the flashlight to the ground. They were standing in broken glass.

"This must be the mirror Gates shot," Danial whispered.

Stedman nodded.

They turned right and climbed the hardwood staircase. The tension in the air thickened as they approached the crime scene. They crept the length of the hall and stopped in front of the master bedroom. Danial's right hand quivered as he reached for the doorknob. The door creaked open. Danial stepped in. The room was pitch dark.

"Where should we look – "

Wham!

Something crashed against the back of Danial's neck. He crumpled to the floor.

Thump!

A shot to the ribs. Danial writhed in pain. He staggered to his feet and threw up his fists. He heard a struggle in the far corner of the room. He swiveled his head searching for the invisible attacker. Light from the window shimmered off the black club as it whirled forward.

Danial lunged.

The club whipped past his left ear.

Danial tackled the assailant and the two men struggled in the darkness. A hand pressed against Danial's mouth. He bit down. The man cried out.

Boom! Boom! Boom!

Shots rang out.

Danial dropped to the floor and froze. The smell of gunpowder billowed through the room. Footsteps thundered a retreat down the hall, then down the steps.

"Danial, where are you?" Stedman yelled. "Are you all right?"

"I'm over here."

Stedman walked toward the voice in the darkness while Danial crawled around searching for the tiny flashlight.

"There it is." He picked it up and shone it on Stedman. A pistol dangled from his right hand.

"Turn that off. You trying to get us killed?" Stedman whispered. "They're still out there somewhere."

"You took the gun from him. How did you – "

"No, I didn't. It's my gun."

"You brought a gun. What were you thinking?"

"I'd rather have a gun and not need it than need a gun and not have one."

* * * * * * *

Wednesday, September 9
7:35 A. M. – Courthouse

Danial sat in the attorney's visiting room in so much pain he could hardly focus. A deep bruise covered the back of his neck. Every time he turned his head searing pain shot up his spine.

He coughed, winced in pain and held his ribs. This was not going to be a good day. Gus Gram would be on the stand in a few minutes, and Danial had nothing.

He began to pray. "Lord, I don't know what happened but You do, and I need a breakthrough here in the worst sort of way. You say in Your Word that if I need wisdom, I should ask for it, well, I'm asking for it – desperately."

Danial's prayer was cut short when the door swung open. Archie stepped in and looked bad. His eyes were swollen from crying, and it took Danial a minute to remember the reason why – Ralph was dead.

"Archie, I'm sorry about your brother. I realize he wasn't much, but he was the only family you had, huh?"

Archie bobbed his head up-and-down as a tear escaped from the corner of his eye. He wiped it away with the back of his hand. His mouth quivered and it looked as though he was about to say something.

* * * * * * *

9:00 A. M.

Judge Williams looked particularly tired and cranky as he ascended to the bench. His eyes were bloodshot and puffy, and his wrinkled skin looked a bit more pale than usual. Danial couldn't tell if he was hung over or sick.

"Is the State ready to call its next witness?"

"Yes, Your Honor. The State calls Jefferson County Coroner Gus Gram to the stand," Lori Franks said.

Lori wore a floor-length-printed dress. It tapered at the waist with white lace around the neck and sleeves. She looked quite beautiful, and Danial noticed the three male jurors were enthralled by her every move.

How can I compete with that?

At the back of the room stood a man in his late thirties; he walked to the front of the courtroom. He was a tall man with jet-black hair combed straight back, with each strand meticulously in place. His dark brown eyes sat back deep in his face. With an average nose and a cleft in his chin, Gus Gram was a fairly good-looking man. He wore a navy blue blazer over a tan pair of pleated pants.

The judge administered the oath. Gram adjusted the microphone and looked comfortable. He had testified at dozens of trials over the years.

"Would you please state your name and occupation for the record?" Lori asked.

"Gus Gram, and I'm the County Coroner here in Jefferson County."

"And how long have you held this position?"

"This is the end of my eighth year. I'm up for election again in November."

"As coroner, it's your duty to determine the cause of death in criminal cases, is it not?"

"It is."

"Do you handle all the cases personally?"

"No. My assistants handle the bulk of the work."

"Was your office called by University Hospital on the night of August fourth, to examine the body of a possible homicide victim?"

"Yes. I received the call at home that evening, and I personally went to the hospital to do an immediate autopsy on the baby."

"Is that standard procedure?" Lori asked as she walked over to the jury box. She leaned against the railing in front of two male jurors.

"No. Ordinarily, my assistant goes to the hospital and takes care of the paperwork, and then the autopsy would take place the following day."

"So why did you make the special trip yourself?"

"Because John and Dorothy Bernhart are friends of mine, and I wanted to make sure everything was handled perfectly. And to be quite honest, I wanted to do everything in my power to help find the animal who did this."

"Would you explain to the jury the results of the autopsy of Baby Jane Doe Bernhart?"

"I examined the baby within an hour of its death. The infant sustained internal bleeding, damage to the organs, and brain trauma. Three ribs were broken, one splintered and pierced the heart. I ruled the death a homicide."

"Your Honor, the State would like to enter the autopsy photos as exhibits B through P."

"Objection!" Danial shouted as he stood. "Your Honor, there is no need to upset the jury with such inflammatory photos. The State is merely trying to play on the jury's emotions. The defense will stipulate the cause of death."

"Overruled. The photos will be allowed in."

Lori walked back to her table and picked up a bundle of enlarged photographs mounted on green cardboard backing, each picture labeled with a brief explanation of the injury in question. Lori handed the stack to the jury foreman who passed them around the jury box. She waited until each juror had the opportunity to review the disturbing images. The gruesome photos universally shook them. A couple jurors were even in tears. Lori seized the moment.

"In all the years of experience as the County Coroner, have you ever seen such a brutal and sinister crime?"

"Objection!" Danial yelled.

"I withdraw the question," Lori said. "I have no further questions."

* * * * * * *

9:35 A. M.

Grandma Bonfini made her way to the Intensive Care Unit, her orthopedic shoes squeaking on the glossy tile floor. Her quiet and warm disposition had grown on the staff, and by this time the nurses were allowing her ten minutes each morning to see Dorothy Bernhart.

This morning Grandma had a sense of urgency. She had just read the story in the Bible where the disciples weren't able to heal a young man. When they had asked Jesus about it, he replied, "These things can only be done through prayer and fasting." Since coming across that passage, the eighty-five year old matriarch didn't eat or drink a thing. She decided to take Jesus at His Word.

Grandma walked over to the bed and placed her bony hands on Dorothy's forehead. She prayed deeply and fervently.

* * * * * * *

9:38 A. M.

"Would you like to question the witness, Mr. Solomon?" Judge Williams asked.

"You bet I would, sir."

Danial stood up, walked over to the jury box and collected the photographs. He wanted their undivided attention. He handed the bundle to Lori and walked to the witness stand.

"Mr. Gram, have you ever seen the defendant before today?"

"Yes, I have."

"You have?"

"Sure. His picture has been in the newspapers for weeks."

"Allow me to rephrase the question. Did you ever have contact with Archie Kisner before the night of August fourth?"

"No, I did not."

"How about his brother, Ralph Kisner?"

"No."

"Is your office responsible for providing the police department with forensic evidence collected from crime scenes?"

"Yes, it is."

"Did you provide the police with forensic evidence in this case?"

"Yes, I did."

"Blood samples, hair fibers, that sort of thing."

"Yes."

"Did you conduct DNA testing to eliminate the possibility of more than one intruder in the house?"

"I didn't see the need to waste the County's funds in such a frivolous manner. The defendant was caught red-handed."

"So, no scientific evidence exists either to prove or disprove the possibility of a second suspect?"

"That's correct."

"Have you ever had contact with a woman by the name of Grace Showers?"

"No."

"Are you sure? She was Ralph Kisner's girlfriend."

"Absolutely sure."

"Would it surprise you if I said I have documented phone records of several calls being made to your office from Grace Showers and several calls from your office to her?"

"No, it wouldn't surprise me a bit. As a public official, I get calls from hundreds of people asking about the death or disappearance of a loved one. I can't be expected to remember the names of everyone who calls my office."

Danial paused and then walked over to the jury box. With his back still facing the witness stand, he asked, "So the conversations you had with Grace Showers had nothing to do with drugs or Ralph Kisner?"

"I don't know who this Grace Showers is, and if she mentioned something about this case or drugs I would have reported it to the prosecutor's office immediately."

"Mr. Gram, you do know I can subpoena Ms. Showers to the stand to see what she remembers from those conversations."

"I recommend you do just that," Gram said, crossing his arms. Danial spun around and charged the witness stand. "Did you hire Ralph and Archie Kisner to search the Bernharts' residence?"

"Objection," Lori said, half -standing. "Mr. Gram is not on trial here."

"Sustained."

Danial leaned into the witness box, nose-to-nose with Gram. "Did you ever purchase heroin or cocaine from Ralph Kisner?"

"Objection!"

"Did you?"

"Make him stop, Your Honor!" Lori screamed.

"Enough!" Judge Williams shouted as he jumped to his feet and slammed the gavel on the bench. "Mr. Solomon! That will be enough out of you. I order you to stop this line of questioning immediately, or you'll find yourself sleeping in the same cell as your client this evening."

"No further questions," Danial said as he backed away from the witness stand, his blue eyes fastened on Gram. Gram glared back with a look of barely restrained rage.

"The witness will step down," Williams said.

Gram reached his right hand forward to pull himself up on the ledge of the witness box and let out an involuntary yelp. He grabbed his badly bruised and swollen right hand, teeth marks still clearly imprinted.

Danial clenched his fists and trembled where he stood.

"We're at a good point to break for lunch," Judge Williams said. "Does the State have anything further?"

"No, we don't," Lori answered. "In fact, the State rests."

At that moment a runner from the Clerk of Courts office entered the room and handed the bailiff a folded piece of paper. The bailiff approached the bench and handed it to the judge.

Judge Williams put on the reading glasses that hung around his neck, unfolded the paper and read the note. He removed his glasses and stood to make an announcement.

"This court will be in recess for forty-eight hours. I just received notice that both Mr. Solomon and Ms. Franks are needed in Judge Spitzer-Clark's courtroom tomorrow morning for some sort of custody hearing. We will re-convene on Friday morning, at which time the defense will present its case, Court is adjourned."

19

11:35 A. M.

The impromptu break in the trial gave Danial some much-needed time to tighten up his defense; it also allowed his wounded body some time to heal. He called Stedman and gave him one simple instruction: Pull out all the stops and find Grace Showers. She may not be much help to Archie, but proving Gus Gram committed perjury may raise enough doubt in one juror's mind to make a difference.

Danial switched gears to focus on the custody hearing. He knew Lori Franks stacked the deck against him, and Spitzer-Clark wasn't afraid to deal from the bottom. He made a quick call over to University Hospital. More bad news, John Simms hadn't found anything he could legally use against Lori. A lot of work needed to be done in a short time; this was going to be a long night.

* * * * * * *

11:55 A. M.

The custody hearing hastened the moment of dread as Spitzer-Clark ordered Erin to appear; Andy and Marianne had to tell her the truth, and they'd have to do it now. Marianne felt like she was having a nervous breakdown and left for her mother's. Andy decided a trip to Dairy Queen would lessen the blow, and he began the daunting task before the car backed out of the driveway.

"Erin, you probably noticed things have been a little tense for Mommy and Daddy recently, haven't you?"

"Uh, huh."

"I know this isn't going to be easy for you to understand, so I'm going to go slow. First of all, you know that Mommy and Daddy love you very much, don't you?"

Erin nodded.

"Well, we have to go to court tomorrow before a judge, because there is a woman who says she's your Mommy."

"That's silly. I already have a Mommy."

"I know you do, but this lady is trying to say the doctors made a mistake when you were born, and now you should go to live with this other woman for a little — "

"I don't want to go away." Tears welled up in her eyes. "I don't want to go away!"

"Don't worry, that's not going to happen. God would never let that happen. He brought us together, and He'll keep us together."

Andy spent the next hour driving around trying to explain the best he could in language a seven-year-old could understand that in spite of how it looked, everything was going to be all right. He knew most of it went over her head, but he did the best he could. Tomorrow was going to be a difficult day to say the least.

* * * * * * *

Thursday, September 10
8:35 A. M.

Danial had only managed about three hours sleep, evidenced by the dark circles under his blue eyes. His neck and back throbbed with pain as he pushed open the mahogany door to Spitzer-Clark's courtroom.

The footfalls of his black wing tips echoed through the cavernous room. He walked toward the front past rows of empty wooden benches. Marianne, Andy and Erin sat behind the table on the right-hand side and nearest the empty jury box. The whole place smelled like Murphy's Oil Soap.

Andy stood and shook his hand; Marianne gave him a hug, then he bent over and gave Erin a kiss on the cheek.

The courtroom doors opened, creaking in protest. In walked Lori Franks along with Gus Gram and Anthony DiAngello. Lori strolled to the plaintiff's table and took off her Gucci sunglasses without looking at Erin; Gram and DiAngello sat in the first row behind her.

Andy leaned over and whispered in Danial's ear, "Hey what's with them?"

"It's just a show of political clout. I'm sure it's meant to intimidate me."

"Is it working?"

"No."

A big bellied bailiff lumbered in from the door behind the bench and said, "All rise, Court is now in session, the Honorable Judge Spitzer-Clark presiding."

Spitzer-Clark strutted in and took her seat behind the bench. She slammed the gavel.

"This court is now in session. We're here this morning to decide the matter of custody for one Erin Lewis. Since we all know each other, let's begin. Ms. Franks you may proceed."

"Thank you, Your Honor." Lori stood at her seat. "I won't take up much of this court's valuable time. I've prepared a trial brief outlining a litany of cases from every level of the judiciary stating that in cases where an infant is erroneously switched at birth, the biological mother has primary rights to custody. I submit, as irrefutable evidence, the videotape from University Hospital, which clearly showed my baby switched at birth by an agent of University Hospital.

"I've also compiled a financial record of my income and investments over the past five years which I believe will show I'm in a far superior position to provide the advantages of life to the child in question than can the Lewis family. Therefore, I respectfully submit I should receive temporary custody until such time as this case is settled through the normal civil process."

Lori sat down and smirked over at Danial. She looked as if she knew something he didn't.

"Mr. Solomon, you may proceed," Judge Spitzer-Clark said.

"Thank you very much." Danial rose to his feet and stood behind Erin Lewis who was seated between her parents. He placed his hands on her shoulders.

"Your Honor, Erin Lewis has lived since the day of her birth with Marianne and Andy Lewis. She is bright and very well adjusted. I believe removing a young child from such a stable environment will do irreparable damage to her psychological development.

"There is little doubt Ms. Franks is in a better position to provide financially for this child. A lawyer usually makes considerably more money than a high school History teacher. However, Andy and Marianne Lewis have other intangibles to offer that Ms. Franks simply cannot provide. First of all, they offer Erin the stability that only comes with a two parent – "

"Stop right there, Mr. Solomon," Spitzer-Clark said in a condescending tone. "This court will not be lectured on archaic sociological principles."

"With all due respect, Your Honor, I have studies that show a two-parent family is the ideal environment for – "

"Statistics can be twisted to say anything. If you have anything else to offer, I suggest you do so promptly."

"Well Your Honor, as a matter of fact I do," Danial said with a touch of defiance in his voice. "I was going over the Local Rules of Court for Custody hearings last night, and it seems that according to Rule Seven C, this court cannot make a ruling on temporary custody until a full investigation and recommendation is made by the Department of Children's Services."

Judge Spitzer-Clark's face turned red. "Five minute recess." She stormed into her chambers to review the local rules. A few minutes later she returned. She didn't bother to sit down, and she kept her eyes riveted on Danial the entire time.

"It appears that Mr. Solomon is correct. Therefore, it is the order of this court that the Department of Children's Services will do all the necessary investigations and will have its report on my desk by this time next week. At that time we will settle this matter once and for all. This court is in recess until next Wednesday morning at nine o'clock. Court dismissed."

She dropped the gavel to the bench and withdrew to her chambers. Before Danial could look around, Lori Franks had stormed out of the courtroom with DiAngello and Gram right behind her. Andy looked completely lost.

"Excuse me if I sound like a complete idiot, but what just happened here?"

"I'm making them play by the rules, and they don't like it."

"And that means . . ."

"Basically, we have another week."

* * * * * * *

9:40 A. M.

Eugene Stedman didn't like how things were stacking up. He arrived at Grace Shower's apartment first thing in the morning. The mailbox was stuffed to over-flowing with mail; even a Social Security Check was mixed in with a bundle of junk mail. An uncashed check at a junkie's apartment couldn't be good news. He examined the post-mark dates on the letters. The oldest ones had been sitting there for over a week.

He walked around to the rear of the house and found the back door unlocked and the refrigerator door still open. A foul stench filled the air, a putrid combination of rotten meat and spoiled milk. Wherever Grace went, she went in a hurry.

Stedman checked with the neighbors. No one had heard from her, and she left no messages. An ominous premonition filled his mind.

She's probably met the same fate as her boyfriend Ralph.

He checked all of her normal hangouts, and the word on the street was plain and simple – Grace Showers vanished into thin air.

* * * * * * *

Friday, September 11
8:05 A.M.

"Mr. Solomon, are you ready to call your first witness?" Judge Williams asked.

"I am Your Honor, but first I'd like to move to have the charges against my client dismissed as the State has failed to reach the burden of proof required by law."

"Request denied," Williams said without giving the request a second thought.

"I then move for a continuance so that the Ohio Supreme Court can certify a conflict."

"What conflict?" Williams asked.

"As you know, when there are two or more conflicting cases on a point of law, a Motion can be filed to the Supreme Court to have the issues resolved."

"What are you talking about?" Franks asked.

"In *Phillips versus Herron*, the Ohio Supreme Court held a viable unborn child is not a person within the meaning of Ohio statute prohibiting the unlawful death of a person."

"I haven't heard of that case. What year did it come out?" Williams asked.

Danial cleared his throat. "Eighteen-ninety-six."

"That's a hundred years old," Williams said. "Request for a continuance denied. You can certify the record on appeal if necessary, Mr. Solomon. Now, please call your first witness."

"The Defense calls Charles Jamison."

"Objection," Lori said. "Mr. Jamison is a Constitutional law professor. The State objects to any such witness on the grounds that his testimony would be irrelevant. Mr. Kisner is on trial, not the Constitution."

"Sustained. Mr. Solomon, call another witness."

"Well, in that case Your Honor, the defense calls Lori Franks to the stand."

"Objection!" Lori yelled, leaping out of her seat.

"Approach the bench at once!" Williams said, his sleepy eyes suddenly alert. The two adversaries bellied up to the bench shoulder-to-shoulder.

"What kind of asinine stunt are you trying to pull, Solomon? I've already warned you with contempt. Apparently, you don't think I'm serious."

"On the contrary, Your Honor," Danial said in as soothing a tone as he could muster. "I've taken you directives very seriously. Regardless of which expert I call to the stand, the State is going to object. So in the interest of time and order, I'll compromise and call Franks as my expert witness. All I want to do is spell out a few scenarios for the jury, and allow Ms. Franks to state whether each scenario is legal or illegal."

"Your Honor, this is obviously a ploy to throw the State off balance, and make a mockery of this court. How could I possibly cross-examine myself?"

"Your Honor," Danial interjected. "The State has already objected to my expert witness, and frankly speaking, I have no other expert at my disposal." Danial looked over his shoulder. "Mr.

DiAngello is also seated at the prosecutor's table. If it would please the State, I could call him instead."

Lori thought, *Solomon would chew that idiot up in no time, then I'd be the one to catch the heat.* Lori shot Danial a glance that singed his eyebrows. "No, I prefer to take the stand. If for no other reason than to see you get disbarred." She turned back to the judge and added, "But, I would like it noted for the record I'm doing this under protest."

"It will be noted," Williams said. He turned his gaze back to Danial. "You sir, are skating on thin ice. Your license is hanging by a spider's thread from my fingertips. Do we have an understanding, Mr. Solomon?"

"Yes, we do."

"Very good. You may proceed."

Lori walked back to her table and explained the situation to DiAngello. Danial waited until Lori had been seated and sworn in before addressing the jury.

"Ladies and gentlemen, you're aware the defense is challenging the contention that it's against the law in the State of Ohio for a layman to kill an unborn baby. In order to prove this contention, I've called Ms. Franks as an expert witness on behalf of the State. I'll simply spell out a situation, and ask her whether such actions are legal or illegal. Do you follow me?"

Several nodded, some sat still, one elderly gentleman in the back row nodded off.

"Ms. Franks, would you agree abortion is defined by the Ohio Revised Code as the purposeful termination of a human pregnancy by any person, including the pregnant woman herself with an intention other than to produce a live birth?"

"I do believe that's the text book definition. Yes."

"So then, would you say it's lawful in the State of Ohio for a woman who is three months pregnant to enter an abortion clinic and terminate the life of her child?"

"Yes, it is."

"Is it lawful for a woman who is eight and a half months pregnant to enter a hospital and go through the gruesome procedure called Partial Birth Abortion we heard Dr. Davies describe a few days ago?"

Lori sat perfectly still, arms crossed and her lips pressed tightly together.

"Your Honor, please instruct the witness to answer the question."

"Ms. Franks, you are presently a witness and under oath. You will conduct yourself accordingly."

Lori pouted for a few seconds then said, "Yes, Mr. Solomon, it's legal."

"Thank you. And am I correct in saying that according to the Revised Code, it is equally legal for a pregnant woman to terminate her own pregnancy?"

"Yes."

"So basically, a woman is entitled to end the life of an unborn child at any time or in any fashion she chooses just as long as it is prior to delivery?"

"Yes."

"But, the State of Ohio says that it is murder for Mr. Kisner to terminate a pregnancy. Could you explain why?"

"Abortion is a procedure a woman chooses to do to her own body. Murder is the unlawful taking of the life of another. I would think a lawyer of your intellect should be able to tell the difference."

Danial paced back and forth in front of the jury. "What I'm going to do now is describe a situation for the jury, and I'd like you to tell me if it's legal or illegal. All right?"

"It's your show." She rolled her eyes.

"Say you're eight and a half month pregnant and on your way to the hospital to deliver your baby. And let's say I'm drunk, and I slam into your car and the unborn baby dies. Would my actions constitute murder or abortion?"

"Murder."

"Why is it murder?" Danial asked with an exaggerated quizzical look on his face.

"It's murder because the woman intended to have the baby."

"I see." He ran his fingers through his wiry hair. "Now let's say you're eight and a half months pregnant and go to an abortion clinic and have the pregnancy terminated. Is that murder or abortion?"

"Abortion."

"Of course," Danial said. "Well, what if you're eight and a half months pregnant and on your way to have the pregnancy terminated at the same abortion clinic. And let's say I'm drunk and slam into your car and the unborn child dies. Would my actions be considered abortion or murder?"

Lori hesitated.

"Ms. Franks, is it murder or abortion?"

"It's murder because it's against the law to drive drunk and take the life of another person."

"But the woman intended to terminate the pregnancy?"

"It doesn't matter."

"So let me get this straight. If I cause the death of the unborn child in question by driving drunk, then it's murder. But, if I'd happen to swerve and miss your car so that you're able to safely arrive at the abortion clinic, and take the life of the unborn child in question, then it is not murder. Is that correct?"

Lori's face flushed. She struggled to control her anger. "You're trying to twist my words to confuse the jury. The fact remains, Mr. Kisner wasn't driving drunk, he purposefully attacked Dorothy Bernhard and killed her child."

"Your Honor, I would like the witness to be considered hostile."

"Ms. Franks, you will refrain from adding commentary to your answers."

"Thank you, Your Honor." Danial turned back to Lori. "Let's go over another scenario that's been in the news frequently as of late.

Suppose a teen-aged girl becomes pregnant and doesn't want her parents to find out. She waits until she is eight months pregnant, and goes into University Hospital for one of those partial birth abortions. Is it murder or abortion if the doctor delivers the baby to the neck, punctures the skull with a sharp pair of scissors, and sucks out the brains?"

"It's abortion."

"Well, what happens if the teen-aged girl goes into labor on the way to the hospital, and delivers the baby in her car in the hospital parking lot before she can have the abortion. She decides to slam the baby's head on the pavement and then throws the carcass in the garbage dumpster. Is it abortion or murder?"

"It's murder, " she said, spitting the words out like venom.

"Why is it murder? In both cases, the exact same baby is equally dead."

"I don't write the laws, I just enforce them."

Danial paused to relish the moment. He finally had Lori Franks right where he wanted her, and he couldn't resist the temptation to savor it.

"Allow me to paint another picture. Suppose I'm a prisoner on death row, and the inmate in the cell next to me is scheduled to die the following day in the electric chair. Now, let's suppose I'm able to escape from my cell and kill the inmate before his execution. Is it murder?"

"Yes, it is." Her lips barely opened enough to enunciate the words.

"And I'd pay the consequences?"

"You would if it happened in my county."

"Well, say my murder attempt fails and the execution goes as planned the following day. Is the State guilty of murder?"

"No."

Danial turned to the jury and said, "Do you see the hypocrisy in the law? Do you see how the State twists the law to make it say whatever it wants? If it's murder for me to kill and unborn baby, then it's murder for a woman to kill her unborn baby. If it's murder for me to kill Mr. Kisner, then it should be murder for the State to kill Mr. Kisner. In either situation, the victim doesn't change – only the executioner. The legality of an action should be determined by the action itself, not by the gender of the person performing it."

Danial's steps echoed through the silent courtroom as he walked back over to the witness stand.

"Ms. Franks, are you familiar with the United States Supreme Court Case *Roe versus Wade*?"

"Every first year law student is familiar with that case."

"Please answer the question."

"Yes, I'm familiar with the case."

"So you're familiar with the language that made abortion legal. For the benefit of the jury, I'll read the exact wording."

Danial walked over to the defense table, opened his briefcase and picked up a copy of the case. He cleared his throat and then began to read:

"The United States Supreme Court speaking in Roe versus Wade expressly held that, and I quote, 'an unborn child is not a person within the contemplation of the constitutional due process protections.'"

Danial walked over to the jury still holding the case in his hand. "Did you hear that?" This is the highest court in the land stating that an unborn child is not a person within the contemplation of the constitutional due process protections. Do you understand the significance of that statement? That means all unborn children have no rights whatsoever. In other words, unborn children are fair game."

He shook his head. "Unfortunately, this absurdity is the law. If the law is wrong, we should change it. Archie Kisner is not guilty of murder because according to our Supreme Court, an unborn child has no rights under our Constitution. They are persona non grata." Danial turned back toward the bench and said, "I have no further questions, and as a matter-of-fact, the Defense rests."

20

Judge Williams shrugged his shoulders and said, "Mr. Solomon, if you're certain you want to rest, then we'll break for lunch and conclude the day with closing remarks."

"I'm certain, Your Honor."

"Very well, court stands in recess until one o'clock."

Lori Franks stepped down from the witness stand, her eyes shooting daggers at Danial. She walked over and whispered in his ear. "If I can prove you were in my medical files, I won't have you disbarred, I'll have you killed."

"Ms. Franks, your reaction to my questions told me more than any file ever could. If you had your way seven years ago, Erin Lewis would be dead right now. And somehow you're trying to come off like you're the victim. Do not be deceived; God will not be mocked. You will reap what you sow."

* * * * * * *

11:45 A. M.

Eugene Stedman raced down one dead-end after another. He had no luck finding Grace Showers, and at this point, he presumed her dead or in hiding. He also had no luck finding his reliable informant, Jack Webster. It seemed like everyone he talked to over the past week or so had mysteriously vanished.

Stedman drove aimlessly through the streets of Steubenville trying to sort everything out. It angered him the police had dismissed Ralph Kisner's death as a drug deal gone bad without even looking into the connection with Archie's murder trial. He replayed his brief conversation with Ralph in his mind over and over. He kept a cigarette drooping from his lips, and his wrinkled face tipped up and back so he could inhale the trail of smoke through his nose.

"I must be missing something. There must be some verifiable connection here, but where? I've looked at this from every conceivable angle. I've searched everywhere for some piece of evidence, but . . . but . . ."

A new revelation struck his mind.

"That's it! One place I haven't looked." He pointed his old truck toward State Route 250.

* * * * * * *

1:03 P. M.

"I trust we've all had a refreshing lunch break," Judge Williams said to the jury. "I believe we can proceed with closing arguments from the State. Ms. Franks you may begin."

"Thank you sir," Lori stood and straightened her orchid pink skirt and matching blazer. She walked over to the jury and made deep eye contact with the two men in the front row. It had always been her philosophy to try the case to just a few particular members of the jury, and then allow them to plead her case during the deliberation process.

"When this trial started a few days ago," Lori began. "I said the evidence would speak for itself. And it did. You heard the testimony of Sergeant Gates. This twenty-one year veteran stated beyond a shadow of a doubt that he caught the defendant in the act of viciously attacking Dorothy Bernhart. The defense didn't even contest this.

"You heard the testimony of Dr. Davies and his explanation of the horrific injuries sustained by Dorothy Bernhart and her baby. You also heard the testimony of the Coroner, Gus Gram, who ruled the death of Baby Jane Doe Bernhart a homicide. So, in the face of such evidence, there is only one logical conclusion you can reach – Archie Kisner is guilty of Aggravated Murder in the first degree.

"As to the other charges in this case, the evidence is equally compelling. There can be no doubt Mr. Kisner assaulted Dorothy Bernhart, he was caught in the act. It's undisputed that Mr. Kisner was illegally inside the Bernhart residence with the intent to commit a burglary. No doubt at all."

She began to pace in front of the jury box, sliding her French manicured hand along the rail.

"Now, Mr. Solomon would have you believe he has found some kind of loop-hole in the law that exonerates his murderous, psychotic client. He wants to divert your attention from the true issues before this court. But, allow me to reassure you no such loophole exists. There have been dozens of similar cases over the past ten years throughout the State, and the result has always been the same – if you brutally assault a pregnant woman and her unborn child dies, you're guilty of murder. You saw the autopsy photos, you saw what Archie Kisner did." She slammed her hand to the rail.

"In just a few minutes the twelve of you will begin deliberating this case, and allow me to ask you this question: Who will speak for Dorothy Bernhart? She can't speak for herself because she's still in a coma, the result of Mr. Kisner's handiwork. And who will speak for Baby Jane Doe Bernhart? She never had the chance to speak for herself. In fact, she never had the chance to have a real name. These two need a voice during your deliberations. Please give them a voice, and return the verdict of guilty on all counts. Thank you very much."

Lori returned to her seat. Anthony DiAngello stood and shook her hand before she sat down. He beamed with confidence.

"Mr. Solomon, you may proceed with your closing remarks," Judge Williams said.

"Thank you, Your Honor, I'll be brief." Danial walked unusually close to the prosecutor's table. He could smell the floral scent of her perfume. Lori refused to make eye contact with him.

"Thou shall not kill – it's one of the Ten Commandments. And the last time I read my Bible, the commandment still applies to everyone, including: pregnant women, doctors, Jack Kevorkian, and the rest of us. However, our State Legislature in their omnipotent wisdom have decided that God must have made a mistake. So they've written exceptions to God's commandment. The question you must decide is who these exceptions apply to?

"Ladies and gentlemen, it's not my intention to mislead you, as Ms. Franks would have you believe. I'm merely pointing out the obvious error in the law. I personally believe abortion is murder. I don't believe in it, I don't agree with it, and I certainly don't like it, but it's the law of the land at this present time. Just because I don't agree with it, doesn't mean I can ignore it. The law is the law.

"The United States Constitution states the law applies to all people. No special class of people are entitled to special privileges under the law. The same law applies to everyone. If we don't like the laws, then we have avenues to change them. Until then, we must live according to them.

"I spoke about the famous case, *Roe versus Wade*. You should read it sometime; it's a rather disturbing case. By stating that an unborn child is not legally a person with due process protection rights under the law means 'non-personhood' applies to all unborn children, not just those who are unwanted." He clasped his hand behind his back.

"It doesn't matter what your opinion happens to be on the abortion issue. You took an oath to uphold the law, and the law is not based on your particular opinion. The question you must answer today is simple yet very profound: Am I convinced that beyond a reasonable doubt it's illegal to kill an unborn child?

"But it doesn't stop there. You're also here to consider reasonable doubt in another direction. Did Archie Kisner act alone?

Was he the one who assaulted Dorothy Bernhart, or was there a second person. You heard both Officer Gates and Coroner Gram say no evidence exists to concretely rule out the possibility of a second person. Remember the open window? The State was never able to explain why the window was left open. So now you must answer a second question: Is it possible a second perpetrator somehow got away?

"If you cannot answer these two questions beyond a shadow of a doubt, then you cannot convict Archie Kisner of Aggravated Murder in the first degree. I thank you for your time, and I pray you'll carefully consider these issues because another person's life is at stake here. Thank you."

* * * * * * *

1:35 P. M.

Judge Williams issued the jury instructions and ordered the bailiff to escort the jury into the deliberation room. The room began to clear. The two deputies slapped the cuffs on Archie and took him to the holding cells to wait for a verdict.

Danial lagged behind at the defense table to collect his thoughts.

"Danial, we just wanted you to know we were here for you," Marianne Lewis said. "And we'll be praying for both you and Mr. Kisner."

Danial spun around to see Marianne and Andy Lewis holding hands directly behind him, both smiling with an unusual look of peace on their faces.

"I can't thank you enough for coming, but what brought both of you down here today?"

"We're taking Erin to a Christian family counselor after school today," Andy said. "With everything she's been through, we thought it best to seek some professional help. But we also came to see Ms. Franks."

"Why in the world do you want to see her?"

They both started to speak. Andy allowed his wife to answer.

"We were doing our family devotions this morning, and we read the Lord's prayer from the Gospel of Matthew. The last couple of verses jumped out at us. 'For if you forgive men when they sin against you, your heavenly Father will also forgive you. But if you do not forgive men their sins, your Father will not forgive your sins.'"

"That passage really convinced us," Andy said. "We need to forgive Ms. Franks for all the pain she has brought to our family, and to ask her to forgive us for holding this animosity against her. It doesn't matter how she responds. Obedience is ours; the consequences belong to God."

"And ever since we decided to follow God's command, He gave us peace in return," Marianne said.

"That's a powerful testimony, but I wouldn't get my hopes up too high if I were you. There's no telling how that woman may respond. But regardless, I know you're doing the right thing."

"So what happens next with Archie?" Andy asked.

"Well, right not all we can do is wait for the verdict. If things go well, Archie will only be convicted of the assault and burglary. If that's the case, the judge will order a pre-sentence investigation and set a date for sentencing. If things go bad and he gets convicted of Aggravated Murder and the death specification, the trial will move into what is called the mitigation phase."

"What happens at the mitigation phase?" Marianne asked.

"The defense is allowed to present witnesses and evidence to try and persuade the jury not to kill the defendant. Unfortunately, I don't have anything to present if the trial would reach that point."

"We'll pray it won't," Marianne said with a smile. "How long will it take for the jury to make a decision?"

"It's impossible to tell. I've had cases where the jury came back in less than an hour, and I've had cases where the jury took over a week. It's impossible to predict."

"We hate to leave you sitting here alone at a time like this," Andy said. "But we really need to catch Ms. Franks before she gets too far away. Let us know when the verdict comes in?"

"Go ahead and go. I'm going to go down and wait with Archie. I'm sure he is on pins and needles."

* * * * * * *

1:51 P. M.

Lori Franks walked into her office to find DiAngello and Gram standing by her desk. In the seven years she worked for DiAngello, he never once came to her office.

"To what do I owe this hallowed visitation?"

"We came down to congratulate you on a job well done," DiAngello said. "You handled Solomon like a pro."

"He can be a crafty one," Gram said. "But he didn't lay a glove on you."

"Thank you, sir. It was easy to see he was trying to confuse the issues. So I just kept pointing the jury back to the obvious facts."

"We also came to reassure you that the wild accusations he made against Mr. Gram are completely unfounded."

"I know, I intend to report Solomon to the Bar."

"Don't worry about that," DiAngello said as he looked over at Gram with a devious smile. "Leave Solomon to us."

The two men walked out of the room. Lori was about to sit down and relax for the first time in two weeks, when someone knocked on the door.

"Ms. Franks, could we speak to you for a moment?"

****

2:02 P. M.

Danial loosened his tie and took off his coat as he joined Archie. The holding cell doubled as a drunk tank and smelled of disinfectant and sweat. Danial sat on the edge of the plastic mattress closest to the cell door and propped his feet up on the stainless steel toilet. This would be the most agonizing wait of his career. At least with most clients, there could be some conversation to pass the time. The silence begged to be filled, so Danial began to speak.

"I've been sitting here wondering what must be going through your mind. This must have been the worst three weeks of your life, and I'm sure the death of your brother has made all this madness seem a thousand times worse. Death seems to be everywhere."

Archie nodded.

"To be honest with you, I spent the first twenty-one years of my life haunted by an agonizing fear of death. I'd lie in bed at night and wonder what the world would be like without me. It managed just fine for thousands of years before I got here, and unless Jesus comes back first, it'll go on for thousands of years without me once I die. I'd lie perfectly still for hours, gripped with the fear of dying. It actually drove me to drink. But that was before Andy told me about Jesus.

"Before I met Andy, I had really screwed my life up big time. It's only by the grace of God, I didn't end up sitting right where you are. Aside from my fear of death, I was consumed by this huge void in my life. I always had a feeling something was missing.

"I tried everything to fill the void. I tried success in sports to feed my ego, but when my sporting days were cut short, the void grew ten times larger. So I turned to alcohol. For years, I drank to the point of unconsciousness, but as soon as I woke up in the morning and the alcohol wore off, that enormous void was back to mock me again.

"I worked as an engineering intern while I worked on my undergraduate degree. I did so well the company offered me a forty-two thousand dollar salary to leave school a year early and begin working full-time. So I've experienced making money and success in the world of business and industry, and even though I excelled at these things, I never had peace in my soul. Did you ever feel that way?"

Danial looked up to see Archie's eyes riveted on him.

"Then I met Andy when I was a Senior at Ohio University, and he explained things to me that I had never heard before. He told me the void in my life was spiritual, and that no amount of physically or worldly things could satisfy that vacuum. He also showed me the road I was running down led to self-destruction, and the only thing I had to look forward to was a life of misery. But more than all this, Andy told me about Jesus Christ.

"Andy said God designed me to bring glory to Himself, and as long as I disobeyed I'd never be at peace. But most importantly, Andy shared with me the Gospel of Jesus dying on the cross for my sins. But I must admit I didn't take all this in at once. Andy even offered to lead me in prayer to receive Jesus into my heat; I said no. But, I couldn't get his words out of my mind. I went out and bought a Bible. I wanted to see for myself if what he said was true. I read the New Testament, and the Word battered down my resistance. I knew I had to do something.

"Finally, I knelt down beside my bed late one night and said this simple prayer. 'Lord, I don't know much about You, but I believe You exist. I also believe what Andy said about Jesus coming down here to die for my sins. I ask You to forgive my sins, and I ask You to come into my heart as my Lord and Savior. I give you my life from this day forward to use in whatever way you see fit."

It didn't matter how many times Danial shared his testimony, he always became overwhelmed with emotion. Every time felt like the first time. Danial looked into Archie's eyes and continued pouring out his soul.

"I can't describe how amazing it felt at that moment; I had been carrying around a ten-thousand pound weight on my back, and all of a sudden, that weight was lifted. All the guilt vanished, and I felt completely new. In fact, I felt born again!

"The next day when I woke up, the entire world looked different. I stopped cursing and taking the Lord's name in vain. But more amazing, the void I had carried around in the pit of my stomach for my entire life was gone. Jesus came to live inside my heart, and when He took His seat on the throne of my heart, I was finally complete. But you know what else? My fear of death disappeared as well. You see, I know for sure that I'm going to heaven when I die. And, with the assurance of eternal life in heaven with Jesus, what could I possibly fear from dying? All death would do is bring me to where I want to go."

Danial pulled a handkerchief from his pocket and dabbed his eyes. He looked over at Archie and asked, "Does any of this make sense to you?"

Archie nodded.

"Would you like me to pray for you to receive this gift of eternal life?"

Archie bobbed his head. Tears streamed down his lopsided face. The Holy Spirit had been working on Archie's heart for weeks, and now God the Father drew another child into His loving hands. Danial led Archie in a short, child-like prayer, and the angels wrote Archie Kisner's name into the Lamb's book of life.

Archie reminded Danial of the thief on the cross who put his faith in Jesus just before death. Even though that horrible sinner had never done a single good deed in his life, the gates of heaven swung open to him because of his saving faith in Jesus Christ.

Danial reached over and hugged his new brother in Christ. Archie froze in his arms. No one had ever hugged him before. A few moments later a deputy banged on the bars with his baton.

"Mr. Solomon, the verdict is in."

21

2:40 P. M.

The jury remained sequestered while the gallery filled with anxious onlookers. Danial stood at the defense table adjusting his tie. Lori Franks pressed through the crowd and made a beeline straight for him.

"We need to talk," she said.

"Call my secretary and make an appointment."

"No, this is personal. I need to talk to you today." Lori's violet blue eyes were glassy. She appeared to be fighting back tears.

"All right," Danial said. "We can get together as soon as we're finished here."

"Thank you very much, Mr. Solomon." Her voice had a ring of sincerity Danial hadn't noticed before. She walked over to her table and composed herself before the jury entered the room.

Mister Solomon? She's never called me 'mister' before. I wonder what's gotten into her. Maybe something Marianne and Andy said to her finally hit home.

Andy reached over the rail and touched him on the shoulder. "Just wanted to let you know we're here."

"What did you guys say to Franks?" Danial asked. "She seems genuinely touched."

"We didn't say anything," Andy said. "We waited outside her office for a long time. DiAngello and Gram came out, but before we had the chance to stand up, two men in uniform came and rushed her away."

"That's bizarre. Then I really don't know what's gotten into her." Danial turned back around to see the bailiff leading the jury into the courtroom.

Usually, he could tell by the look on the jurors' faces as to which way they had voted. This jury must have been great around the poker table, because their faces were like stone; not a single indication as to what the outcome would be. Once the jury took their seat, the judge brought the proceedings to order.

"Foreman, has the jury reached a verdict?"

"We have Your Honor."

"And is your decision unanimous?"

"It is Your Honor."

"Very well then, please hand the decision to the bailiff for my review."

The foreman handed a small folded piece of paper to the bailiff who quickly relayed it to the judge. Williams unfolded the paper; his expression didn't change as he read the decision. He simply nodded to the foreman and continued the proceedings. His many years on the bench had calloused him to jury surprises.

"The defendant will rise for the reading of the verdict."

Archie and Danial both stood. An aura of electricity filled the air. A thin layer of sweat covered Archie's forehead. Andy and Marianne Lewis joined hands and began to pray silently. They asked for mercy not justice. Lori Franks composed herself and eagerly awaited the most important verdict of her legal career.

Behind the Prosecutor's table, Gus Gram rubbed his chin. Anthony DiAngello slowly rocked back and forth from foot-to-foot as he fastened the bottom button of his double-breasted Armani suit.

Judge Williams scanned the courtroom. "As to the charge of aggravated burglary, how do you find?"

"As to the charge of aggravated burglary," the foreman said, "we the jury find the defendant guilty."

A sigh rippled through the room, and then silence.

"As to the charge of aggravated assault against Dorothy Bernart, how do you find?"

"As to the charge of aggravated assault, we the jury find the defendant guilty as charged."

Again a sigh rippled through the room.

"And as to the charge of aggravated murder with accompanying death specifications, how do you find?"

"As to the charge of aggravated murder and the attached death specifications, we the jury find the defendant, Archie Kisner guilty as charged."

A cheer from the gallery rent the air. DiAngello reached over and hugged Lori Franks; she beamed from ear-to-ear. Gus Gram stepped over the waist-high railing and also hugged her. The pinnacle of her career had arrived. On the other side of the courtroom, the picture looked much different.

Archie slumped down into his seat. He may not have understood a lot of things, but he clearly understood the meaning of *guilty*. Andy pushed through the crowd and stepped through the swing-gate. He placed his right hand on Danial's back. "How can you be so calm at a time like this?"

"To be honest with you, I expected the verdict. The arguments I used were highly technical and really geared toward the Appeals Court. I didn't expect a jury to follow my reasoning, but in order to address these points on appeal, I had to get them in now. So things actually went as I planned."

Judge Williams pounded his gavel on the bench. Even though the verdict was in, the proceedings were far from over. The jury needed to again be impaneled to hear the mitigation phase arguments, and Judge Williams didn't plan on wasting a single minute. With the jury coming back in record time on the verdict, he now hoped they would be equally expedient in recommending the death penalty. He actually looked forward to sentencing Archie to death. It was the ultimate power-rush to decree the death of a prisoner. It made him feel like the Roman Emperors of old who would give the thumbs down on a condemned man. And with the verdict coming in on a Friday, a sentence today would give him front-page coverage in the Sunday papers all across the country. With his bid for re-election only a few months away, Williams needed to ride the free publicity for all it was worth.

"Order in the court," he shouted, banging the gavel. "We still have unfinished business here. The gallery will be seated and come to order, or I'll have the courtroom cleared."

Silence fell over the courtroom as the white-haired judge addressed Danial.

"Mr. Solomon, you may begin your mitigation arguments."

"Your Honor, the defense has no witnesses to call so what I would like to – "

Danial felt a tug on his arm. He looked down to see Archie Kisner pulling on his coat sleeve. Archie pointed to the witness stand and said, "I want to talk up there."

Archie didn't articulate words well. He spoke deliberately, each word slurred. But his oratory captured everyone's attention. Lori Franks' eyes shot wide open. Gus Gram's chin fell.

"Your Honor, I'd like a ten-minute recess to confer with my client."

"Absolutely not," Williams thundered back. "You've had two months to confer with your client."

"But sir, this is the first time he's actually said anything since I took this case. Obviously, you can see the difficult position I'm in."

"You'll use your allotted time now or you'll forfeit it."

The cardinal rule for questioning a witness is to never ask a question you don't already know the answer to. But Danial really had no choice but to put a witness on the stand with no idea of what he would say. However, desperate times called for desperate measures.

"Your Honor, the defense calls Archie Kisner to the stand."

Archie Kisner shuffled to the stand like a frightened child. His brown hair matted to his head with sweat; his face flushed, which made the scar running across his forehead turn deep purple. His pants were too big around the waist and a bit too short, his white socks showed. He didn't have a belt, so he reached back and held the pants up by the back belt-loops as he walked.

The bailiff carried the courtroom Bible to the stand and said, "Raise your right hand. Do you swear to tell the truth, the whole truth and nothing but the truth so help you God?"

"Yessir."

"You may be seated," Williams said. "The witness is yours Mr. Solomon."

"Would you please state your name for the record?" Danial asked.

"Archie Kisner."

"Since the purpose of the mitigation phase is to let the jury get to know you better, why don't we start with your childhood. Would that be all right?"

"Yessir."

"But, before we get into all that. Do you mind telling me why you haven't said a word until right now?"

"He says he kill me if I say anything, I don't want to die so I believed him."

"But why wait till now? You could have talked to me this morning or even yesterday."

"Ever since you told me about that Jesus feller lovin' me and dyin' for me, and that I could go see Him in heaven when I die, I ain't afraid of dyin' no more."

Danial couldn't help but smile. "I guess that's as good a reason as any for breaking your silence. But for now, let's talk about you for a little while. Do you remember much about your parents?"

"Yessir, they were nice people. I like them."

"Do you remember how old you were when they died?"

"Naw, I'm really not too good with figures. I was a pretty small feller."

"Why don't you tell the jury how your parents died."

"Well, my mom went to work one day and never came home. Seems some drunken feller hit her with a car. Dad was pretty sad about it. Shot himself."

Danial paused to allow the full weight of the tragedy to sink into the jury's collective mind before he continued.

"That's a horrible thing. How did you find out your dad killed himself?"

"I came home from school," Archie paused and took a deep breath. "Found him in the garage."

"I know this must be a terribly difficult thing for you to talk about so I won't take you any further in that direction. Let's move on to your relationship with your brother Ralph. From what I understand, you spent a few years in several different orphanages before Ralph became your legal guardian."

"Yessir."

"Tell me about your relationship with Ralph."

"Ralph was my brother," Archie said while bobbing his head up-and-down and rubbing his hands nervously.

"I know Ralph was your brother, but how did he treat you? Was he mean to you?"

"He wasn't too mean . . . most of the time," Archie said stammering over his words.

"Did he ever hit you?"

"Only when I did bad . . .I did bad things a lot I guess. Sometimes, I would do things I didn't remember, and Ralph would hit me, but he always said I had it comin'."

"What do you mean doing things you didn't remember?"

"Well, sometimes he would run out of money, and Ralph would say it was my fault, and he would hit me or kick me. Or sometimes he would drink a lot of beer, then hit me. But I'm bad so I . . . I deserved it."

"He told you, you were bad?"

"Yessir. He always said I was bad."

"Tell me about that scar on your head, did Ralph do that to you?"

Archie froze in his seat like a deer in the headlights. His head twitched to his left, and he rubbed his hands more vigorously. "Ralph told me I ain't supposed to talk about that."

"Ralph isn't going to hurt you anymore, so it's all right. You can tell me."

"Are you sure?"

"I'm sure."

"Well, that was my fault too. The lady that lives downstairs . . .well . . . she made some cookies and Ralph put them on a plate, and I ate a couple. Ralph got mad and hit me with Duke."

"Hit you with Duke? What's a Duke?"

"Duke is the baseball bat we keep by the door in case there's trouble."

Gasps rippled through the gallery.

"Order," Williams said. "I'll have order. Continue Mr. Solomon."

"Let's jump ahead to the events of the past two months. I'm sure a lot of people here today, including myself, would love to hear from your mouth what happened on August fourth. Why don't you start by telling us how you came to be in the Bernart residence that night?"

"Ralph came home after dinner and said he got us a job. He told me we had to go find something, says I had to be real quiet."

"Did he say what you were looking for?"

"He told me we were looking for some sort of box of something. I really didn't figure that one out. I didn't want him to get mad at me so I didn't ask him to tell it to me again. So we got in the car and drove to the hospital. Ralph had to talk to some guy – "

"Sorry for interrupting you," Danial said. "But which hospital did you go to?"

"That big red brick one."

"Do you mean University Hospital?"

"I'm not real good with names and such, but I think that's it."

"Please continue."

"Ralph came outside, he laid a couple of pieces of paper on the seat. Then we drove up a street with a lot of big houses on it. I had never seen such big houses. Well, anyway, we parks down the street, and Ralph says I had to be quiet cause we were going to walk in the woods. But before I got out of the car, I stuffed those papers in my pants."

"What did those papers say?"

"I don't know." Archie lowered his eyes. "I can't read. But I figured papers must be important, so I brought 'em in case Ralph needed 'em. He never did I guess."

"Please continue."

"When we got to the house, Ralph broke the door, and we walked in, and me and Ralph starts looking for whatever that was we were looking for. I never did figure out what it was. But we didn't find it. Ralph said something about a safe or something being upstairs, and he told me to look behind the pictures on the walls downstairs. I didn't find nothing. I was going to go upstairs to find Ralph when a man yelled at me to freeze."

"What did you do then?"

"I froze. Then he didn't say nothin' and when I looked down the stairs he wasn't there, so I got scared and ran upstairs to find Ralph." He looked up to see Gus Gram glaring at him through squinted eyes.

"Then what happened?" Danial asked.

"I ran down the hall, and I heard some noise."

"What was it?"

"Ralph was hitting and kicking some woman. It made me so mad, I pushed Ralph off of her. He yelled at me and said we had to jump out of the window, but I couldn't do it. I just couldn't do it."

"You couldn't do what?" Danial asked. He leaned on the side of the witness stand just a couple of feet away from Archie.

"I couldn't leave that lady. Ralph shouldn't have hit her. She wasn't bad like me, why would he do that?" Archie said through his tears.

"What did you do next?"

"I tried to help her. She didn't look like she was breathing so I tried to do that thing on her I saw on that TV show with them doctors. I blew air in her mouth and that didn't work. I figured I was doin' it wrong, so I hit on her chest like I saw on TV, and then that police feller came in and pointed his gun at me." Archie sobbed, his chest heaved.

"So you were trying to help her?"

"Yessir."

"I don't have any further questions. You can step down."

Archie plodded heavily down the steps. He reached back to hold up his pants, tears streamed down his cheeks. Everyone in the courtroom was silently stunned by his compelling and honest testimony. The jury seemed to be the most profoundly affected. Just minutes ago they wanted to kill this man, and now they didn't know what to think. Archie walked about halfway back to his seat when Danial stopped.

"I've got one last question, just to clear the matter up in my own mind. Was Ralph the one who told you he would kill you if you said anything?"

"No."

"If it wasn't Ralph, who was it then?"

"It was that man over there." Archie pointed at Gus Gram.

The emotionally charged courtroom exploded. Some were shouting at Gram, some were shouting at Archie, and the judge shouted at everyone. When things finally quieted down, Lori Franks sat in her seat speechless.

Anthony DiAngello stood and said, "This is all very moving drama, but this is nothing more than a desperate man's attempt to save his own skin. The fact remains everything he said is completely unsubstantiated and self-serving. He doesn't have a single witness to corroborate his testimony – "

"Yes he does," shouted a woman from the back of the courtroom.

Everyone spun around to see who made the outrageous remark.

"And who might you be?" DiAngello asked.

"I'm Dorothy Bernart."

22

4:35 P. M.

Judge Williams slumped back in his chair and watched the courtroom come unglued. He shook his head and poured himself a glass of water. This morning's papers reported Dorothy in critical condition, still clinging to life in a coma. Now here she stands, the picture of health. He picked up the gavel, but before he dropped it a collective hush fell on the crowd.

Danial jumped to his feet. "Your Honor, the defense would like to call Dorothy Bernhart to the stand."

Judge Williams, still a little stunned, said, "Why not."

Dorothy Bernard walked down the center aisle. She wore a black beret to cover her head shaved from surgery, a turquoise button-down shirt with the collar out over a black blazer, and a pair of pleated pants. She nimbly climbed the steps to the stand, took the oath, and sat down. She looked remarkably calm, quietly awaiting the first question.

Danial wasn't sure what direction to aim the questioning, so he walked over and said, "Why don't you tell us how it is you came to be at the courthouse at this moment in time?"

"Everything has happened so very fast," she said, her voice high-pitched and child-like. "I was sleeping one minute and the next thing I knew I woke up with Grandma Bonfini's hand on my forehead. This may seem odd, but I never knew I was in a coma. I woke up feeling like I'd slept though a prolonged nightmare, but from what I'm told my nightmare is very real."

"I'm afraid it is."

"I may still be in shock but it feels like all this happened years ago, and I've already gone through the grieving process."

"But you do remember what happened the night of August fourth?" Danial asked.

"I remember it well. It was the last night of calling hours for my husband. My doctor ordered me to stay home. I guess the stress of dealing with John's death was too much for me, and I started to hemorrhage. My doctor feared I'd go into labor prematurely if I didn't rest. I tried to sleep but couldn't, then I hear some noises coming from downstairs. People were in and out bringing over dinner, so I really didn't concern myself. The next thing I knew, some lunatic is screaming in my face."

"What did he say?"

"Where's the safe? Where's the safe?" Dorothy said, her voice choked with emotion.

Eugene Stedman quietly slipped in the rear entrance of the courtroom with two tall men wearing dark suits and one wearing sunglasses. He motioned to get the bailiff's attention, and handed him a note.

"I told him we didn't have a safe, but he didn't believe me. I tried to run past him to the bedroom door, and he knocked me down and started punching me and kicking me. Then I heard some gun shots and got really scared. I knew I was going to die. The last thing I remember was that man over there." She pointed at Archie. "He came and pushed the other man off me and held me in his arms. That was the last thing I saw until this morning."

Murmuring rumbled from the gallery.

"I know this is rough on you, but I really need to ask you some questions about your husband and some of his activities at University Hospital. Would that be all right?"

"Sure."

"Mrs. Bernhart, do you know that man sitting in the front row behind the Prosecutor's table?" Danial turned and pointed at Gram, whom had his chin tucked and peered out through lowered eyebrows. He whispered something to Mrs. Bernhart under his breath.

"Yes, I do. His name is Gus Gram."

"Do you happen to know if your husband had any illegal dealings with Gus Gram?"

"Absolutely not! My husband was a good and decent man."

"I'm sorry ma'am, but are you absolutely sure? I have reason to believe Mr. Gram had something to do with your assault."

DiAngello elbowed Lori Franks to do something. She shrugged him off. DiAngello stood and shouted, "Objection! Gus Gram is not on trial here."

"Shut up and sit down," Judge Williams thundered back. "The witness will answer the question. I intend to get to the bottom of this matter one way or another."

"I know all about Gus Gram. He approached my husband on several occasions. John didn't like him or trust him for that matter."

"Did you husband ever meet with him?"

"After a while John worried Gram would get vindictive or maybe set him up if he didn't give in, so he met with him once . . . only once."

"Do you know the contents of that conversation?"

"Yes, I do. When John came home from the hospital that night he looked visibly shaken. He said Gram wanted him to offer cocaine to his wealthy patients."

Pandemonium erupted in the gallery.

Gram shoved DiAngello. "Do something you idiot!"

DiAngello stood and shouted over the crowd, "Objection! This is hearsay!"

Judge Williams smashed his gavel violently on the bench. "Order!" He waited for silence then asked, "Mrs. Bernhart, is there anyone who can corroborate what you've just said?"

"No." She shook her head. "No . . . wait a minute . . . my husband tape-recorded the conversation."

"He what?" Williams asked.

"Yeah, he took his pocket Dictaphone with him. He wanted to protect himself."

"Do you have the tape?"

"No, I don't sir. My husband had it with him when he died. In fact, he was on his way to the FBI office when his car went over the side of the embankment."

"In that case, I'll be forced to sustain the – "

"Hold it," Stedman shouted from the back of the courtroom. "I have the tape right here."

Gram spun around in his seat. The color drained from his face when he saw the old detective holding a small clear tape in his right hand. Gram dashed toward the fire escape door near the jury box.

"Bailiffs, stop that man!" Williams shouted.

Two bailiffs seized Gram by the arms.

"Court is in recess," Williams said. "The jury will leave the room. DiAngello, Franks, Solomon, and you men in the back, come to my chambers at once."

* * * * * * *

4:55 P. M.

The impromptu assembly crowded into Judge Williams chambers and sat around the oval conference table. Williams took his place at the head of the table. Anthony DiAngello sat directly to Williams' right. His forehead glistened with sweat, and he unconsciously twisted his West Virginia University class ring. Lori sat next to him, looking remarkably fresh and perky considering everything that just transpired. Danial sat next to her; his heart thumping against his chest.

Directly across the table from Danial sat Eugene Stedman looking like he had just conquered the world. It had been a number of years since he had been invited into a judge's chambers for something so vitally important, and a measure of pride filled his heart. The two men in dark suits sat next to Stedman.

Williams glanced at the two unknown men.

"Who are you?"

"I'm Agent Mears and this is Agent Choice, FBI"

"And the reason you are here is?"

"We're here to arrest Gus Gram for drug trafficking and murder," Mears said.

"Murder?" Lori said.

"The murder of whom?" Williams asked.

"The murder of John Bernhart, and the suspected murders of Ralph Kisner and Grace Showers."

"Hold on, hold on," Williams said. "I think we've gotten ahead of ourselves. Will someone explain to me what's going on here."

Stedman spoke up. "Yesterday, it dawned on me that maybe what the Kisner boys were looking for wasn't a box of drugs, but maybe something else. And as I considered the possibilities, it occurred to me that I'd never inspected John Bernhart's car. So I drove up to 250 Auto Wrecking, and sure enough, his black BMW hadn't been touched since being hauled in there two months ago.

"I asked the manager for permission to look through the car. I told them I was looking for parts. I borrowed the underbelly inspection mirror and examined every square inch of the bottom of the car. Someone had cut three of the break lines and punched a hole in the fourth. No doubt someone had sabotaged the car so it could stop during slow city driving, but fail at high speeds. John Bernhart was murdered."

The more Stedman spoke, the more uncomfortable DiAngello became. He looked physically ill.

"I next went through the car interior. In spite of being pretty bent up and containing a little broken glass, the car wasn't in bad shape. I looked in every conceivable space and found nothing. However, as I lay across the front seat on the driver's side, I noticed the cassette window in the stereo depressed. I tried to eject it, but it's one of them new-fangled electronic contraptions that won't work without the power on. So I bought the stereo and took it home. I put some juice to it, the tape jumped right out. I listened to it, then called the FBI. First thing this morning, Mears and Choice showed up."

"But where do the murders of Kisner and Showers fit into this?" Williams asked. "I didn't even know this Showers girl was dead."

"We've been watching Gram for sometime now," Agent Mears said. "We received some reports of excessive campaign spending the last time he ran for office. When Bernhart came up dead, we started digging a little deeper. Then low and behold Ralph Kisner came up stinking, and we had to make a move, but we had to make sure all our bases were covered. So, we tapped everyone's phones, even the payphones around town." Agent Mears paused to make sure everyone still followed him. "After the Kisner killing, we stumbled onto what sounded like a coded phone conversation between Gram and some questionable Pittsburgh heavies. The name Showers camp up, but we thought it was part of the code. Unfortunately, we didn't put it together in time. They fished her out of the Ohio River at the Pike Island Dam before sunlight this morning." He lowered his eyebrows.

"We arrested two hit men from Pittsburgh about twenty minutes ago, and traced them back to Gram. We were waiting for the hearing to end so we could arrest Gram. Didn't want to interrupt and make a scene."

DiAngello's face turned ashen white. Lori thought he was having a heart attack.

"Are you all right, sir?" she asked.

"I'll be fine, just a lot of excitement for one day. I need to get some air and a drink of water."

"No one leaves this room until this is settled.," Williams said. "This is what we're going to do. When we walk back into that courtroom, the State is going to drop the death specification from the indictment, then I will dismiss the jury."

"Your Honor, couldn't we just have a recess and still seek the death penalty next week sometime?" DiAngello said.

"No, we will not," Williams said. "What kind of idiot are you? Weren't you paying attention out there? The victim in the case said the man you are trying to kill didn't harm her, and may have saved her life. You're not going to make a fool out of me. When we go back in there, you will drop the specifications, and I'll dismiss the jury. Do I make myself clear?"

"Yes, Your Honor," Lori and DiAngello said in unison.

"Solomon," Williams said. "As soon as the jury is gone, you're going to move to have the court dismiss the murder conviction on the grounds of newly discovered evidence. I'll grant the request, and we'll set a date for sentencing for sometime in October when all of this has had a chance to die down. The media all over the country will be carrying this story as soon as this thing hits the AP" He shook his head. "That'll be another nightmare altogether.

"Anyway, at that point I'll clear the courtroom, and you Federal boys can get rid of that dirt-bag Gram nice and easy, and we'll call it a night." He jammed his fists into his tired eyes. "I don't know about any of you, but I've had about enough excitement to last me for a while. Now, let's walk back into court all orderly like and take care of business."

The meeting broke up and the group reassembled in the courtroom. Everyone did exactly as Judge Williams instructed, and within twenty minutes the courtroom was cleared. Agent Choice slapped the handcuffs on Gram who looked utterly defeated. As they escorted him out of the attorney's entrance he yelled back to DiAngello, "I'm not going down alone, buddy. Not by a long-shot!"

23

5:20 P. M.

When all the smoke cleared and everyone else had deserted the courtroom, Danial walked over to Lori and asked, “Do you still want to get together?”

“Sure. That’s of course if you’re still up to it?”

“I’m up to it,” Danial said with a disarming smile. “Please don’t take this wrong, but it has been about eighteen hours since I last ate. Would you like to talk over dinner?”

“Sounds good to me, but on the condition you let me buy.” Lori looked up at him with a silly expression on her face. This was a side of Lori that Danial had never seen before. In fact, this was a side of Lori no one had ever seen before.

They drove separately to *The Greenery*, a restaurant on sunset Boulevard. Danial asked for a table for two, and the maitre d, thinking them a couple, seated them in a romantic spot in the corner, a sky-light above allowed the fading glow of the day to cascade down upon their faces.

The waiter came over and lit the pink candle in the middle of the table. They sat looking at each other then looking away, then fidgeting, and then looking at each other some more. Lori finally mustered the courage to speak.

“Mr. Solomon, what I want to talk to you about is very personal, and I’d like your word that what is said here tonight won’t go any further.”

“You have my word on it, and since this is personal feel free to call me Danial.”

“Thank you . . . Danial. This may sound unbelievable, but you’re the only person I trust enough to discuss this with – ”

“Me?”

"Especially, after a particular thing happened this morning; I've not been able to get it out of my mind." Lori paused and bit her lip. "What I'm about to say has got to be completely off the record."

Before Danial could answer, the waiter strolled over and handed him a wine list. He handed it right back. The waiter stood waiting to take their orders.

"I'll have the New Orleans stuffed shrimp," Danial said. "With a baked potato, salad, and a large Pepsi."

"I'll have a bowl of French onion soup and a Chef's salad," Lori said.

They both looked impatiently at the waiter as he scribbled down their orders, then scurried away.

"I assure you that whatever you say is completely off the record," Danial said.

"I'm serious, because if you repeat what I'm about to say, I'll deny it and call you a liar."

"You've made your point, now please go ahead. What's on your mind?"

"All right. I hope you understand this is awkward for me." She took two exaggerated deep breaths. "I'm ashamed to admit this, but I overheard the conversation you had with your client today."

"When?"

"While the jury deliberated."

"You what! That's impossible – "

"If you'll let me finish – "

"How?"

"I'll explain everything. It's why I had to swear you to secrecy. DiAngello has all of the holding cells bugged. He rationalizes it by saying nothing we overheard can be used against the defendant, so it's no harm, no foul. It's just information."

"Information! I'll tell you what it is, it's a violation of the very Constitution he has sworn to uphold."

"Look, I'm not saying it's right. I'm sure that once the FBI is finished investigating DiAngello, this and a whole lot of other things will come out in the wash. But what I'm trying to say is I heard what you told Kisner. I really heard what you were saying." She stared across the table at Danial like a little girl pleading for validation from an overworked father.

"I'm sorry, go ahead."

"When you were describing the things you were frightened of when you were younger, it sounded like you were reading my diary. I know that pain you talked about; I know that void you described; I know the endless search for meaning in life; and believe me, I know the fear of death. But what I don't know is this Jesus you spoke about."

Danial nodded.

"Don't get me wrong. I've known all about Christmas and Easter since I was a kid. I know Jesus supposedly rose from the dead, I just don't know what that's got to do with me. I mean it happened a couple of thousand years ago." Her eyes shifted to the flickering candle. "All I know is I'm tired of living the way I'm living."

She let down her guard for the first time in over twenty years. She ripped off her mask of self-confidence and superiority and began to cry.

"I'm tired of hating myself, I'm tired of merely existing. There has to be more to life than this. I'm financially independent, I have influence, but I don't have peace, and I really don't have any joy."

Danial listened intently with compassion in his eyes.

"I've watched you closely these past two months," she said. "You never let things bother you. And to be honest, I've done some questionable things to shake you, but you're like a rock."

"I'm not a rock. I'm only standing on the Rock. It's only through Him that I have peace and joy. Without Him, I'm nothing."

"That's my point. You believe that . . . you sincerely believe that."

"I do."

"I heard the way you spoke to Kisner today. You had nothing to gain from him, but you poured out your heart anyway. It's like you have so much peace that you're always trying to give it away."

"I can't help but share what He gives me."

She dropped her eyes. "Well, I wish you'd share some with me."

With that opening Danial shared the glorious Gospel of Jesus Christ with her. Beginning with the basic definition of Grace, Danial carefully explained step-by-step, God's plan of salvation. They were so engrossed in conversation, they didn't notice the waiter place their order on the table. Lori asked several analytical questions, and each time Danial answered with the Scriptures. He cited verses with authority as if citing cases during an oral argument; this was language Lori could understand.

As the minutes ticked by, Lori could feel a strange sensation racing through her body like heavy, constricting chains falling from her heart.

At the end of forty-five minutes, Danial reached his hands across the table in an inviting fashion. Lori placed her tiny hands in his, and the two bitter adversaries approached the throne of Grace together. At precisely 6:45 P. M., Lori received the Lord Jesus Christ into her heart.

They sat quietly looking at each other. Lori dipped her spoon into the French onion soup, raised it to her lips, then spat it back out.

"It's cold," she said. "Waiter! This soup is ice cold."

The waiter scampered over to the table.

"I'm sorry ma'am, but we can't guarantee the soup will stay hot for more than thirty minutes." He smiled and looked at his watch.

"Has it been that long?" she asked.

"It has Madam."

"Boy, the time has flown by."

"It's been over an hour since you were seated."

"Would it be possible to have both meals warmed up," Danial said. "And I promise we won't let them get cold again." He paused then added, "Our thankfulness will be evident in the gratuity."

The waiter picked up the two platters and hurried back to the kitchen.

"If you don't mind me asking, why did you take the Kisner case to begin with?" Lori asked. "I mean, once you found out it was going to be a capital murder case?"

"It started out as a favor to Andy, and I kind of got caught up in it. But if you were thinking I took it because I believed Archie innocent, you're wrong. I was just as surprised as anyone to find out he didn't do it."

"Then why stick it out?"

"I saw this case as an avenue to the United States Supreme Court, maybe a crack at overturning *Roe versus Wade*."

"I don't see the connection."

"I met a few times with Reverend Stone from the Greater Ohio Valley Pro-Life Society. I wanted to make sure I wasn't being counter-productive. But the way the facts were stacking up, I didn't see much of a chance to win this case, so I found a way to win even if I lost."

"By attacking the law itself?"

"Well, if my line of defense didn't work, and Archie got convicted of aggravated murder, I could challenge the Court of Appeals to either overturn the conviction, or grant due process protection to unborn children. Obviously, no court in the land would be in a hurry to overturn a grizzly murder conviction. So I would have had them over a barrel. They could release all the muggers, rapists, and drunk drivers who ever killed an unborn child by harming the mother, or they could overturn *Roe versus Wade* and make all unborn human life sacred. If you put them on the horns of a dilemma, they can't have it both ways. But it wasn't meant to be."

"At least not yet," Lori said. "Have you considered representing someone on death row who has the same type of case?"

"Actually, I never gave it much thought. When I woke up this morning, the thought of Archie being found not guilty seemed impossible. But as far as that goes, the possibility of you and I sharing dinner seemed a whole lot more impossible."

Lori laughed.

Danial took a drink of his Pepsi with his right hand, while still holding the stem of his last stuffed shrimp in his left. His face grew serious.

"What is it?" she asked.

"In all the excitement, I completely forgot about another matter we need to address."

Lori's face grew equally serious. "What is it?"

"Erin Lewis."

* * * * * * *

7:05 P. M.

"What do you think of Dr. Thompson, Erin?" Andy asked as he gently brought the old Ford sedan to a stop at the busy intersection at Market Street.

"I thought he was nice. But he was kind of nosey."

Marianne and Andy chuckled at her innocent reply.

"What do you mean by that?" Marianne asked.

"He asked a lot of questions. Didn't you think he was nosey too?"

"That's what counselors do," Andy said. "They have to ask a lot of questions so they can find out how to give us the best advice."

"Well, if that's what he's supposed to do, then I guess I liked him all right."

The light turned green, and Andy stepped down on the accelerator. Marianne pushed a cassette tape into the stereo and the voice of Twila Paris singing *How Beautiful* fluttered out of the speakers.

Andy thought to himself, that now the trial was over, Franks would step up the pressure on the custody case. Spitzer-Clark is just dying to snatch Erin away. Thank God Danial found a way to get more time.

Andy looked over at his wife. She stared out the window at the barge full of coal churning through the murky Ohio River.

I don't know how Andy keeps himself so calm. After everything that happened in court today, I was a nervous wreck at Dr. Thompson's office.

How did our lives get so out of control? Everything is so crazy now. I can't bear the thought of losing her. Lord, I can't take this any longer. I'm begging you to deliver us from this nightmare. Please do something to show me everything is going to be all right. I know it's wrong to ask for a sign, but I'm at the end of my rope here. Please give me something I can hold on to.

Erin could tell they were getting close to home by the blinking, white lights lining the sides of the cooling towers of the Brilliant Power Plant. It wouldn't be long now until she would be tucked safely in bed.

It took twenty-five minutes for Andy to negotiate the winding trajectory of Route 7. Fifteen minutes later, Erin splashed around in the bathtub without a care in the world. Andy went through the mail; he came across a plain white envelope. It had no stamp or return address. He tore it open, unfolded the letter and read the few words scribbled in a woman's handwriting.

"Thank you Jesus!" he shouted at the top of his lungs. "Oh, praise the Lord!!"

Marianne ran into the kitchen. Andy stood speechless with a toothy smile that spread from ear-to-ear.

"What is it?" Marianne asked.

"The Providence of God, my love! The Providence of God!"

Andy handed the letter to Marianne; she read it. Her lips quivered, her voice trembled. "Does this mean it's over? Is it really over?"

"That's right, babe. It's over. No one will ever break up our family. We will be together forever."

Marianne and Andy Lewis hugged and kissed until a beautiful little girl interrupted them, dripping wet and wrapped in an over-sized, terry-cloth towel. The trio laughed and cried and prayed until late into the night. They were a family, and a family they would stay.

* * * * * * *

7:10 P. M.

"Oh that," Lori said, her voice filled with embarrassment. "Ever since the last hearing, I've been tormented to no end about that little girl. A voice in my head kept telling me I was doing a terrible thing. I didn't believe in a personal conscience until a few minutes ago, but I guess that was God talking to me.

"I made up my mind after hearing you talk to Kisner to drop the whole custody thing. Erin should stay where she belongs, with her parents. I sent a letter to them by courier this afternoon. I told them I dropped the case, and I offered them my most sincere apology. First thing tomorrow morning, I'm going to go down to the courthouse to withdraw my suit. I also intend to apologize to the Lewis family in person, that is if they'll see me."

"I'm sure they will be thrilled to see you. I hope this doesn't sound condescending, but I'm really proud of you."

"You shouldn't be. I didn't have the best motives when I started that whole escapade. But now I just want to do the right thing, especially for that little girl. Although, I must admit I'd love to see her once in a while."

"I'm sure that can be arranged."

"By the way, you were right about the delay," Lori said.

"What are you talking about? What delay?"

"The delay in Sergeant Gates responding to the silent alarm. His partner said Gates insisted it was a false alarm so he went and bought a cup of coffee at the quick Stop first."

"I don't recall seeing that in the Discovery."

Lori shrugged her shoulders. "Sorry."

They finished their meals, the waiter cleared the table and brought the check. True to his word, Danial left the biggest tip the waiter had ever received, a fifty dollar bill tucked inside a tract entitled, "Where Will You Spend Eternity?"

Danial helped Lori on with her coat and as they were walking out the waiter rushed over.

"Thank you so very much, you're too kind."

"Don't mention it," Danial said. "Tonight's a very special night."

"An anniversary perhaps?"

"More of a birthday," Lori said.

"You two make a really nice couple. I wish you all the best in the future."

"Oh we're not . . . ah . . ." Lori stammered, the corners of her lips curling into a smile.

"We're just . . . uh . . . friends," Danial said.

They slowly shuffled to the parking lot and hesitated before going their separate ways. Lori stuck out her hand.

"Thanks for everything."

Danial grasped her hand and gently shook it. "You're welcome."

They gazed into one another's eyes, clenching each other's hand tightly. Lori withdrew her hand and stepped back.

"I'll see you around," she said.

"Yeah, I'll see you."

Danial turned toward his car.

"Wait," she said.

He turned back around to see her standing with her arms stretched out wide. "Can I have a hug?"

Danial stepped forward and held her close. It was a good fit. She looked into his eyes and said, "What do you suppose is happening in heaven right now?"

"The angels are rejoicing, my friend, the angels are rejoicing."

THE END